PRAISE FOR ELISSA WILDS AND
BETWEEN LIGHT AND DARK!

"A smart, sexy read . . . a magical delight!"
> —*New York Times* and *USA Today*
> Bestselling Author C. L. Wilson

"Elissa Wilds has created a sizzling story line to entertain and challenge her readers and does not disappoint. Sexy characters and tense plotting makes for a read that is fun, fascinating and unforgettable."
> —*New York Times* and *USA Today*
> Bestselling Author Julie Leto

"This is a fascinating romantic fantasy . . . subgenre fans will enjoy stepping into Wilds's world . . ."
> —*Midwest Book Review*

"A striking debut . . . Wilds's imagination is impressive. Readers should look forward to new offerings in the future!"
> —*RT Book Reviews*

THE JOINING

"It begins with us holding each other," he said.

She blinked. "Okay . . . and?"

He scooted close to her on the couch and pointed to his lap. "You will need to sit here, facing me."

She jerked away from him. "Get out! This is a come on!" Her eyes narrowed with suspicion.

"I assure you it is not. It works best if our chakras line up. We could embrace standing up if that would be more agreeable to you."

She bit her lip. A moment later, she shook her head. "No. That's silly. We should be comfortable." She stood over him, lifted one shapely leg, and planted herself in his lap. "Now what?" she asked. Did her breath catch just a little?

His thighs heated and burned where she sat, and his pulse raced. His stomach muscles tightened, and he willed himself to relax.

"Now you must lean close and place your hands on my shoulders. The most important thing is to relax into the sensations you are feeling and not to close up when you sense my energy merging with yours."

"How will I know when we're merging?" she asked.

"You will know."

Other *Love Spell* books by Elissa Wilds:

BETWEEN LIGHT AND DARK

DARKNESS
RISING

ELISSA WILDS

LOVE SPELL NEW YORK CITY

*For my two favorite boys: Jett— we wrote this one together.
First with you in my belly. Then with you in my lap.
Michael—without you I'd never get a word written. I love you
both so much.*

LOVE SPELL®

September 2009

Published by

Dorchester Publishing Co., Inc.
200 Madison Avenue
New York, NY 10016

ISBN 10: 0-505-52792-8
ISBN 13: 978-0-505-52792-9
E-ISBN: 978-1-4285-0739-5

The name "Love Spell" and its logo are trademarks of Dorchester
Publishing Co., Inc.

Printed in the United States of America.

10 9 8 7 6 5 4 3 2 1

Visit us online at www.dorchesterpub.com.

ACKNOWLEDGMENTS

I'd like to thank my editor, Alicia Condon, for getting me and all my weirdness, and for always having such great ideas. Thanks to Cheryl Wilson for encouragement and support I can count on. And of course, I couldn't survive without the fabulous P-Squared Plus: Jean Mason, Cheryl Mansfield, June Bowen, Erica Ridley, and Linda Hurtado. Only we could turn a water spout into a positive omen! Thanks to all the members of Tampa Area Romance Authors for making this writing thing a lot less lonely.

And finally, I must express my gratitude to my family and friends who continue to love and support me. To name each one of you individually would be a book in and of itself, but you know who you are. I'm blessed to have you in my life. And I darn well know it.

DARKNESS RISING

Mobius strip: a continuous, one-sided surface formed by twisting one end of a rectangular strip through 180 degrees about the longitudinal axis of the strip and attaching this end to the other.
  —*Webster's American Dictionary*, College edition

When it is dark enough, you can see the stars.
  —Charles Beard

PROLOGUE

Light Realm

A century after her death, his beloved walked the Earth again. It was Meri. She'd come back from the dead to taunt him. The resemblance was striking. Wavy, dark hair, wide-spaced eyes with long, spiky lashes, and plump lips that had fit his own so perfectly, he'd spent what seemed like an eternity aching to taste them again. He sucked in a harsh breath. He was a god. But his heart had turned traitor, had turned *human* on him, long ago.

Mobius, Light God and Director of the Divine Council, crouched before the magical mists of the peering pool, the portal via which the gods could observe those on Earth. The swirls of colorful mist—pink, turquoise, and soft green—contrasted sharply with the bright light of the otherwise stark, white room. He blinked and looked deeper into the pool.

Normally, he would leave the task of checking on the Earth Balancer to the god Helios or the goddess Willow. They were both able to keep the members of the Divine Council abreast of the situation on Earth. But the last Council meeting had been rife with a fear uncommon to the gods.

A fear so palpable that it had drawn him to the peering pool to see for himself what he could of the situation on Earth.

"The gods are dying."

Mobius had turned to the god Helios after he'd uttered those horrible words and immediately attempted to wipe them from his thoughts. *Gods dying? Unheard of!*

"There has been a new influx of evil on Earth. The Umbrae's hold on mankind is increasing," Helios had said, his deep voice filled with concern, the broad features of his ebony-skinned face edged with worry. "It is time to formulate a new plan. The Earth Balancer is losing ground."

Now, Mobius peered deeper into the pool, willing the device to show him more of the Earth Balancer. The translucent tendrils of mist shifted and faded until, once again, he had a clear view of his subject.

She sat alone in a darkened room, perched in front of a mirror, her hands fisted, jaw clenched. Her black hair twisted around her shoulders and curled over her face as she bent her head, hiding her face temporarily from his view. Shudders racked her body, and a soft groan escaped her lips. Her breathing became ragged, and she began to shake her head from side to side as though to ward off some secret pain.

An image flashed through Mobius's mind's eye. A memory from long ago: Meri's body spasming in his arms as unspeakable grief consumed her. Oh, how he had tried to console her, even as a piece of his soul was ripped away and lay dying. He'd had no idea then just how much worse the pain could get. Mobius bit back an agonized groan.

Now he pictured another scene, one forever woven into the very fabric of his being. Meri's body crumpled and broken, her beautiful gray eyes, once full of life, dull and empty. He had no wish to remember, but the vision washed over him anyway, along with a familiar accusation. *You killed her. Because of you, she is dead.*

His chest constricted as he struggled to remain in the present. Long moments passed before the searing sensation in his midsection became a dull ache. He blinked and focused again on the Earth Balancer. What he saw made his breath catch.

She lifted her head and fixed her gaze on the mirror. Sweat trickled down her cheek as she struggled to control her inner turmoil. It was her eyes that caught him, though. Eyes that ought to be the sparkling silver of a Gray God were instead inky wells of blackness. Devoid of light, they shone with the taint of the evil permeating Earth, the evil that had destroyed his beautiful Meri.

Theirs had been an ill-fated love and a passion doomed from the start. But since the moment he'd left Meri on Earth and returned to the Light Realm, he'd been consumed by regret. He'd thought there would be no chance to make amends. *Until now.*

Chapter One

Earth
Tampa, Florida

This is the last one I'll reclaim today. Aurora glanced at the man lying prone at her feet and sighed. Exhaustion weighted her limbs. She lifted her hand to his head and pressed lightly on his blond hair, steeling herself for the expected burst of current. The initial charge was slightly uncomfortable. Lately, though, the discomfort had increased to the point of pain.

After eleven years of healing people infected by the evil of the Umbrae, she ought to be used to the strain it put on her. She wasn't. Or to the effect being half goddess, half witch, and mostly human had on her life. *Or rather, my lack of a life.*

The man's body lurched and shook as she utilized her power to pull the blackness from his heart and mind and soul. Cloudy, murky matter twisted out of him from three of his chakras: the crown, the heart, and the solar plexus.

He groaned and writhed, saliva dripping down his chin. Heat arced through Aurora's body, accompanied by a quick but biting lance of pain. She gritted her teeth and shot another blast of energy into the man. A moment later he coughed, sputtered, and went still. She pulled her hand from the man's head. It was done. She'd reclaimed another Finder.

"Aurie, are you okay? Can I get you anything?"

Aurora gulped air and willed her heartbeat to slow, then turned toward the voice. Her mother stood a few feet away, hovering in the doorway of the hotel room, her short dark hair disheveled as though she'd run nervous hands through it more than once that day.

Her mother, Laurell, had not been happy about this particular Field Trip, the term Aurora had coined for her travels to different parts of the country to battle the Umbrae.

The members of her coven, Hidden Circle, took turns accompanying her. They went wherever their resident psychic, Dawna, and their empath, Wayne, detected the most dark activity, the areas where the demonic Umbrae had been most active in turning people.

Aurora sighed and stared at her mother. The woman had been a bundle of nerves ever since they'd arrived in Tampa that morning.

"Can I get you anything?" her mother asked again, her gaze awash with concern. "Would you like some water?"

"Water," Aurora whispered with a frown. She'd felt the effects of this reclaiming more acutely than was usual. "That would be great."

Her mother nodded and started toward the bathroom. The sound of water running followed by a grunt of disgust echoed off the bathroom walls.

"Aurie, you don't want to drink this water. It stinks. I saw a vending machine down the hall." She disappeared out the door.

Aurora glanced around the run-down motel room they'd chosen for its cheap rate, and more importantly, its remoteness. No sense putting innocent bystanders in danger.

A sharp rap sounded at the door, and she hurried over to open it. A tall, wiry man stood on the other side. He scratched his five-o'clock shadow, studying her.

Elissa Wilds

"Aurie, are you okay in here?" the man asked.

Her lips twisted wryly. She must really look like crap. She glanced toward the mirror at the end of the bed. Her stomach twisted. Did they know? Did her secret show?

The man at Aurora's feet stirred and mumbled something unintelligible. With a sigh, Aurora reached down and touched his cheek, stilling his movements.

"I'm fine, Wayne. Mom went to get water." She motioned toward the man on the floor. "We need to get this one out of here before he wakes up looking for an explanation."

Wayne stepped into the room. "I'm on it."

He scooped the man up with a grunt, amazing Aurora, as usual, with a strength that belied his sixty-something years.

Wayne started toward the door, dragging the man with him. "You should pack while I'm gone, though. I'm sensing something weird around here."

"Weird how?" Aurora asked.

He shrugged. "Bad, but not Umbrae. I don't know how to explain it. But I don't think we should hang around ta figure it out."

He paused in the doorway, glancing left to right, no doubt to make sure no other guests were about. Fortunately, the dump of a motel was pretty empty. *No one else wants to camp with roaches.*

The man he held suddenly came to life. His eyes popped open, and he blinked rapidly, struggling to focus.

"Where am I?" the man asked.

"You're in wonderland, Alice," Wayne quipped, yanking the man to his feet and pulling the door shut behind them. Their footsteps echoed on the concrete walkway, fading as they moved farther away from the room.

Aurora stood from the bed and glanced briefly again at the mirror. She frowned. Her eyes still held the slightest tint of blackness, the color they turned when she utilized her power. She blinked, and her eyes flashed silver once more.

Aurora bit her lip and started packing. She hated to leave without reclaiming more people. But if Wayne said trouble was brewing, she knew better than to question him. No one picked up the dark energy of the Umbrae like he did.

And besides, her tattoo had been itching and burning all morning. Aurora turned and glanced over her shoulder at her reflection in the mirror.

The open back of her halter top bared her left shoulder so that the yellow, blue, and red lines of the tattoo were clearly visible. A sun and a moon mating. She'd gotten the tattoo to cover up a large, unusual birthmark. Not that the mark had actually been there since birth, but she didn't know what else to call it.

Over time, a form had etched itself into her skin, becoming clearer with each year until an almost perfectly shaped half-moon merging into a sun had appeared.

She'd been self-conscious about the birthmark, so she'd decided to get herself a tattoo.

Recently she'd been experiencing strange sensations in the skin beneath the tattoo whenever danger lurked nearby. Her own personal warning signal. A warning signal that was suddenly burning her skin something furious.

Chapter Two

The hairs on the back of Aurora's neck stood up. Her gut clenched in anticipation. She wasn't alone.

The door to the hotel room crashed open with a resounding thud. A man stood in the doorway, tall and wiry with limp black hair that looked like it could stand a good wash and lips twisted into an ugly sneer. He wore black from head to toe.

His gaze pierced her with the deep dark of a starless midnight sky. In that moment, Aurora wished she didn't have the supersensitive sight she'd inherited from her father. Because even from a few feet away, those eyes projected a vile, menacing evil.

"What do you want?" she demanded, willing the shiver from her limbs. Why should she fear him? She was the Earth Balancer. No one could hurt her. She held her hands out, poised to send a blast of elemental energy if he so much as twitched.

"I have come for you, Earth Balancer." His voice was deep and gravelly. His hands fisted.

That counts as a twitch. "I don't think so," Aurora hissed just before a blast of crimson light shot from her palms and struck the man at chest level. He staggered, groaned, but quickly regained his footing. Then with dizzying speed, he leapt forward and threw his body against hers. They tumbled to the ground.

The sudden impact took the breath from Aurora's

lungs. She gasped for air and shoved at the man's mid-section, willing her fingers into claws of sheer energy, slicing into him from the inside out. The man's back arched for a moment. His face twisted with a flash of pain, but instead of moving off of her, he reached forward and grabbed her around the neck. He leaned in close.

His hands raked her head, and she let out a yelp at the sharp sting of pain. Pulling hair? The guy did not fight fair!

Aurora grasped his hands and yanked them from around her neck before pushing the man away and flipping him to his back. She straddled him and held his hands above his head. Thank Goddess for her superior strength. No mere mortal could fight her. But he was strong. He managed to free one wrist from her grasp and struck her in the cheek. A blast of pain shot through her, and she fell backward.

Confused, she scrambled to her feet. He followed suit. How could he move as fast as she? How did he match her strength? Who—*what*—was he?

He started to charge her again, but at that moment another man burst onto the scene.

This man was tall and broad, with fiery, shoulder-length hair, a strong, square jaw, and piercing amber eyes. His full lips thinned as his gaze fixed on her attacker. Aurora stared at the stranger, unable to speak. Her flesh tingled with a strange recognition. Why? She'd never seen him before in her life. Out of the corner of her eye, she noted her attacker had frozen in place and stood staring at the red-haired stranger, just as mesmerized as she.

Long moments ticked by before the black-haired man seemed to come to his senses. With a loud grunt, he was on her again, this time grabbing for her throat at the same moment as he dug one knee into her midsection.

Before she had a chance to claw his heart out, the red-haired man appeared next to them. He lifted her attacker bodily, tossing him into the wall like a sack of potatoes.

The black-haired man didn't stay down for long, though. A second later he let out a roar and hurled himself at the redhead.

The two men wrestled, muscles straining as each fought to gain the upper hand. The man with the black eyes put enough distance between them to grab the other's hand and twist his arm behind his back. He laced his arm around the redhead's neck in a choke hold. She was at a loss. Should she help the red-haired man? How did she know he wasn't out to get her, too? Should she run?

The redhead grunted, lifted his free hand, and managed to grab the dark man's arm, yanking him forward and onto his back with an amazing show of strength. The man lay dazed for a moment, then struggled to sit up. The red-haired man pressed his hand to his opponent's forehead, his fingers caging the man's face.

He pushed his weight forward, leaned into the hold, and white current burst from his hands. The dark man cried out in pain, twitched, then suddenly lay still.

Aurora's rescuer stood, chest heaving, eyes glowing with white light so fierce it hurt to look at him. The light quickly dissipated, though, and his eyes turned tawny once again.

"You killed him?" Aurora glanced at the man lying prone at her feet, the second man to fall there in the past hour.

He shook his head. "No. He has been momentarily stunned. A result of the onslaught of white light against his darkness."

Aurora frowned. "I could have taken him, you know."

His lips curled in a sardonic smile. "No, I do not know that."

Aurora's back stiffened. "Look, I'm not just some helpless chick."

"I know who you are."

"Really? How?"

"Everyone in the Light Realm knows of the Earth Balancer. It was we of the Divine Council who conceived of you."

Aurora didn't like the arrogance she read in his face. "Actually, I think my parents conceived me."

There was something familiar about the man. Despite her annoyance at his attitude, she was drawn to him. She knew she'd never met him before, but for some reason she had an irresistible urge to reach out and twine her fingers through all that red hair, to tug his mouth to hers. At this thought, heat burned her cheeks. What was wrong with her? *I'm just depleted from the battle.*

"Who are you?" she demanded.

"My name is Mobius."

Mobius? Director of the Divine Council? "Why are you here?"

"Because your mission is in jeopardy. A new threat has emerged."

She frowned and motioned toward the man on the floor. "You mean him? Why did he attack me? And what the hell *is* he?"

Mobius's jaw clenched. "I am not certain why he attacked you. And as for what he is . . ." He paused and ran his fingers through his hair, a perplexed expression crossing his face.

The muscles in his arms bunched beneath the black T-shirt he wore, drawing her gaze. Damn, he was good looking. Why couldn't she stop staring at him? The energy between them pulsed and grew. What the hell? He was an absolute stranger and yet she was so inextricably drawn to this Light God, she didn't think anything could break through her fascination with him.

"He's the same as you," he finally said. "A Gray God."

Except, maybe, for that.

Mobius couldn't imagine anything more torturous than the flight back to Grave's Manor, Aurora's home in Wisconsin. Wayne and Laurell occupied two seats in front of him, and he sat stiffly beside Aurora, careful not to touch her. A couple of times, their arms fought for the same armrest and she glared at him, all but shoving his limb out of the way so she could rest her own there. She had the bearing of a goddess, including the sense of entitlement and arrogance of someone accustomed to getting her way.

He gave up the armrest willingly, though. Touching her elicited sensations too dangerous to dwell upon.

Now that he'd seen her in person and experienced her presence firsthand, he knew for certain. Source help him, she was Meri come back to life. Meri reincarnated. Meri, just as beautiful and obstinate and powerful as ever.

"How is it that Grays are leaving the Light Realm to hang out on Earth now?"

She smelled of jasmine and spice. He remembered that scent. His chest tightened. Mobius took a sip of the water the flight attendant had brought him earlier.

"It would not make sense for a Gray, or any other god for that matter, to spend too much time on the Earth plane. We cannot survive here in god form for more than a few days. A Gray would have to take human form, and even that would last only a few months."

"That guy wasn't human in any way."

"No. He was still in his god form. But completely turned by the Umbrae."

"Why was he here?"

Mobius raised his eyebrows. "Clearly, to kill you."

Aurora shifted in her seat and tilted her head, confusion fluttering across her features. "I don't get it. My father was a Gray. I'm a half Gray myself. I thought they—we—were the good guys."

"In the Light Realm, yes. On Earth, however, it's more difficult for Grays to resist the lure of their shadow selves. Your father has not spoken of this? I believe he has experienced that inner battle firsthand."

She seemed to think about his question for a moment, then cleared her throat and swiftly changed the subject. "And you? What part do you play in all of this?"

"I'm here to help you."

She raised her black, perfectly arched eyebrows. "I'm not sure I need help."

"I'm quite certain that you do," he said.

Her spine stiffened noticeably. "How exactly do you plan to be helpful?"

"I'm not certain yet exactly what my role will be," he finally answered. He hesitated to tell her he would be focused on her protection. He had the feeling she would not take that admission kindly.

Sitting this close to her, he could study her in detail. She was even more beautiful in person. Those silver eyes, those plump lips. He ached to touch them. First with his fingers. Then with his mouth and tongue.

And then . . .

"You okay?" she asked.

He shifted in his seat. "Yes."

"You don't look it. You look tired."

Not exactly, he thought. But he was grateful his desire wasn't evident to her. "Fighting that Gray was a bit draining. I haven't yet adjusted to being in human form."

"Oh," she said. "That's rough."

"You are not tired from the fight?"

She shrugged. "Nope. I guess my girl power is just that strong." But as she spoke, her gaze slid from his, and he had the distinct feeling she did not speak the truth.

Before he could question her further, she made an abrupt change of subject. "So, you didn't kill that Gray back there."

Mobius shook his head.

"Why not? I mean, he did try to kill us."

Mobius sighed. He hated to admit his weakness. Between seeing Meri again, live and in the flesh, and the shock of finding her being attacked by a Gray that should have died eons ago, he had not thought his course of action through. He had never killed another god. And truth be told, considering his regret over unfairly banishing this particular Gray to Earth, he wasn't certain that given the chance again, he could kill him. But Aurora didn't need to know all of these reasons.

"I am in human form," Mobius said. "Powerful, yes. But not more so than a being in god form."

"Oh. So, since I'm half god, I might have had a chance?"

She was still trying to convince him she didn't need him. "It's unlikely you could have defeated a Gray in his god form. At least not on your own."

"But I'm a goddess."

"Who is half-mortal."

Aurora grimaced. She clearly didn't like being reminded of her mortality. Mobius waited for her to point out the obvious. That together they might have killed the Gray. She didn't.

Instead, she stood and waved her hands at him. "Scoot those long legs of yours. I have to pee. Oh, and when I get back, I want you to tell me how you were able to conjure up plane tickets for all of us like that. If it's a spell, I want you to teach me."

He started to tell her that gods didn't need spells, and it was simply one of his personal powers—to conjure minor items from nothing—but she was already heading down the aisle toward the restroom, full hips swinging in tight blue jeans, turning more than one head as she made her way.

Chapter Three

Graves Manor
Lake Geneva, Wisconsin

Aurora's father, Axiom, engulfed Mobius in a bear hug and flashed a grin so wide he could have swallowed bugs. Aurora observed the exchange with interest. She had never seen him interact with any of the gods.

"You have not changed," Axiom said, taking a step back and eyeing Mobius.

"You, however, have aged, my friend. How odd to see you with lines around your eyes and white in your hair." Mobius responded with an equally healthy smile.

"Now don't you give him grief about his age, Mobius," Laurell quipped, entering the foyer of Graves Manor and circling her husband's waist with her arm. "He barely has any gray hair, and the few lines around his eyes are what we like to call laugh lines. They're a good thing."

She tilted her head to Axiom. "Aging is a small price to pay for the privilege of remaining here on Earth with Aurora and me," she told him with a teasing smile.

Axiom chuckled and gestured toward the kitchen. "Come and eat something, Mobius. You can explain your visit over some dinner. Most of the coven members are already here in anticipation of your arrival. The others are on their way."

"I called from the airport," Laurell explained.

"Good," Mobius said. "It's better if they are here."

"Aurie, you come too," her mother called, waving her toward the kitchen. "Your dad tells me Hill has made something special."

The scent of spices and cheese drifted to Aurora's nose, and her stomach grumbled. When the group got together for Full Moon rituals and Sabbat celebrations, they took turns preparing feasts that all looked forward to.

Aurora followed her parents and Mobius through the kitchen to the dining room. A sparkling chandelier cast shadows across the cream-colored walls and hardwood floors. Someone had lit nag champa incense, and its spicy, slightly sweet scent filled the room.

Thumper, a chemist in his early thirties with soft, blue, bespectacled eyes, was already seated at the massive mahogany table. He was the group's computer guru.

Beside him sat Hillary, a smooth-skinned, heavyset black woman who was a nurse-practitioner and the coven's resident healer.

Hillary had insisted on fixing dinner: chicken Parmesan, thick crusty garlic bread, and salad. Dawna and Lynn had not yet arrived, and Wayne was busy checking the perimeter of the property for any dark entities.

Mobius's gaze washed over Thumper and Hillary, then Laurell and Axiom. "Where are your High Priest and High Priestess?"

"Reese and Fiona recently handfasted. They're on their honeymoon," Laurell said.

Mobius frowned. "It would be best for the entire coven to be together. We may need Reese and Fiona's power in the days ahead."

"We can't reach them. They're backpacking through Europe and purposely left their cell phones behind so they could have some time alone together for once," Aurora told him.

Mobius raised his eyebrows.

"We have been battling the Umbrae for the last eleven years, my friend. The coven members must go on living their lives even as the fight continues," Axiom explained.

"Of course," Mobius said.

After all the introductions had been seen to, Aurora took her seat. Mobius slid into the chair next to her. Did he choose to sit beside her on purpose? She couldn't be sure, but she had noticed the way he looked at her on the plane. He'd been checking her out. And she'd been annoyed with herself for being pleased that he found her attractive. *It's not as if I can or would date him.*

Although she longed to have a normal life, to date and to fall in love, it wasn't meant to be. She'd learned that the hard way. Her life had been predestined and dedicated before she was born. Before her conception, even.

Still, he was striking to look at. All that thick shiny hair, layered with hints of yellow and orange, like the flames of a Beltane bonfire. And his gaze—amber colored, gleaming like eyes she'd before seen only in felines. Square jaw. High cheekbones. A body just too hard and beautiful to believe. He was wearing a plain blue T-shirt and jeans—nothing special, but she could see he was solid, all muscle.

Again, this sudden and fierce attraction. She sighed. *Get ahold of yourself, girl.*

"Bread?" Mobius's voice tugged her from her thoughts. She blinked. He held a basket of garlic bread and stared at her with interest. Did he know what she'd been thinking?

She snatched the basket from his hand and quickly averted her gaze. "Thanks." *Don't blush.* Her cheeks ignored the command.

Over dinner, Mobius explained the situation in the Light Realm. The Light Gods were falling ill of some unknown disease, and the Council believed it was tied to the sudden influx of negative energy on Earth. Humans and gods were connected by way of their shared parentage; they all emerged from Source, the gods' term for the energy that moved through all living things.

For a time, it had seemed that the Earth Balancer's efforts to restore humans who had been turned and to dispel Umbrae were paying off. All of the Light beings had sensed a shift on Earth. A shift that in time would take the evolution of humankind higher and would relegate to second place the Dark beings forever.

However, in the past several months, the Umbrae had begun multiplying, suddenly able to turn humans at a rate such as the Council had never seen. And the level of evil on Earth had risen.

This was not news to the coven.

Any witch who possessed even an ounce of intuition could feel the change. Lately, the very air seemed heavy with menace.

The problem was that the Council had been unable to pinpoint the exact source of the rising darkness, but it seemed inevitable that the Umbrae would plan an attack on Aurora. She was all that stood in the way of the Umbrae's domination of humankind.

"And how did you know Grays were involved?" Axiom asked.

"I didn't. Not until I saw the one that attacked Aurora," Mobius responded. "We will need to get a message to the Light Realm."

"How will you accomplish this without a Liaison?" Axiom asked, referring to the mediums who sometimes acted as go-betweens linking humans and the gods.

"It is not the same as during your mission, Axiom. We

no longer need to hide the trail of the Light Gods from the Umbrae."

"So one of the Light Gods will travel here periodically?" Laurell asked.

"I will likely make contact via the Astral Plane myself," Mobius agreed. "Or one of you can travel to the Light Realm directly."

"You'd need to be in god form to travel to the Light Realm," Axiom pointed out.

"One of us *is* in god form," Mobius said. "Granted, it will require at least one preliminary visit in her spirit body in order to make her ready to transport there at will without leaving her physical form behind."

He motioned toward Aurora, and suddenly all eyes were on her. She glanced around the table from one witch to the next, finally returning her gaze to Mobius, who chewed his chicken thoughtfully.

"You mean I can go to the Light Realm?" It sounded too good to be true. She'd long wished to see for herself where the goddess half of her came from.

"If need be, yes," Mobius said.

"If Aurie is in such danger, maybe we should send her there now. For protection," Laurell suggested.

Aurora's eyes narrowed. "I won't run and hide," she burst out.

Mobius rested one hand on Aurora's, his fingers massaging her tightened fist. Aurora immediately stilled. Her hand tingled beneath his. She glanced at him, but his profile was to her as he addressed the rest of the group.

"Aurora is right. She is needed here. I'm convinced she will be even more instrumental in stopping the Umbrae than we know."

At least he agreed with her. She'd been raised and trained to fight. She'd never backed down from a challenge. She certainly wouldn't start now. Realizing his large fingers still engulfed hers, she pulled her hand from his, suddenly self-conscious.

She scooped up her fork and began cutting her chicken, though for some reason Mobius's presence so nearby made it difficult for her to focus on her food.

"So, why exactly are you here?" Axiom asked, his gaze questioning, his brow knitted. Aurora knew that look. Her father suspected there was more to Mobius's story than he had divulged.

"I thought I made myself clear. The Council agreed the coven could use some assistance. So, here I am."

Axiom frowned. "No, I mean, why you? Why not another of the gods? I am surprised the Council allowed you to come. You are too important to the Light Realm to place yourself in such danger."

Mobius shrugged, but the rigidity of his spine belied his nonchalance. "It was my decision."

Axiom's eyes narrowed, but before he could say more, the rest of the coven arrived.

Dawna burst into the room, pushing her shoulder-length ebony hair out of her pale face, her eyes wide with alarm. "Sorry we're late, but we've had a helluva day."

Her girlfriend Lynn appeared behind her, resting one hand on Dawna's shoulder, her short, choppy blonde hair tousled from what appeared to be more than the wind. Her face mirrored the concern on Dawna's.

"We were attacked by Finders," Lynn said.

"Where?" Aurora gasped.

"We were at home. Lynn was meditating with some of her crystals, and I was on our front porch, talking to Reba. From out of nowhere, two Finders busted through our back door, guns blazing."

"Fortunately, we were able to take them with a bit of fire energy, but not before they shot the place up pretty good," Lynn said.

Laurell stood, her long black skirt swishing as she crossed the room to the other two women. She reached out to touch the crimson stain on the side of Dawna's face. "Your blood or theirs?"

"Mine, but the other guy looked worse."

Laurell turned and motioned to Hillary. "I think she might need stitches."

Hillary hurried over to inspect Dawna's cheek. "Yup. At least a few."

Something scurried near Dawna's feet. A small, brown rodent appeared between the witch's ankles and squeaked to make its presence known.

Hillary jumped back. "Rat!" she cried, her voice panicked.

Dawna laughed. "Naw. That's Reba. My familiar." Dawna bent and held her hand out to the creature. The squirrel climbed into Dawna's palm, scurried up her arm, and rested on her shoulder, her little head bobbing from left to right. Her tiny body visibly trembled.

"It's okay, Reba. No one here will hurt you," Dawna assured the animal.

Dawna had the ability to talk to animals, a talent she'd discovered in her early twenties by communicating with birds. Over the years, she'd made contact with the insect kingdom, small rodents, dogs, and cats. There were always one or two animals that fell in love with the raven-haired witch and moved in. This time, it was Reba.

"I don't understand why the Finders attacked," Aurora murmured.

Finders didn't just attack without a purpose.

Mobius sighed. "This is yet another indication that I made the right decision coming here. It's best if the coven stays together for now, rather than living in your separate dwellings."

"Done," Thumper said. Thumper had obtained a

dual degree in chemistry and computer engineering. He worked as an independent computer consultant and set his own hours. His chemistry degree came in handy when the coven needed a potion or two for dealing with the Finders.

"I'm in between jobs right now, so that's not a problem for me," Dawna said.

"I'll see if my partner can't take my clients for the next week or two," Lynn agreed. Lynn was a family therapist, and it was always difficult for her to get away from her practice.

Wayne was retired, and Hillary was a widow, living on her husband's pension. As for Aurora, she had never had a job. Or gone to school. She'd lived most of her life secluded in Graves Manor or traveling to fight Umbrae. She'd found it difficult to make friends outside the coven. In fact, she'd never done anything but vanquish Umbrae and reclaim turned humans. She frowned at this thought.

She was bothered by the fact that there was absolutely nothing else in her life besides demon hunting. *But that's what I'm here to do. It's why I exist.* This knowledge stirred a familiar ache in her gut.

Mobius's next words yanked Aurora from her thoughts. "And I will be Aurora's new best friend. I will not leave her side until we have conquered this latest threat."

Now, why did that announcement infuriate her just as much as it thrilled her?

Chapter Four

"I must ask you a difficult question," Axiom said as he settled into a chair across from Mobius in the library at Graves Manor. "Which is it that you really want? To be my daughter's bodyguard or to bed her?"

The dim light of the table lamp next to Axiom's chair cast shadows about the room and over the angles of his face. His deep silver eyes seemed to hold an almost ominous gleam.

Mobius shifted uncomfortably in his seat. "You know I have the utmost respect for you and your family. That holds true for Aurora as well."

Axiom ran his hands over jeans-clad legs and tilted his head to one side, studying Mobius for a moment. Then, he stood and crossed to a small bar in the corner of the room. He lifted a glass from the counter and uncapped a crystal decanter. The sound of the amber liquid he poured from the bottle broke the charged silence.

"Brandy?" Axiom offered a glass to Mobius, who took it, although he had no idea what the fluid was. He lifted the glass to his nose and inhaled the slightly acidic, sweet scent.

After pouring himself a glass, Axiom settled once again into his chair. He took a small sip and sighed. "Mobius, I see how you look at Aurie."

"Speak plainly, Axiom." Mobius's words came out a

bit rougher than intended. He did not like to be on the receiving end of a reprimand, and he sensed one coming.

"Please know that I fully understand your predicament. Before I came to Earth on my own mission, I had no idea what pleasures could be had with a mortal woman. Those pleasures can be quite tempting. And you, having been here before and tasted of that desire . . . of that passion . . ." He paused and drank more of his brandy, a gulp this time. "Well, I can certainly understand wanting to experience such delights again."

Mobius's jaw tensed. "Of course I've thought of what it would be like to mate with a mortal woman again." He would not bother lying to Axiom, who would sense whether or not he spoke the truth. "And Aurora's beauty and power could certainly be an intoxicating combination."

Axiom's gaze darkened with warning.

"However," Mobius was quick to add, "I would never jeopardize our friendship. Or my mission. I cannot afford to be distracted. Neither can Aurora." Mobius took a deep swallow of the brandy and coughed as it burned his throat.

"Easy, old friend," Axiom said. "Best to sip this particular drink."

Mobius grimaced. "I assume it's an acquired taste?"

Axiom gave a half smile and nodded in response before finishing his own drink in one final swallow and setting down the glass. "Why do you feel it's in Aurora's best interests for you to be so close to her? She has the protection of the coven."

"The coven may not be enough to withstand the present threat. That's why I'm here." Mobius set down his own glass. He knew the next point of discussion would open up old wounds that would prove painful for them both. Dread laced his gut.

"You mean the Grays?" Axiom prodded.

"Yes."

"I assume you have a theory as to why Grays would be attacking Aurora? Or, for that matter, why they would even be on Earth?"

Mobius sighed. "Somehow the Umbrae have enlisted and turned them."

Confusion fluttered across Axiom's face. "I should think a Gray in human form would still be no match for Aurie."

"They remain in god form."

"But they'd be dead within days," Axiom insisted.

"That would normally be true. However, I believe the Umbrae have found a way to alter the Grays so that they fully embrace their shadow sides."

Axiom shook his head. "I still cannot fathom what would cause a Gray to leave the Light Realm and assist the Umbrae."

Mobius rose, crossing to where Axiom sat. He had purposely waited to explain the situation with the Earth-bound Grays. He wanted to speak to Axiom without an audience.

He knelt in front of his friend, placing one hand over Axiom's, hoping to lend comfort and reassurance, and scrambled for the right words. "My friend, I believe these are Grays from times of old. Those who existed before the Council realized that the Grays' mixed energy is not to be feared."

Axiom's hand tensed beneath Mobius's palm. "You mean the Grays who were banished to die on the Earth plane?" His words came out strained, an old hurt filling his gaze.

Axiom still resented the prejudice he himself had experienced in the Light Realm while trying to attain a seat on the Divine Council.

Mobius had never felt more ashamed of his own role in that initial banishment than he did at that moment. It was something he wished he could change, but could not. Instead, he'd done everything in his power to further the interests of the Balancers—the Grays—once he'd become Divine Director.

It was because of him that Axiom had been chosen to head his own mission to Earth. Others on the Council had doubted the wisdom of his choice. Old fears died hard. Prejudice died harder.

"How do you know these are the same Grays?"

Mobius recalled the face and form of the Gray who had attacked Aurora. The long dark hair, the square jaw, all the features had been all too familiar to Mobius.

"I recognized the Gray who attacked Aurora. He was one of the original banished."

Axiom sighed and pulled his hand from beneath Mobius's. He ran his fingers through his coal black hair. "Perhaps he is the only one of his kind?"

"If the Umbrae have found a way to turn a Gray to their side, do you think they would stop at just one?"

Axiom's lips thinned with frustration. "No. It is no wonder they would turn against the Light. The Light turned against them."

Mobius sensed his friend's pain. He could offer no solace to Axiom. He could not undo the past.

Mobius stood, and Axiom began pacing the room, his agitation clear. "How is it that the Grays have survived all this time? How is it that they are reemerging now?"

"I imagine the Umbrae found some way to keep them alive until they perfected a process to turn them," Mobius responded.

Axiom continued his frenetic movement across the floor, his steps wearing tracks in the thick carpet.

Mobius halted him with a hand on his shoulder. "Axiom, please know I regret my part in the banishment of the Grays. I was—"

Axiom waved his words away like pesky insects.

"No. No apologies. You've more than made up for your earlier mistakes. You behaved no differently from all the other well-intentioned Light Gods of that time. I have long since forgiven you."

Mobius swallowed, allowing the tension to flow from his body. This was a conversation long overdue, and he was more than pleased to have it done.

"And," Axiom continued, "you are right about Aurora needing your protection. A turned Gray is dark and powerful. The only thing that can stop such a being is one of equal power. And that, my friend, is you."

Mobius nodded. "The problem is, I'm in human form now. Not as strong as I would be in god form. However, my force combined with Aurora's is something else entirely."

Axiom smiled wryly. "A force even a turned Gray will find difficult to defeat."

Chapter Five

Aurora woke to the sound of hissing in her ear. At least, to her sleep-befuddled mind it sounded like hissing. As she came fully awake, though, the noise disappeared. She sat up and kicked the sheets aside, glancing around the darkness of her bedroom, half expecting to see a snake coiled somewhere nearby.

A half-moon sent slivers of light through her window, illuminating just enough of the room to hold the shadows at bay. Still, webs of darkness occupied the corners of the space and hovered there like watchful ghosts. Why this sudden unease that made her skin crawl and her heartbeat accelerate?

Her shoulder burned beneath her tattoo. She was safe inside her bedroom at Graves Manor. What kind of danger could there be here?

She'd been dreaming. Strange, disjointed dreams of Mobius. His face smiling into hers with tenderness. His hands on her skin, rough calluses teasing soft curves. Making love. Fighting. Crying.

Then the landscape had changed. Dark, disquieting images had infiltrated. Horrific visions of death, cruelty, and rage. People performing acts so vile, no one should ever have to bear witness to them. Rapes. Molestations. Murders. She shuddered now, her stomach clenching as the images filtered back through her consciousness.

Aurora scooted to the side of the bed and lifted to her

lips the glass of water she habitually kept on her night-stand. She took a sip and willed her pulse to slow.

A moment later, pain lanced her gut. She gasped, and the glass slipped from her grasp and crashed to the hardwood floor. Her vision filled with more of the ugly scenes. A group of men laughing as they looked on while a woman was violated. Her cries echoed in Aurora's ears. She felt the man's rage and anger toward the woman he raped, his belief that the woman had taunt-ed him, then turned him down. Now she'd get what was coming to her.

A mother holding a pillow over her small son's face as she suffocated the life out of him. Aurora choked on the mother's selfishness and greed. Her beauty had been ruined by the child she'd never wanted. The one man she desired refused to stay with her because he wanted no children of his own.

Aurora cried out, a harsh, anguished plea to the shad-ows threatening to infiltrate her very soul. "Stop!"

She couldn't take much more. This was far worse than the brief images that flashed through her mind when she reclaimed someone. Those visions, ugly as they were, were brief, fleeting snapshots of moments in time. These visions emerged full-bodied and lifelike. It was as though she were committing these atrocities her-self. As though her own body, her own hands, were committing the crimes.

She barely registered her bedroom door opening and closing. It wasn't until a tall, broad figure crossed the room, sat on her bed, and pulled her into an embrace that the images cleared enough for her to realize she wasn't alone. A surge of energy ran through her body, full of power and softness at the same time. The images disappeared completely. *Mobius*.

She breathed in the scent of her rescuer. A clean, fresh-out-of-the-shower smell. She buried her face in his bare chest and sighed in relief. His flesh felt hot against her cheek, and she allowed her hands to trail to his sides and rest lightly against his waist. Her heartbeat finally slowed to normal.

Safe. She wanted to stay there, wrapped in him.

It felt good to be held; it was heaven to relax into him, to let go even momentarily of the need to be the strong one, the powerful Earth Balancer.

Mobius rubbed circles on her back, and she leaned farther into him, sighing inwardly. After a few more moments, he pulled back and cradled her cheek. He lifted her head, and she blinked, still not quite awake. Had the horrible visions been a nightmare? Was she still sleeping now? *Are you part of my dream?*

His gaze roved her face. He peered into her eyes, his own amber orbs deepening to topaz, as his forehead wrinkled with concern.

"What is it?" she asked, her voice a breathy whisper.

"You have been battling the pull of the Umbrae."

She shook her head. "I had ugly dreams. That's all."

He sighed. "It's much more than that."

Aurora shifted away from him, suddenly embarrassed at her need to hold on to him. The fog of sleep and the remnants of the visions had passed, and now she wondered at his presence in her room.

As she moved, her thigh crumpled a notebook she'd left there. She must have fallen asleep without putting it away. Normally, all of her artwork remained safely hidden in her chest of drawers. It was a secret passion she shared with no one.

Mobius noticed the notebook and scooped it up. Before she could stop him, he flipped through its pages, taking in the sketches of her mother, Graves Manor, a towering oak tree on the property where she loved to nap. He paused on her self-portrait.

Although there was almost no light in the room, she

knew that with his heightened god vision, Mobius could see just as well as she. Glancing at the picture, she tried to view it through his eyes. An attractive woman stared back at her from the page with eyes that revealed painful emptiness.

"These are good. You're an artist?" he asked.

"I dabble. Mostly just sketches like these. Sometimes, I use charcoal." Her palms itched to grab the notebook from his hands. She'd never shared her work with anyone, and she didn't want the first person to see her sketches to be a virtual stranger. She felt naked all of a sudden. She didn't like that feeling.

His brow rose. "You have talent."

The compliment filled her with a quiet joy, but the way he studied the picture made her uneasy. *What does he see?* She couldn't take it anymore.

She snatched the notebook from his hands and stuffed it beneath her pillow. "It's nothing," she snapped. "Why are you in my room?"

"I heard you cry out." He glanced down at the floor, where she'd dropped the glass. "And other noises."

"You heard me?"

"I'm staying in the room next to yours." He cocked his head to the side. "For your safety."

She bristled at his words. "I don't need a bodyguard." She became suddenly aware that she was wearing only her panties and a thin T-shirt that came to just above her knees.

She stood, skirting the shards of glass as she moved to the dresser, intent on finding a pair of shorts. A wave of dizziness overcame her, and she braced herself with her hands on the dresser.

Mobius appeared behind her and placed one hand at the small of her back. "Are you alright?"

She nodded and waited for him to say something else. Instead, his fingers traced the outline of the tattoo on her left shoulder. The burning sensation had faded.

"This tattoo is beautiful."

"Thanks," she said, grateful for the distraction of banal conversation. The dizziness was starting to pass. "I got it to cover my birthmark."

"A moon and a sun merging. How appropriate. The god and goddess, and the connection between the two. Being the Balancer, you are a perfect blend of Light and Dark."

"Yeah. I liked the symbolism of it, too." She moved to twist away from him. His hand clamped over her shoulder and held her in place.

He lifted his hand and a fresh glass of water appeared in his palm.

Her eyes widened, but she took the glass and drank the liquid greedily, grateful for the steadying influence of the drink.

"How did you do that?" she asked.

He shrugged. "In addition to the usual god powers of speed, strength, and heightened eyesight, I have the ability to bring things into being with my thoughts."

"Really? So you can just think of, say, a jet plane, and make one appear?"

"Not exactly. I can only create minor items. Like a glass of water, or those plane tickets you asked me about before."

"Oh." She handed the glass back to him and turned to the dresser. "Thanks for the water, but I told you, I don't need your help."

He touched her cheek for the second time that night and lifted her head to the mirror. "Don't you?"

She peered at her reflection. Even in the dim light, her eyes were giant black orbs engulfing her pale face. She hadn't been using her powers. She hadn't been performing a reclaiming. *My eyes shouldn't look like this.*

"What's happening to me?" Her words sounded strained to her own ears.

"The rise in dark energy on Earth is wreaking havoc with your shadow side. It's trying to take over."

Aurora shook her head, wishing she could will his words away. No. She was strong. Her light energy was powerful enough to keep her shadow side in balance.

As though he heard her internal thoughts, Mobius sighed. "You can't deny this, Aurora. Tell me, how long have you been having symptoms?"

She turned slowly around to face him. Her mind raced over her recent weakness after reclaimings, the way her eyes failed to return to their normal state as quickly, her nightmares.

"Aurora?" Mobius prodded.

She rubbed her hands over her eyes, resigned. "I don't know exactly. A month? Maybe a little longer?"

"And it's getting worse?"

She breathed deeply and let out a ragged sigh. "Yes. Much worse."

"Then I know what we must do."

Hope surged inside Aurora. Maybe this problem wasn't such a big deal after all. "You know how to fix this?"

Mobius nodded. "We need to take you to the Light Realm."

Chapter Six

"So let me get this straight," Laurell said, stepping forward and placing one hand protectively on Aurora's arm. "You're both going to leave your bodies here and astral-travel to the Light Realm?"

Aurora nodded and smoothed her hands over her jeans-clad legs, willing them to stop trembling. Why was she afraid? Mobius had assured her the journey would be event free and that she'd be safe.

The group had gathered inside an upstairs bedroom at Graves Manor. Aurora stood next to her parents, watching a myriad of emotions flicker across her mother's face.

Mobius sat on the edge of the king-size bed that took up one corner of the room; it was surrounded by quartz crystals of varying shades and sizes. Earlier, Lynn, who was an expert in the magical use of crystals, had led the entire coven through a ritual charging of the crystals to add additional protection for Mobius and Aurora.

Although a protective circle already encased the property itself, Hillary, the group's acting High Priestess, had thought it a good idea to go the extra mile.

"This is the best way," Mobius said. "It's very similar to what you might call astral travel. And in fact, we have to cross through the Astral Plane to get to the Light Realm."

"And your bodies, they'll continue to function while you're gone?"

"It will be as though they are in a deep sleep. Laurell, you are worried, yes?" This from Axiom, who circled his wife's waist with one arm and tugged her close.

"It's just that I don't have a good feeling about Aurie leaving."

"Neither do I," Dawna said, stepping up behind them. The group turned to face the thirtysomething brunette, whose eyes, heavy with purple eye shadow, widened with worry. As the group's resident psychic, her take on the situation was important.

"What are you picking up?" Laurell asked.

"I'm not sure, exactly," Dawna murmured. "You're positive nothing can get in or inhabit your bodies while you're gone, right? Or prevent you from reentering them?"

Aurora's skin crawled at Dawna's words. *Get in my body?* She hadn't thought of that possibility. A vision of some other entity walking around in her flesh and speaking with her voice while she hovered outside of her body frantic for reentry made her stomach twist with nausea.

Mobius lifted his eyebrows and shook his head vehemently. "That is a common fear about out-of-body travel. I can assure you, this is not possible. The body has a way of protecting itself from such attacks. Besides, your spirit is never completely separated from your physical form. Your silver cord connects you wherever you are."

"Silver cord?" Aurora asked.

"The energetic tie between your physical and etheric body. It's always connected so you can find your way home."

Laurell's hazel eyes finally lit with understanding. "You know, I remember my astral visits years ago during the mission to bring Aurora into being. I never felt unsafe, and no one ever tried to mess with my body." She paused. "Of course, I was only making brief trips to the Astral Plane. I might have been gone maybe ten minutes."

Axiom smoothed a lock of chestnut hair from his wife's forehead and gave a reassuring smile. "My goddess, there is nothing to fear here. Aurora's journey will be just as safe as yours."

Axiom turned to Aurora then. "I only wish you had come forward about your symptoms sooner, Aurie. Perhaps I could have helped you before it required such measures as this. I do have experience with these things."

Aurora glanced quickly away from her father's penetrating gaze. Embarrassment tickled her insides. She probably should have said something to him sooner. She had considered talking to him about the problem, but had been procrastinating. She just hadn't wanted to believe she couldn't handle the situation herself.

"It would not have mattered, my friend," Mobius responded to Axiom's admonition. "The level of dark energy is so high right now, I doubt any of your techniques would have effected more than a temporary remission. In fact, the sooner we get Aurora to the Light Realm and back again, the better. We've much work to do in order to prevent the Umbrae from turning enough humans to permanently injure the gods and goddesses."

"And if that happens?" Aurora wanted to know.

A shiver of fear flickered through Mobius's big body. "If that happens, Source help us all."

Chapter Seven

North of Tampa, Florida

The cave reeked of something rancid. Rhakma had been on the Earth plane for several weeks now, but he had yet to become used to the pungent odors that assailed him at every turn.

Of all that he had dealt with in order to become acclimated to Earth—the bright lights, the harsh noises, the jumbled mess of human thoughts that reached into his mind when he didn't have his ward in place—it was the scents that overwhelmed him most. He hated the smell of humans.

The harsh, cloying perfumes and deodorants they wore to cover up their animal-like odors only made the situation worse.

He knew that if he had taken on a human body, he wouldn't be so affected by these things. The dense matter of the human form wasn't as highly attuned as his god form. But he would need the extra strength his god form provided in the days to come.

And besides, there was no longer any need to be transformed. Nilram, the current leader of the Umbrae, had perfected his techniques for allowing gods to retain their spirit forms on Earth.

It had worked well with the Balancers, the Grays cast out of the Light Realm. It was working well with him, too, although he hated having to assume some of Nilram's energy in the process. He was revolted by the idea of mixing the Umbrae's demonic matter with his own once-pure form.

His solar plexus twisted at the thought, and if he were human, he'd have been sick to his stomach. But, thanks to Nilram, he wasn't human. He was a god. A god who could survive on Earth indefinitely.

He walked farther into the cavern carved into one of the few hills that existed in this part of Florida, a state characterized by flat lands and palm trees. But, some sixty miles north of Tampa, there were small hills and chunks of wooded land with no inhabitants for miles. The Umbrae liked this area. The humidity and the dampness of the soil seemed to please them.

The cave was dank. The damp soil made squishing noises under his feet as he moved farther inside. He was greeted by blackness until he entered the thousand-square-foot room where Nilram spent much of his time when on Earth. He had no idea whether the Umbrae leader had a gender, but it was easier just to refer to Nilram as a he.

Battery-powered lanterns lit the inner chamber. The light was for the benefit of the Finders who congregated here. It certainly wasn't for him, the Grays, or the Umbrae, who could see quite easily in the dark.

Today, several Finders, three men and a woman, reclined on plastic crates turned into makeshift chairs, seemingly oblivious to the intense heat he knew they must be feeling at midday. Sweat poured out of their pores, and they stank.

Nilram stood in the center of the room at a table. As usual, Rhakma was taken aback by the appearance of his newfound ally. Nilram's form stood at least seven feet tall, his body made up of hundreds of Umbrae; he was one big mass of the squirming, scaly, putrid creatures. Somewhere near the middle of his body was a face, a hideous misshapen form containing two red eyes and a gaping mouth with razor-sharp teeth.

The worst thing about Nilram was that he stank worse than any human or Umbra Rhakma had ever encountered. Like rotten eggs times one hundred. Still, with the help of a turned Gray God, Nilram had rescued Rhakma from his exile on the Astral Plane. For that he was grateful.

Having such a powerful ally to aid in his revenge against the Divine Council, which had banished him to the Astral Plane and stripped him of his seat on the Council, would prove invaluable. For that, he would bear the stench.

"Were you able to obtain the sample I requested?" Rhakma asked.

Nilram turned at his words, and his mouth twisted into a half smile that only made the demon leader's appearance even more hideous.

"Yes. I have a hair sample from the Earth Balancer," Nilram said, his voice a ragged whisper. The thing had no vocal cords.

"Excellent. Might I ask how this was accomplished?"

"The Gray who battled her obtained it during their fight."

"Good. Then all is in order."

Nilram moved closer to him, drifting over the uneven ground as only a creature who lacked feet and moved on the air could. "How is this hair useful to us?"

"Patience. All will be made clear in time. In the meanwhile, continue your efforts to turn more humans and weaken the coven. Send more Finders."

"And if the coven hides in one of their circles?"

"Create a reason for them to leave. They cannot resist saving humans, can they?"

"What about the Earth Balancer?"

"She will not be able to help them. She will be"—he paused and gave a small, satisfied smile—"vacationing."

Chapter Eight

It's no big deal. I'm just going to leave my body. It will be here waiting when I get back. Aurora closed her eyes and took deep, steadying breaths, trying to remember the instructions Mobius had given her. After a few moments her limbs grew heavy and her breathing became slow and steady. A buzzing sound filled her ears. Her body hummed and vibrated. Then, it was as if she soared outside of herself.

She floated to the ceiling, then through it. She made certain not to turn and look back at her body. Mobius had said doing so would immediately pull her back to it.

Suddenly she was moving so quickly her vision blurred and dizziness overcame her. Scenery whirled by: clouds, blackness, and then a barren landscape of orange rocks and red sky.

She turned her head to Mobius, who stood next to her. He tugged her hand. "This is the Astral Plane. We don't want to stay here long. Umbrae are able to move freely here."

"I'm not afraid of Umbrae," she reminded him.

"No, but I would rather they did not know you were not on Earth at the moment."

She nodded her understanding, and with a swiftness that left her breathless they rose again. Moments later a bright light engulfed them. Aurora had to shield her eyes; it was painful to look into. A whooshing noise filled her ears. She squeezed Mobius's hand, reassured by his presence. An invisible force tugged and pulled her up, up. And then suddenly the noise stopped and stillness surrounded them.

She found herself lying on a solid surface that was cool beneath her fingertips. She no longer held Mobius's hand. Annoyed with herself for the sudden nervousness that washed through her at that realization, she sat up abruptly and experienced another wave of dizziness.

She blinked open her eyes. Mobius stood over her, holding out his hand. Disoriented, she took his hand gratefully, and he helped her to her feet.

Cool air tickled her skin. Not too hot. Not too cold. Perfect. The breeze held the barest slightly sweet scent, like flowers just about to bloom. All around her light shone. Not the blinding light of minutes before, but a calming, pleasant whiteness that encompassed all the space around them. They stood on a surface that glittered like sparkling crystals.

"Welcome to the Light Realm." Mobius's deep baritone broke the silence.

Aurora tucked her long hair behind her ears and tilted her head to the side. "Is this it? No angels with harps? No people dancing by in heavenly bliss?"

Mobius chuckled. "This isn't the heaven humans think of. Angels exist, yes, but they are in the Angelic Realm. Spirits of people do exist here, but they are in a different part of the Light Realm. And they are only here for brief periods of time between lives, while they experience their re-visionings and decide which Earth life to assume next. Didn't your father tell you what to expect here?"

Aurora nodded. "He told me some of this when I was a kid, but my memory is a little foggy. I always thought maybe it was sort of hard for Dad to talk about. I know he doesn't regret his decision to stay with my mom, but I think he misses the Light Realm sometimes."

Mobius sighed. "That is understandable." He smoothed the white robe he wore. When had he changed from his jeans and T-shirt?

Aurora glanced down to realize she wore a similar garment. "Hey, what's with the fancy threads?"

"You don't like the robe?"

She shrugged. "It's okay, I guess. I'd prefer something with more color, though."

"Then think it differently."

Aurora flashed a half smile. Oh, right. That part about the Light Realm she remembered. The inhabitants of Earth had not yet fully realized the power of conscious will. Everywhere else in the universe, you could literally think things into being.

She immediately envisioned her robe a bit more formfitting. And crimson colored. She loved the color red. She added some silver threading for a little bling.

"What do you think?" She motioned to her attire.

Mobius's amber gaze darkened with appreciation and roved from her head to her feet and back again. Did he linger on her ample chest? "Your robe is—attractive."

She lifted her eyebrows, but said nothing. Attractive? That's all? What had she expected? She should probably be relieved that he hadn't said anything about her need to hold him the night before.

In the light of day, she'd been embarrassed by her display of weakness. Did he know that in those brief moments when he'd held her, she'd wanted him to do a whole hell of a lot more than just put his arms around her? If he did, he wasn't letting on. Which was probably for the best. It was pointless to let herself go there. She couldn't get involved. Even if she knew he was interested. And she wasn't entirely sure of that. A few brief hints of lust in his gaze weren't enough evidence to go on.

"So, what now?" she asked, uncomfortable with the silence that had once again set in.

"It's time for you to meet some members of the Council and for you to be assessed for the taint of darkness. We must heal you."

Chapter Nine

Willow sensed Mobius's presence outside her private chambers in the Light Realm. The weather goddess set aside what she had been reading, a text etched into rose-quartz tablets, and mentally bade him enter. A moment later, he appeared at her side with the Earth Balancer in tow. Willow stood, smoothing her purple robe, not bothering to hide her surprise at their presence.

"Mobius. You have returned rather sooner than we had expected." She glanced at Aurora. The girl was attractive, with her long ebony hair, bright silver eyes, and full mouth. "And you have brought the Earth Balancer with you? I'm confused. Are you both not needed on Earth?"

Mobius nodded. "We ran into a problem. Aurora's shadow side is threatening to emerge."

Willow frowned. She strode quickly to Aurora's side and placed her hands on either side of the other woman's cheeks. Aurora started at her unexpected touch, but did not attempt to move away.

Willow peered into Aurora's eyes and scanned her auric field. Inky black shards of negative energy swirled amid the yellow, blue, and pink shades in the girl's aura. An unusual amount of dense energy. Seeds of darkness waiting to burst into life. If Aurora had remained on Earth, it would have been only a short while before she experienced a full-on assault.

"My friend, you were right to bring her here. I will arrange for her to be bathed in the Violet Fire."

Mobius nodded.

Aurora's eyebrows rose. "Violet fire?"

"Yes. But the chamber will not be ready immediately. We have been utilizing it to help heal some of the affected gods and goddesses."

"Is it working?" Mobius wondered.

"Not entirely. But it is helping to delay the progression of their weakness, which is something. Avina is looking better."

Mobius sighed. "That is good news at least."

"Fire?" Aurora asked again, this time directing her question to Mobius. Her face was etched with concern.

"I'll explain momentarily," Mobius said. Then to Willow, "Is there anything we can do in the meantime to help Aurora? I am concerned that, although it is certainly more difficult for the darkness to touch her here, the Light Realm is no longer completely immune to it."

"Given the gods' recent influx of illness, I think your concerns are warranted," Willow agreed. Then she added in an undertone that only Mobius would hear, "You should perform a harmonization with her in the meantime. You could share some of your power with her."

Willow didn't miss the way Mobius's jaw tensed at the suggestion, nor how he shifted from foot to foot with discomfort. She'd thought he would leap at the chance to share some intimacy with the girl. Though he might try to hide it, his interest in Aurora was evident to Willow. She'd known him too long and too well to be mistaken.

"Give me a moment," Mobius said to Aurora before taking Willow by the arm and leading her out of earshot.

"What is it?" Willow asked. "Surely you have thought of this yourself? It might be helpful to her."

"The thought had crossed my mind. But I promised her father I would keep my relationship with her strictly platonic."

Willow could only imagine the Gray God, whom she had once known, as a human father protecting his daughter's chastity. How strange it must be for Mobius to be forced to acquiesce to Axiom's demands. Mobius was not much used to taking orders from others. She smiled at the thought.

"This is not an amusing matter, Willow." Mobius's eyes darkened with frustration.

Willow placed one hand on his arm, soothing him with her touch. "Come, now. Harmonization is not the same as the sexual relations of humans. At least, it doesn't have to be. Many of the gods engage in it simply for the power surge it affords. You direct the way the current flows and how the session goes. Keep it—how did you put it? Oh yes, 'platonic.'"

Mobius ran one hand through his hair, and it flowed over his broad shoulders in soft waves. His brow furrowed, his agitation obvious. It was clear to Willow that he was not certain of his ability to conduct a harmonization with Aurora without the process taking on a more earthy quality. In times such as these, she was reminded of what had happened during Mobius's prior mission to Earth. His sexual relations with the mortal woman called Meri no doubt had made it difficult for him to separate the gods' form of energetic connection from the more base form practiced by humans.

She herself had once fancied experiencing harmonization with Mobius, but he would have none of it. She suspected his refusal was motivated by more than his desire to keep his relationship with her one of friendship. She believed he still yearned for the lovemaking of one particular mortal woman and even perhaps preferred it over what he could experience with a goddess of the Light Realm.

She watched him carefully now, wondering at his thoughts. His lips twisted and he glanced over his shoulder at Aurora, who watched them with interest.

Finally, Mobius spoke. "A harmonization it is, then."

Mobius showed Aurora his personal chambers with a mixture of apprehension and excitement. He wasn't certain why the thought of bringing her to his private space should make him nervous. Or why he watched her so closely, alert to every change in expression on her lovely face, every raised brow, pursed lip, and murmur of interest. She wandered from one corner of the space to the other, running her fingers over the massive amethyst slab where he spent time relaxing.

Her gaze lingered on the bookcase carved of quartz where he kept records of Council meetings, human revisionings, and other work-related documents.

He saw his chambers with new eyes, looking at the white walls, the clear, smooth, crystal floor, and wondered how it appeared to Aurora.

In her ruby red gown she stood out in the space like a bright flame in a cavern of ice.

"So, you can create anything you want here with your thoughts," she said, turning to face him.

"Yes."

"And this is the best you could do?"

Mobius frowned. "What do you mean?"

She shrugged. "I don't know. How about a throw rug or two? Or maybe some kind of artwork on the walls? Something soft to sit on?" She twirled around, hands raised as though to encompass the entire room. "I mean, really, it looks like all you do is work in here."

Mobius shifted uncomfortably. Her comment hit a little too close to home. He was not ashamed that his existence was devoted to protecting the gods of the Light Realm and humans on Earth. He was a protection god. He existed for that purpose. But something about the way Aurora said the word *work* made him think of Meri. *Meri, who showed me just how much more there could be. With her. On Earth.*

"Show me how you would make it different."

She seemed to think about this for a moment. Her full pink lips pursed and her forehead wrinkled as she glanced once more around the room.

She closed her eyes and took a deep breath. Suddenly the walls turned a warm beige color. Plush rugs in shades of plum, red, and gold appeared on the floor. An L-shaped couch with inviting, overstuffed cushions replaced the amethyst slab. And the lighting dimmed as candles appeared about the space, lending a soft glow.

Mobius started at the abrupt change. The effect was striking. Aurora sighed her pleasure at her handiwork and settled onto the couch.

"Not bad, huh? Much cozier." She grinned. He noticed an attractive crease in her left cheek when she smiled. Meri had had the same dimple. "It's pretty cool to be able to do that just by thinking of it. Too bad I can't do that on Earth."

Mobius crossed the room and took his seat next to her. "You can. It just doesn't happen as quickly. It requires prolonged focus and intent in order to achieve a particular outcome on Earth."

"The whole quantum-physics create-your-own-world thing, huh?"

"Yes. Your scientists who study such things are the closest to understanding how this works."

Silence ensued. A rare awkwardness overcame Mobius. He was not used to experiencing nervousness, but what he was about to suggest to Aurora made him uneasy. Never mind that he intended a harmonization only with the purest intent—her healing—in mind. It had been a long time since he'd harmonized with anyone.

"So, you didn't answer me. Do you like my decorating?"

"If it makes you more comfortable, then I am happy with it. But why the candlelight?"

He could see the flush on her cheeks in the glow cast by a candle on a nearby table. "I wasn't trying to get romantic, if that's what you're hinting at. It was just so bright in here, and I love candles. Especially scented ones."

As if on cue, he smelled sage and citrus. No doubt from the candles. He sensed her unease and held one hand up in surrender.

"I didn't mean to imply anything with my question."

She shifted slightly away from him. He could read the discomfort in the stiffness of her spine and the way she did not meet his gaze, but instead seemed to be focused on some unknown object over his right shoulder. This was not going as he had planned. He needed her relaxed and at ease for the harmonization to work. But how to broach the subject?

Mobius sighed. He'd never been one to mince words before. Why should he start now?

"Aurora, I believe we should attempt a harmonization." *There. I said it.* He waited for her reply.

Her forehead crinkled with confusion. "I'm not much of a singer."

He shook his head. "No. You misunderstand. A harmonization is a way for two gods to exchange energy with each other and strengthen the power of each."

She tilted her head to one side, black hair swinging and framing her face like the wings of a blackbird, making her large, wide-set eyes stand out even more in her beautiful face.

"Oh. Well, if it will help me fight my shadow side, why not? What do I have to do?" She leaned forward eagerly.

"It begins with us holding each other," he said.

She blinked. "Okay . . . And . . . ?"

He scooted close to her on the couch and pointed to his lap. "You will need to sit here, facing me."

She jerked away from him. "Get out! This is a come-on!" Her eyes narrowed with suspicion.

"I assure you, it is not. It works best if our chakras line up. We could embrace standing up if that would be more agreeable to you."

She bit her lip. A moment later, she shook her head. "No. That's silly. We should be comfortable." She stood over him, lifted one shapely leg, and planted herself in his lap. "Now what?" she asked. Did her breath catch just a little?

His thighs heated and burned where she sat, and his pulse raced. His stomach muscles tightened, and he willed himself to relax.

"Now you must lean close and place your hands on my shoulders."

She did as instructed. He circled her waist with hands that were suddenly unsteady.

Get hold of yourself, he silently commanded. His hands stopped their telltale trembling. Fortunately, Aurora hadn't seemed to notice his agitation.

"Now," he continued, "close your eyes and envision all of your chakras opening and twirling clockwise. As you do this, breathe out slowly, and I will inhale your essence. When I exhale, you breathe me in."

A light flowery scent of jasmine with a hint of something spicy drifted on the air and tickled his nose. He found her perfume more than pleasing. "The most important thing is to relax into the sensations you are feeling and not to close up when you sense my energy merging with yours."

"How will I know when we're merging?" she asked.

"You will know."

Chapter Ten

Aurora leaned into Mobius, ignoring the way her insides clenched at being so close to him. There was nothing to be nervous about. What they were doing wasn't sexual. Mobius had said the process would increase her power and help her resist the pull of her shadow side.

Then why am I so damn aware of what his body feels like beneath mine?

Hard, strong shoulders bunched beneath her fingers as Mobius shifted in his seat. His robe was smooth and soft to the touch, but also thin, so that the heat emanating from his flesh warmed her palms.

She recognized a similar heat starting at the base of her spine and slowly crawling upward through each of her chakras. Her limbs grew limp, heavy, and her head fell back in a state of utter relaxation. Next, a tingling sensation settled in, tickling her skin. *Ummmmm.* The sensations were yummy—energizing and relaxing at the same time.

An incredible expansiveness filled her. She remembered to direct and share some of that energy with Mobius. She willed the sensations toward him and immediately received a jolt of current in return.

She was melting. Turning to mush and falling into Mobius. Or was he falling into her? She could no longer tell where she began and he ended. They were one being.

Something was building inside her. The sensations changed and became more intense, spiraling up and then down through her body in waves. The pleasure was like that of a building orgasm, only fuller, deeper, encompassing her whole body, mind, and spirit.

Her breath came faster, harder, and a moan escaped from her lips. She became keenly aware of her bottom resting against Mobius, aware of the hardness of him beneath her. She found herself sliding against that bulge, suddenly aching for some kind of release.

This desire blurred with the bizarre perception that her body and Mobius's were one and the same. She dimly registered the texture of his robe beneath her forehead where it rested against his shoulder. Drawn by a force she couldn't control, she lifted her head slowly, and her mouth trailed up his neck, his cheek, and hovered over his mouth.

The energy ripped through her with a dizzying speed, making her almost desperate to reach orgasm. She sensed Mobius tensing beneath her. She tried to open her eyes, but they were heavy as lead. Instead, her mouth was pulled to his with a weight she couldn't resist.

Her lips touched his—first briefly, then, as more energy racked her frame, harder. She kissed him with a ferocity she'd never before known. She wanted to consume his mouth, and her lips and tongue roved his as more energy spiraled through her, making her press her breasts against his chest. Her nipples immediately came awake.

Mobius groaned and kissed her back. He tasted of her lips with an equal fervor. His hands crept low over her back, cupped her bottom, and pressed her harder against him.

The ache that settled between her legs seemed to fill her whole body like one giant well of need. She wanted more. She needed more. The feeling was building inside her, growing, expanding, surging through her blood and rushing from limb to limb. Just when she thought she couldn't take it anymore, that she couldn't ride the wave of desire one second longer, the most powerful orgasm she'd ever experienced exploded through her.

Surprised by the sudden, fierce sensation, she gasped and dimly noted that Mobius bucked beneath her, the length of his swollen shaft pressing at the door of her most intimate of places.

She barely had a chance to catch her breath before he abruptly lifted her off him and set her aside. The harmonization was over.

Aurora blinked and sank into the couch. She needed to catch her breath and clear her mind. That was not at all what she'd thought the harmonization would be like. Hadn't he said it wasn't sexual? Wait—he'd said his invitation wasn't a come-on. He hadn't said *anything at all* about sex. Still, he should have warned her. Her cheeks burned. She couldn't believe she'd kissed him like that. Or rubbed herself against him. *Goddess!*

"Why didn't you tell me it would be sexual?" She glared at him. She didn't like being caught off guard.

Mobius put more distance between them on the couch and ran his fingers over his face. His fiery hair was disheveled, as though his fingers had run many tracks through it. Had he done that—or had she? His mouth was swollen. She touched her own lips. Hers, too.

"A harmonization isn't normally that . . . physical," he responded. "I didn't anticipate how your mortal side would react to the energy. You interpreted it as sexual and therefore acted accordingly."

"So it's my fault?" she replied in a voice thick with sarcasm.

"It is no one's fault."

But she *was* the one who had attacked him. Why had she done so? A strange urgency had filled her, an energy so strong it could not be denied. Yet somehow she knew it to be just a distant echo of a much more powerful force. A force she had experienced with Mobius once, long ago.

She blinked. Now where had that idea come from? She hadn't even met Mobius until a few days ago.

Aurora shoved these errant thoughts from her mind. She didn't want to think about them at the moment. She also didn't want to think about how much she'd enjoyed touching and kissing Mobius. She glanced at his face, his square jaw, straight nose, large amber eyes, and those lips . . . full and soft. *He's pretty and all man at the same time. Er—all god.*

"And you had no idea I would react as I did?" She couldn't keep the accusation from her eyes. She remembered how he'd looked at her before. She might not have a lot of experience with men, but she knew when one found her attractive. Mobius definitely desired her.

Mobius's jaw clenched. "I have sworn to treat you with the utmost respect and to guard your life with my own. I would never coerce you or any woman into intimacy with me."

Aurora sighed. Shame lanced her gut. She hadn't meant to insult him. She'd just been eager to take some of the blame off herself and to assuage her embarrassment at her behavior.

"I'm sorry. I guess I was just wondering whether you might be curious about what it's like to have sex with a mortal woman." This was the truth. She had wondered about how gods reacted to such things. Her mother had explained to her that gods didn't mate as humans did. Aurora had always thought it sort of romantic that her father had never been with anyone but her mother.

Mobius swallowed. She didn't miss the way his gaze

grew distant and glazed. "I have been with a mortal woman before. I do not need to experiment."

Aurora's eyebrows lifted. "Really? So, you've been to Earth before?"

"Yes. This is not my first mission." He cleared his throat and stood, turning his back to her. "In fact, before joining the Divine Council, I had been involved in many missions in many realms."

Her curiosity was piqued. "How many different realms are there?"

"There are planes of existence all around us. Multiple universes and vortexes leading to other realms and life-times."

Her head hurt trying to wrap her brain around that. "But scientists have not been able to prove there is life on other planets."

Mobius turned back around. "I'm not referring just to planets, but to multiple levels of existence occurring in any moment in time in the same space."

The change in subject seemed to relax him. Was it just her imagination or had the brief subject of his prior mission to Earth struck a nerve? She wanted to know more about that mission, but sensed this wasn't the time to press.

"Hmmmm. Interesting. But no life on other planets, huh?"

Mobius shrugged. "Just because humans cannot see something with their mortal eyes or test it with their instruments does not mean it doesn't exist."

He sat back down beside her, the tension in his limbs seeming to wane. He peered at her face, his gaze roving over her with intense scrutiny.

"What is it?" she asked.

"The harmonization seems to have helped your situation for now. I can sense a slight retreat in your dark energies. Your aura is clearer."

She nodded. "Well, that's something."

She wished she could see auras as well as Lynn and Dawna could. Lynn, in particular, was highly adept at reading subtle energy fields. Apparently Mobius and Willow could see auras, too.

Mobius rose again and reached a hand out to her. "There is more of the Light Realm to show you. Would you like a tour?"

Was it so easy for him to brush off their heated encounter? She was still reeling from her reaction to the harmonization, to him.

He watched her, his face an emotionless mask. Apparently it was very easy for him. She sighed inwardly and took his hand.

Thumper, who at thirty-one years old really preferred to be called his given name, Evan, but couldn't seem to convince the coven members to honor that request, absently flipped the channels on the television set in the living area of Grave's Manor. Nothing on but garbage. What else was new?

He glanced at the clock. Midnight. It was his turn to keep vigil over Aurora and Mobius. It had been two days since they'd left their bodies to visit the Light Realm.

Yesterday, Laurell and Axiom had hovered around the bedroom where the two lay inert, protected by the circle of crystals surrounding them.

Evan wondered at the need for such measures. Seemed like overkill. Then again, they'd been dealing with the Umbrae and their Finders for years now. Just when they thought they knew all the Umbrae's tricks, the demons came up with a new way to wreak havoc. So, maybe the round-the-clock watch was a good idea after all.

Hillary had insisted on taking turns watching over

Aurora and Mobius. That way, everyone could get some rest. If they had let her, Laurell would have remained on watch constantly, barely getting up to go to the bathroom or eat. Hillary would have none of that, though. The fifty-something acting High Priestess of Hidden Circle Coven had an air of wisdom about her. She commanded respect. Which was probably why Fiona and Reese had left her in charge during their absence.

It was also why, when Hillary insisted Laurell and Axiom get out of the house for the evening, they'd agreed. Evan had strict orders to call if any problems arose. The two had gone to dinner and a late movie. They'd be back soon. Hillary had returned to her house to get magical supplies and clothes for a long stay at Graves Manor. Same for Lynn and Dawna.

After Lynn and Dawna had been attacked and Mobius had insisted they stick together as a group, no one had thought to argue with the god. He seemed to know what he was talking about.

Wayne, who traveled light, was snoring away in a guest room upstairs. Evan was glad to see him getting some rest. He'd been coughing and hacking a lot lately and claimed he had the cold from Hades. No doubt he was wearing himself thin. He'd been doing almost constant perimeter checks on the protection circle.

Evan wondered at Wayne's energy level. He moved like a man half his age. And he was a hell of a shot with a gun, which came in handy from time to time. Fortunately, they hadn't needed his prowess much. Elemental magic and witchcraft spells seemed to work just fine against most of their foes.

Evan stood and dropped the remote on the couch. Time to check on his charges. He climbed the stairs and entered the bedroom where the two lay. He stepped toward the bed. The quartz crystals surrounding it lit and flashed, reading his intentions. They would sense if his purpose was dark, and he would be unable to move past them.

The crystals winked out again. He leaned forward and peered at Aurora's closed lids. Her eyes moved rapidly back and forth beneath them, as if she were dreaming. Her breathing was steady and even. A glance at Mobius assured Evan the red-haired god fared equally well.

He turned to leave, and Aurora's muffled moan drifted to his ears. He spun back around. He watched her closely for a few minutes. Her chest rose, and she gasped for air. Her hands fisted, then relaxed. At the same time, Mobius's body displayed the same movements. But then, both were still again, and their chests rose and fell with even, steady breaths.

Evan blinked and lifted his wire-rimmed glasses. He rubbed his eyes and set his glasses back on his nose. He was tired, that was all. His eyes were playing tricks on him.

He glanced once more at the two on the bed, resting peaceful as babes, and headed back downstairs.

As he reached the bottom of the steps, the front door opened and Laurell and Axiom came through, wearing grim expressions.

"What is it?" Evan asked.

Axiom's jaw clenched, and his silver eyes flashed. "Have you seen the news?"

Evan shook his head.

"Dawna called my cell phone to tell us," Laurell said. "Apparently there was an attack on some local women at a shopping mall in Madison. One of them is in critical condition at the hospital."

"That's awful, but shitty stuff like that happens. Why does it have you two so out of sorts?"

"The attack wasn't of the normal sort. Not just some

thug who wanted their purses," Laurell said. "The women described the man as moving with superhuman speed, having eyes black as night, and being monstrously strong."

Evan's eyes widened as realization dawned.

Axiom's fists clenched and he said the words before Evan could. "A turned Gray."

Chapter Eleven

"Her aura is clearer. You harmonized with her?" Willow's turquoise gaze swept from the top of Aurora's head to her toes and back again.

Mobius nodded. "Yes, but the effects will likely only be temporary." Mobius glanced at Aurora, who stood near the re-visioning room, eyeing the large blank screen the gods used to view the memories and life of a human who had died. The device hovered in the air, awaiting its next use.

Aurora appeared to have fully recovered from her initial shock at the turn of their harmonization. Her face had lost its flush, the swelling of her lips had diminished, and she seemed more interested in learning about the Light Realm than about Mobius.

He, on the other hand, couldn't stop thinking about their kiss, or the way her curves had felt beneath his hands. He struggled to push these thoughts away. He had to get control of himself. That brief exchange had brought to life memories of Meri and their lovemaking. Dangerous memories best left unexplored.

"When will the Violet Fire chamber be ready?" Mobius asked Willow, focusing on the issue at hand.

Willow, who had been watching Aurora, turned back to him, her golden hair shimmering as it curled over her shoulders. "Not for a bit longer. Perhaps you can utilize this time to visit some of the gods and goddesses who have fallen ill. It would do them good to see their Director checking in on their well-being."

"Excellent suggestion," Mobius agreed. "Aurora, would you like to accompany me?"

"Sure," she said.

"Then I will show you how we travel in the Light Realm. Just by thinking of where you wish to be, you can instantaneously appear there."

"Really?" Her eyes widened.

"Yes. Right now, think that you would like to be in the Healing Quarters. I will do the same."

Aurora complied, and a second later the two teleported into the Healing Quarters, a section of the Light Realm created to keep the ailing gods and goddesses comfortable. Massive beds covered with plush white blankets were surrounded by airy gauze curtains just thick enough to provide each patient with privacy. The room smelled of relaxing lavender.

"Mobius, it's good of you to come," a soft voice called from one of the first beds he passed. Avina. Goddess of justice.

There's nothing just about her falling ill. He lifted the curtain away from her bed and stepped inside, Aurora following.

"I sensed your presence," Avina murmured. She sat upright in the bed. She wore a shimmering silver robe, but its sparkle did nothing to hide the circles under her eyes or the hollows in her cheeks. Her normally topaz-colored eyes were as black as coal, shaded by the same darkness that had tried to get hold of Aurora.

Mobius perched on the side of the bed and took her hand. "You're looking well."

Avina ran her free hand through her ebony hair. "You never were a good liar, Mobius." She gave a soft smile. "But that is what makes you such an honorable and just Director."

Mobius forced himself to return her smile, although he really felt like cursing. It was difficult to see a goddess as strong as Avina confined to a bed.

As though reading his thoughts, Avina gestured toward her bed. "Strange to see a goddess bedridden, isn't it? Did Willow explain we have to sleep now? It's our connection to the humans and the taint of the darkness on us all."

Mobius had not heard this part. Gods did not normally sleep. They didn't need to. "No, I did not know."

Avina yawned. "I'm tired much of the time. The only thing that seems to keep me going is bathing in the Violet Fire."

Before Mobius could respond, Avina seemed to notice Aurora for the first time. "Is this who I think it is? The Earth Balancer?"

Aurora stepped forward and held out her hand. "Aurora. Nice to meet you," she said.

Avina released Mobius's hand and took Aurora's in both of her own. She peered at Aurora as though inspecting every feature individually. "Beautiful. And so much strength." She sighed. "But I hear the Umbrae have tainted you as well?"

Aurora withdrew her hand and grimaced. "Not exactly," she said. Mobius was quickly learning that any reference to weakness put Aurora instantly on the defensive.

"We have the situation under control," Mobius reassured Avina.

"I've heard another rumor, Mobius," Avina said, worry flickering in her almond-shaped eyes.

"Yes?"

"That there are Balancer gods on Earth who have been turned and are working against us."

Mobius nodded. He had just informed the Council

of this development, and already the word had spread. "It is true."

Avina leaned back against her pillows. "Interestingly, the Grays in the Light Realm have not been affected as yet. Since they are the main reason we are able to keep the Umbrae away from us, I thank Source for this."

Avina's last words grew softer, more distant, and a moment later her eyes fluttered shut. The need for rest had overtaken her.

Mobius stood. "We should go."

He stepped through the curtain back into the main room. The fabric fell into place with a soft swish. Aurora stifled a yawn and rubbed her eyes. Mobius read her weariness in the slump of her shoulders.

"I want to meet some of the Grays," Aurora said. "I want to meet some of the gods and goddesses that are like my dad and like . . ." She didn't finish her sentence, but Mobius heard her unspoken words. *Like me*.

"Soon. For now, you need to rest."

Aurora shook her head. "I'm fine. And I'm tired of everyone around here gawking at me like I'm some sort of circus freak."

"They are simply reading your energy. They wish to be helpful."

Aurora shrugged. "Yeah, I know. I just get tired of all the scrutiny. My entire life, I've been different from everyone else. I guess I thought in the Light Realm, I'd fit in." The admission burst from her mouth, and then she immediately clamped her lips shut and glanced away. A pink tinge colored her cheeks.

Mobius touched her arm, suddenly understanding the importance of introducing her to the Grays. "After you rest, we will meet with some of the Grays."

She nodded and shrugged with feigned nonchalance. "No biggie."

* * *

Damn the Umbrae. Damn the turned Grays. And damn his own helplessness.

Axiom paced, his shoes scraping against the hardwood floors of the dining room of Graves Manor. Another day had passed since Aurora and Mobius had departed for the Light Realm. So far, the two seemed safe enough. But they were not the ones he was worried about.

In the past twenty-four hours, the news reports had been filled with stories of attacks on innocent humans by creatures all bystanders described in the same manner: fast, eyes black as night, viciously strong. *Grays*. But what was the common thread linking those who were attacked? Was there a common thread? And how was he going to visit all of these victims to erase the memory of the Grays from their minds? The last thing they needed was a mass panic.

"It's no coincidence they're attacking people in cities near Graves Manor," Lynn said.

"They're trying to draw us out of the protection circle," Thumper agreed, sticking his hands in his jeans pockets and joining Axiom as he paced the room.

"More likely they're trying to draw Aurora out," Dawna said, stroking one finger over the back of her familiar. The little chestnut-colored squirrel scurried from her shoulder to her lap, waited for some petting, and then scampered back to Dawna's shoulder.

Axiom stopped in his tracks and his gaze roved over the various members of the coven. He could not dispel the sense of unease that had started in his stomach the night before, when they had received the news about the first Gray attack. That same unease continued to crawl up his spine now.

"I can fight a Gray. I have the same speed and strength they do," Axiom said.

Laurell jumped from her seat and was at his side in an instant. "Uh-uh. No way. You're human. They aren't. You can be killed."

"We are all human here. The entire coven is at risk. It has not stopped us from fighting before." Axiom circled his wife's waist with one arm and offered what he hoped was a reassuring half smile. "You worry too much, my goddess."

Her eyes narrowed, and she ignored his attempt to placate her. "We can't just go charging off in search of Grays to fight. And we aren't putting anyone at risk if we can help it." She fixed Axiom with a pointed stare. "That includes you, husband."

Dawna nodded, her thick hair swinging over her shoulders. "She's right. We need a plan."

Wayne, who had been sitting in his chair quietly sipping a Jack and Coke, tilted his Stetson to the side and sighed. "I can sense where those Grays are just as easily as I pick up on the Umbrae."

Axiom's eyebrows rose in question. "Really? How?"

Wayne took another swallow of his drink before answering. "No offense, Ax, but they have the same stench."

Axiom knew Wayne was afraid that insulting the turned Grays would somehow be a slight to him as well, since he had once been a Gray God of the Light Realm. "None taken. The turned Grays no longer bear any resemblance to those of my kind."

He released his hold on Laurell and crossed the space between him and Wayne. "What exactly do you mean by *stench*?"

Wayne shrugged. "It's hard to explain. When I pick up on the Umbrae, there's a particular feelin' I get in my gut, but I also smell 'em coming. They smell like—"

"Sulfur," Laurell finished for him.

"Spoiled eggs," Dawna added. They'd all had run-ins with the Umbrae over the years. There was no mistaking the smell when one of their kind was present.

"Yeah," Wayne agreed. "Only difference is, you guys can't smell them until they're on top of you. I pick 'em up from miles away."

Axiom thought a moment. "Ever since Aurora was old enough to be able to reclaim those turned, we have been hunting Finders and the Umbrae. And we have continued to do so in the same manner."

"By going where Dawna and Wayne say the most activity is," Laurell offered.

"Yes. And I see no reason to change how we handle the Umbrae now. We cannot wipe out this threat without locating the source of it," Axiom said.

"I'm not sure I get what you're saying, Axiom," Thumper interjected. "Do you think we should take another Field Trip?"

"Yes, but we need to determine the appropriate place to focus our efforts," Axiom said. "And I think it is obvious where that place might be."

Wayne spoke up again. "Where we saw the first Gray. Tampa."

Laurell folded her arms over her chest and glared. "I have a bad feeling about this."

Axiom touched her arm. "Our goal right now is simply to find out how the Grays are being turned. If we can answer that question, perhaps we can determine a way to stop this madness."

Chapter Twelve

She dreamed again of Mobius, of simple times.

She laughed with him over breakfast, and later splashed through waves to reach him in the ocean. She was swept into his arms for a hug, a kiss. . . .

His body lay next to her, bared to her gaze, his skin hot from their recent lovemaking. He spooned her, and his fingers trailed her arm, sending shivers over her flesh.

"I love you," he whispered, and the words warmed her like rays of sunlight. "But I cannot stay."

Aurora's eyes fluttered open. It took her several moments to get her bearings. She lay in bed, surrounded by silky sheets of crimson and bronze. A bed she'd mentally created in Mobius's quarters. He'd insisted on her staying close so he could keep an eye on her.

She sat up. The dim lighting she'd created in order to facilitate rest made the space shadowy, but even shrouded in darkness, Mobius's home had an air of lightness and peace about it—the same energy present in all of the Light Realm.

Guess that's why it's called the Light Realm.

Mobius's voice, barely more than a whisper, tugged away the last remnants of her slumber. She left the bed and followed the sound to where Mobius lay on the far side of the room, his large frame draped over the couch she'd created previously. His thick mane of hair curved over his shoulders and glowed dark red in the dim lighting.

His head was tilted to the side, resting against the back of the couch, and his eyes were closed, dark lashes spiked over his cheeks, long enough to make any woman jealous. His full lips were relaxed, his breathing deep and even.

The words that came out of his mouth, however, caused her own breath to catch, and Aurora almost couldn't believe what she was hearing.

"If I were more powerful, if I were a goddess, you'd want to stay with me for always," Meri whispered against Mobius's chest as he held her tight. They lay in bed, snuggled close beneath the patchwork blanket Meri had stitched. The night breeze drifting through the worn floorboards of their cabin carried a slight chill. Meri shivered in his arms. He rubbed circles over her flesh, willing some of his warmth to her.

"You are a powerful witch, my beloved. None would argue with your abilities."

She leaned on one arm and rolled her eyes at him. "My skill in witchcraft is far from superior. I am good with herbs, and I can talk to spirits, but I am not yet well schooled in elemental magic."

He frowned. How could she not see her own strength? "You are a great healer. And you help trapped spirits make peace with their Earth lives and move on. These are important skills." He offered her a reassuring smile. "And your elemental magic is improving."

"Yes, but if I were a goddess, I could travel with you to the Light Realm." She let out a ragged breath. "Your precious Light Realm."

The last sentence came out edged with disdain. He knew she was only trying to hide her hurt, and he hated that he'd caused her pain.

"My beloved, you know I must go. Let's not waste this last night with talk of things we cannot change." He ached to hold her, kiss her, and breathe in her sweet scent. He couldn't get enough of her. He wanted to brand her into his memory so he could always think of her and their time together and embrace what moments of peace he could. For he knew that once he left her, he'd never truly experience joy again. How ironic that the mission he'd failed at so miserably had shown him the only true happiness he'd ever known.

"I know, I know. The Grays. You have to go and make things right," she murmured, burrowing down farther beneath the covers as she spoke, so that her words were muffled.

Yes. He was needed on the Council. Who knew? He might even be Divine Director one day. Then he'd truly be able to make a difference.

"Please, Meri." He pulled the covers back down to her shoulder and lifted her chin, forcing her eyes to meet his. Sorrow filled her gaze.

"Say you love me," she whispered. *"Say it again and again so that I can remember your words in the days to come and wrap them around me like a blanket."*

"Meri," Mobius whispered in a voice thick with sleep. "I love you." He shifted, and his brow furrowed in frustration. "But I cannot stay."

The hairs on the back of Aurora's neck stood. The exact same words she'd heard in her dream. Mobius was having the same dream that she'd had? Wait a minute. *Gods don't need to sleep.*

She shifted closer to him, torn. Should she wake him? Was this an indication that Mobius, too, was being affected by the taint of the Umbrae? He murmured something unintelligible and moved, sinking farther into the cushions.

A lock of hair slipped over his brow. There was something so vulnerable about Mobius asleep. It was more than knowing that normally this god wouldn't be pulled into slumber. His face was softer, sweeter.

Unable to stop herself, she reached out and pushed the hair off his forehead.

She gasped when his hand suddenly tightened over hers and his eyes popped open, his amber gaze penetrating and intense.

"What are you doing?" he demanded.

"I was trying to wake you up," she said. "You were sleeping. I thought gods didn't sleep."

Fortunately, this remark immediately took his attention away from her wayward fingers, and he dropped her hand and bolted upright.

He blinked and glanced around the room before his gaze settled back on Aurora. Confusion flickered over his face. "I can't have been sleeping."

"You sure were. You were dreaming, too."

Mobius ran his hands over his eyes. "Dreaming?" he murmured, his disbelief evident.

"About someone named Meri."

These words seemed to jolt him out of his confusion, and alarm sprang into his gaze. "I spoke of Meri?"

Aurora nodded. "Who is she?" And how was it that he'd whispered words to this unknown woman that she herself had heard in her own dream? She didn't ask him this question, though. She didn't want to admit to him that she'd been dreaming of him.

Clearly, she was attracted to him, and it was coming out in her dreams. But he didn't need to know that. And she wouldn't allow her feelings for Mobius to grow. She had no business harboring an attraction to him.

Nothing good can come from going down that road.

Mobius's eyes grew distant. "She is a woman. A woman from my prior mission to Earth."

"Tell me about the mission," she urged, her curiosity piqued.

He cleared his throat. "Perhaps another time."

Aurora's eyes narrowed. "Why do I get the feeling you're hiding something from me?" This was the second time he'd spoken of his prior mission with that pained look in his eyes. And the second time he'd failed to elaborate.

Mobius tilted his head to the side, regarding her with interest. "I will tell you more about my time on Earth when you explain why you hide your sketches away and why"—he leaned in close, his gaze boring into hers—"you have such sadness in your eyes. What is it that you want? Has your short life on Earth been so disappointing to you?"

Aurora jerked back from him as if she had been slapped. It was as if he'd reached inside her and spied her most secret thoughts.

She shifted her gaze from his. "You wouldn't understand."

He touched her hand and rubbed reassuring circles. "Try me."

She should refuse to discuss the matter further. She should distract him with idle chatter or—or even a kiss. But for some reason she wanted to tell him. He managed to pull her in and make her feel that she could confide anything to him and he wouldn't be surprised or judgmental. Like an old friend. A very sexy old friend.

She cleared her throat. "I hide the sketches because I'm afraid people will think they're silly."

"Why would they think that?"

She shrugged. "I'm supposed to spend my time kicking ass and planning my next Umbrae attack, not dabbling in art."

Mobius frowned. "People don't expect you to be nothing more than a demon-fighting machine."

"Actually, yeah, they do." It was all she'd ever been. All she knew how to do. *What I was born, conceived to do.*

"You truly believe that?"

"Yes." She bit her lip and blinked away the moisture that suddenly clouded her vision. Dammit, she would not cry. What was wrong with her? Why was she getting so emotional? She'd accepted her life purpose a long time ago. This wasn't some new realization.

"That is no way to live."

She glared at him. "What the hell do you know about living, anyway? All you do is work."

He sighed and eyed her warily, seeming to realize this was not an argument he could win. "I think you should get more rest, and I will consult with Willow to see if she can determine why I fell asleep."

"I'll go with you," Aurora offered, grateful for the abrupt change in subject.

He shook his head. "No. Rest. I will return shortly."

A moment later, he disappeared from sight in movements as quick as her own. It was a little disconcerting to be around someone who shared her powers. Her father still possessed the ability to move with godlike speed, but he didn't use his abilities unless in battle or emergency situations. The gods and goddesses in the Light Realm had no qualms about utilizing their abilities all the time.

After all, they weren't trying to fit into a world of humans.

With Mobius gone, Aurora sank back into the couch. The cushions seemed saturated with the earthy, clean scent of Mobius. *Or maybe I'm just more aware of it than I would normally be. No—don't go there.*

The laughing blue eyes and crooked smile of her ex-boyfriend Corbin flashed before her mind's eye. Those same eyes had turned hard, and the smile became a grimace of fear when Corbin had realized Aurora was not really human. She'd met him in a bookstore during one of the few private moments she'd been able to steal away from her work with the coven.

He'd treated her like a normal girl, and she'd *felt* normal for the first time in her life.

But the relationship hadn't lasted for long. Just long enough for her to be hurt badly when Corbin ran. She'd had to have her father step in and erase Corbin's memories of his time with her, lest he alert the rest of the world to the presence of the Earth Balancer. The mission was too important to be compromised.

And Aurora went back to being the girl that no one could accept for who she really was. She sat upright, and her spine stiffened. She refused to wallow in self-pity.

She was the Earth Balancer, the savior of mankind. That should be, *would* be, enough.

Celene, goddess of healing, tapped one finger against her right temple, her cerulean eyes narrowed in concentration. She examined him with such concentration that Mobius had to force himself to stay still and not squirm under the scrutiny.

He was not used to being under such close inspection from another god. Willow had enlisted Celene's assistance when she scanned Mobius's aura and found nothing to explain his earlier fall into slumber. Then she'd abruptly left the examination room, stating she had something else to attend to.

Celene pushed her curly brown hair from her face and shook her head. She let out a sigh of frustration. "I have scanned you several times and cannot find any indication that you have been afflicted by the same dark energy as the other gods."

"Have I stumped you then?" Mobius asked, not certain if he was happy or discouraged not to have a definitive answer about his situation.

A crooked smile crossed Celene's face. "Come now, Mobius. You know I do not give up so easily." Mobius returned the smile.

It was true. Celene's specialty as a goddess was healing. She could ferret out conditions and causes of illness better than any other god or goddess who specialized in the same modality. She had a tenaciousness that drove her to dig deeper and look harder.

"I know you are here with the Earth Balancer. How is she faring?"

"She is weakened by the increase in dark energy on Earth. We have scheduled her to visit the Chamber of Violet Fire," he said.

Celene's eyes narrowed with interest. "That is certainly a good idea. I think you should visit it as well. Just as a precaution." She shrugged. "You will be going back to Earth soon. Your strength should be reinforced first."

Mobius shifted with discomfort. It was not the Violet Fire that made him uneasy; it was a peaceful, calming force. However, the period after a cleansing by Violet Fire would leave him temporarily weakened, as were all who bathed in its rays. The force of the cleansing would detoxify and remove impurities from his energy field, but he didn't like the idea of even a temporary reduction in his powers.

Celene touched his arm. "You know it is the best course. And you and the Earth Balancer will both be perfectly safe during the entire process. You are in the Light Realm, after all. What could possibly harm you here?"

Mobius sighed. There must be some reason he had been overcome by sleep earlier. Perhaps a Violet Fire cleansing was in order. "Schedule me for a session as soon as possible."

Willow returned to the room then. She crossed the space to where Mobius and Celene reclined on a massive rose-quartz slab.

"The Chamber is available now for the Earth Balancer."

Celene grinned. "Wonderful. Mobius will receive his healing after her, then."

"You're sure I'm not going to be lit on fire?" Aurora asked, glancing at Mobius, who stood at her side while Willow held open the door to the Violet Fire chamber and waited for Aurora to enter. Aurora peered dubiously at the tall, cylindrical crystal chamber before her. At its base, tiny bubbles of light shifted and gleamed like diamonds.

"It is a painless process," Mobius assured her.

Aurora bit her lip and stepped toward Willow. *Might as well get it over with.* She started to enter the chamber, and Willow stopped her with one hand on her arm.

"You must disrobe first. You must be in your purest form before entering."

Heat flooded Aurora's cheeks. She glanced over her shoulder at Mobius. "Uh, privacy, please?"

Mobius blinked, and an unreadable expression crossed his face. Did he look disappointed? Embarrassed? She couldn't be sure, but discomfort seeped from his every pore. He backed out of the room, leaving her alone with Willow.

Aurora started to remove her clothes, but Willow cleared her throat and caught her attention.

"What?" Aurora asked.

"You may remove them with your mind. You have learned to do this, yes?"

Oh, right—she was in godland now. She could do everything with her mind. Not that she thought Willow would judge her, but Aurora was extremely self-conscious as she willed her clothes away and stepped gingerly into the crystal chamber. Not many had seen her naked. Her mother, a couple of the females in the coven, and her one boyfriend.

Her body type wasn't the skinny, almost-starved frame so popular on Earth. She had curves and hips and a rear end. She wasn't comfortable with her nakedness, no matter who was viewing it. Willow barely seemed to register Aurora's nudity, however. She patted her reassuringly on the shoulder and ushered her into the chamber, closing the door behind her with a swift sweep of one slender hand.

"Aurora, close your eyes and stand as still as possible. Continue to remain relaxed. Breathe slowly and deeply. You may experience sensations you've never felt before. It's nothing to fear. Just open your mind and your heart and let the fire inside you." Willow's words drifted over the air, soft as butterfly wings.

Aurora stood in the center of the chamber and felt a slight brush against her skin. Her eyes flew open, and out of nowhere straps of thin mesh appeared. They wrapped themselves around her waist, her chest, her ankles and pulled taut.

Panic surged. "What is this? Restraints?"

"Nothing to worry about," Willow called. "Just a precaution so that if you're overwhelmed by the treatment, you will not fall."

Great. She had to worry about falling? Wasn't this process supposed to be painless? A moment later, eyelids shut, fists clenched at her sides in expectation, a strange sense of calm came over her.

A low hum filled her ears, the sort of vibrational noise made by crystal singing bowls being played. The air filled with a scent she could not place. Possibly citrus and sage and something sweet. The humming grew louder until it filled the space around her and took on form. She could swear it touched her body and surrounded her.

She tried once to open her eyes, but found she couldn't make them budge. Pressure built and swelled from her feet, crawled over her legs, her midsection, her torso, neck and arms, and finally her face. Sparks of light danced and flashed in her mind's eye, her own private fireworks display. First, crimson, then burnt orange, gold, apple green, sky blue, purple, white, and always a brilliant violet glow pulsed within each of these other colors until they all blended and her vision filled with the purple hue.

Her form seemed to expand, as though she'd grown to fill the entire chamber, the room which contained it, the entire Light Realm. The universe itself. Pleasure, first subtle, then sharp, consumed her being. She cried out at the intensity of the sensations riding her skin. She vaguely registered dampness on her cheeks. Tears of joy.

Aurora swayed, imagining herself dancing with the energy that moved through her.

A moment later, the mood shifted, the hum took on a more ominous tone, and amid the pleasure, dark visions came.

Chapter Thirteen

Mobius paced outside the Chamber of Violet Fire, waiting for Aurora to finish her treatment. Why was he experiencing such agitation in his limbs? Why had the thought of seeing her naked unnerved him so? At the thought of her disrobing, his pulse had sped and his libido had spiked. A libido he had no business indulging.

Gods don't have sex. Gods don't desire mortal women. He sighed at this thought. *Not true. They desire them. They just don't act on it.* The mission to Earth that first he and then Axiom had embarked upon had been an exception to that rule. They'd assumed mortal form. The lovemaking had been part of the mission. Necessary.

He'd thought he could forget his time on Earth. That he could push it to the recesses of his memory until it faded away. The problem was, his memories were not just made of desire but of love. Love for a woman. Meri. *Aurora.*

He groaned inwardly. He had to control these foolish thoughts. He and Aurora could not be lovers. He had made his choice many Earth lifetimes ago. He would make things right by protecting Aurora, helping her and the coven prevail against the Dark, and then he would return to the Light Realm where he belonged. He did not deserve anything more than that.

A commotion inside the chamber caught his attention

and yanked him from his thoughts. Footsteps scurried. Aurora's voice cried out.

He reacted swiftly, appearing within the chamber in an instant. The Violet Fire had been turned off. The crystals at its base sat lifeless and dark. Willow knelt inside the chamber, quickly removing the harnesses from Aurora's inert form. Celene appeared from out of nowhere as though sensing something amiss. The dark-haired goddess rushed to assist Willow, with Mobius close behind.

"What happened?" he demanded as the two goddesses removed Aurora from the chamber and laid her on a nearby crystal slab.

Her lashes, black as night, were dark crescents against her pale cheeks. Her features were ashen. His chest tightened at the sight. Realizing she was still naked, he immediately clothed her in a white and silver robe, not wanting her to feel any more vulnerable when she woke than she already would. He knew enough about Aurora to realize she did not like being vulnerable. Of course, neither did he.

"The treatment was going well until the Violet Fire started to purge the taint of the Umbrae. Her shadow side was difficult to bring into balance. The shadows tried to cling," Willow explained, rubbing a moist cloth over Aurora's forehead.

Celine held her hands over Aurora's head and drifted them through the air over her body from head to toe. "The treatment was a success. It appears to have taken more out of her, however, than we had expected."

"She'll be alright?" Mobius asked, a wave of helplessness coming over him as he observed the two goddesses caring for Aurora.

As if to answer his question, Aurora began to stir. She murmured softly and rubbed one hand over her eyes. Her lids slowly lifted, and her silver gaze penetrated his own.

"What happened?" she asked.

Mobius touched her arm reassuringly. "The process overwhelmed you."

She grimaced. "That's putting it lightly." She sat up too quickly and went pale.

"Careful. Abrupt movements might make you dizzy right now," Celene warned, taking Aurora's arm to assist her.

Aurora waved the goddess's ministrations away. "I'm fine." She swept her feet to the side of the crystal slab.

It was just like Aurora to refuse help. Mobius let out the breath he didn't know he had been holding.

"I will take her back to my chambers to rest."

Willow shook her head. "I'll take her back, Mobius. It is best if you have your Violet Fire session now while the chamber is available."

Although he wanted nothing more than to stay with Aurora and keep close watch over her well-being, Mobius knew Willow was right. He'd better get his own healing tended to. Just in case.

"Very well."

Willow led Aurora out of the room while Celene stood and presented Mobius with a small smile.

"Well, Director, something I never thought I'd tell you to do . . ." Her eyes twinkled with humor.

"What might that be?"

"Disrobe."

By the time Mobius returned from his treatment, Aurora had been pacing the floor of his chambers for what seemed like hours. Her movements were jerky and brisk. Her experience in the Chamber of Violet Fire had left her disoriented. She felt raw and naked in a way she didn't like. The purging portion of the treatment had dug the most vile images of destruction and death from her, and she'd had to live them in full, horrifying color.

And part of her, some small corner of her shadow side, had liked, even reveled in, the evil urges that had engulfed her during the moments she'd been caught in the dark visions. That realization unnerved her. She glanced at her hands and realized they were shaking.

"You should be resting," Mobius said.

"I don't think I can." She crossed to the couch and sat, then pressed her hands between her knees.

He perched next to her and touched her hand. His forehead crinkled with concern. "You look unwell. You really should lie down."

She shook her head. "Uh-uh. If I close my eyes, I'm afraid I'll see them again."

"See what?"

"The evil of the Umbrae, the Finders, all the terrible acts committed by people who've been turned." She hated not being able to control the quiver in her voice. The strain of the past few weeks was starting to take a toll on her.

"You should not have those visions again. Certainly not while in the Light Realm. Not after the Violet Fire treatment," Mobius assured.

"What about when we return to Earth?"

"I do not know. The pull will be strong there. But your power is reinforced after the treatment. That should help."

She bit her lip. "If I'm supposed to be feeling more powerful, why am I so tired?"

"There's a brief period after the treatment during which you are stripped clean of all impurities and your aura is regenerating."

"Oh." Not very reassuring, but at least the weakness was a temporary disability. "Did they figure out what's wrong with you?"

"No. It is possible that I, too, have been affected by being on Earth." He paused and tilted his head to the side, studying her. "You really should rest, Aurora." His expression stern, he pointed toward the bed.

Aurora sighed. She really didn't want to close her eyes. The events of the past days had worn her nerves thin, and she didn't entirely trust that if she slept she wouldn't have horrible dreams again. Or dreams of Mobius. She didn't know which she found more disconcerting.

"Tell you what," she suggested. "I'll lie down, if you keep talking to me." She moved over to the bed and nestled amid the satin sheets.

"Talk to you about what?"

"I want to know all about your prior mission to Earth."

Was it just her, or did that request make Mobius uneasy?

The human woman beneath him writhed with pleasure. Her bloodred hair, unnaturally dyed to hold such a hue, sprawled across the tan-colored pillows of the bed. Her Cupid's bow lips parted, and she gasped as Rhakma entered her plump body again and again. Harder. Deeper. His rhythm was harsh, his thrusts cruel.

He drove himself into her with a speed and depth that only a man who was not a man, a man who was a god, could do. He had already used this woman, this Finder, in every possible way, had already committed upon her every sexually depraved act he could pull from the darkness that had taken up residence inside him since he'd merged with Nilram. But though he knew he hurt her, she loved it. She reveled in his defilement of her.

He reached out and twisted her erect nipples between his fingers.

"Oh, more," she gasped. He pulled harder, and the twin peaks of flesh turned purple. His face twisted with disgust for her. Her body reeked of sex. Of her own desire. She stank. Just as all humans stank.

He did not allow himself to feel orgasm. In his god form, a harmonization would be the closest he would get to the sexual ecstasy of humans. And he would not waste a harmonization on a human. Not that he couldn't give in and have an orgasmic release if he wanted to, but the idea held no real appeal for him. It was the act itself of defiling her that fueled him. Nothing more.

She tried hard to please him. The pathetic thing seemed so bent on his pleasure that she would do anything, present him with any part of her body for his use. Even now, as he withdrew from her, she sat up, leaned over, and tried to take his erection into her mouth. He shoved her away.

"Enough," he growled. She pouted like a petulant child. He ignored her.

Earlier, while the female slept, he'd visited the Astral Plane and made contact with his ally in the Light Realm. Something important had occurred. A vital moment in his ultimate plan to punish those in the Light Realm had come.

"Nilram!" he cried out. A moment later the air shimmered and stretched, and a clawlike hand reached out and pulled the scaly, putrid countenance of his co-conspirator through.

Nilram's red eyes, pinpoints in his writhing mass of a body, focused on him. "I do not like being summoned as if I were a servant," the thing said in its usual hoarse whisper.

Rhakma ignored Nilram's words. He did not care what Nilram liked. Instead, he smiled and said, "It is time."

Chapter Fourteen

Aurora lay on the bed, her head propped on one elbow, and waited. Mobius sat stiffly next to her, seeming to gather his thoughts. He shifted a few times and arranged his silver robe in an uncharacteristic display of nervousness. Mobius, nervous? Now her curiosity was really piqued. When the length of the silence became unbearable, she cleared her throat.

He blinked as though just realizing how long the silence had stretched on. "My mission was similar to your father's. I was to mate with a human woman and bring a being into the world that would fight the Umbrae."

"But it didn't work?"

Mobius shook his head.

"Why not?"

"The Council had the right idea in believing that we needed a being who was both god and mortal, one able to remain on Earth indefinitely and fight the Umbrae. But we did not realize that this would not be enough."

"Tell me about the child."

Mobius's amber gaze turned pensive. "Unlike you, he was not of mixed energies. He was pure light. He was—" Mobius paused. His gaze grew distant, pained. "He was beautiful. A perfect blend of Light God and mortal. But his tiny body wasn't able to fight the Umbrae. It was up to me to protect him, but I failed."

Aurora sat up and folded her hand around his. "I'm sorry."

He kept speaking as though he hadn't heard her, and his voice took on a raw, edgy tone. "It wasn't until later that we, the Council, realized the potential of the Balancers, the Gray Gods. It was then we understood that the child hadn't stood a chance. One bright spark of light against such impenetrable darkness. He would have been able to fight the darkness once he was grown, but he never made it that far. If my mission had been successful, the plan was to create more of his kind. But it was clear the Umbrae would wipe out any such children before they were strong enough to fight."

He breathed in deeply, then exhaled. "And that was my failed mission."

Aurora frowned. "What happened to the woman? The mother of the child? She was a witch, right? Like my mother?"

Mobius's jaw clenched. "She died."

"Her name was Meri?"

"Yes."

She held his hand tighter, her throat constricting as she realized just how much Mobius had lost on that mission. He had clearly loved this woman. And the child.

"You aren't a failure, Mobius. You did exactly what you were sent to do. It's not as if the Council, or you, had any idea what to expect from the mission. You tried something that didn't work, but—"

Mobius tore his hand from hers and jumped to his feet, silencing her. "A protection deity who fails to keep safe not one but two innocents is a *failure*." His eyes narrowed, and his chest heaved with barely restrained anger and frustration.

Aurora, who was not prone to weepiness or extremes of emotion, felt his hurt as though it were her own. It was as if she herself had known these two innocents who had died unjustly. Tears welled in her eyes.

She experienced momentary embarrassment at her reaction to Mobius's story, but pushed it away when she realized how he was struggling with his own emotions right then.

What a pair we are. Each of them was so used to their role as the strong, powerful one—the one who saved everyone else—that sympathy shamed her and grief shamed him. A pang of regret swept through her that she'd pressed him to talk about the mission. She'd brought up painful memories.

She stepped closer to Mobius and placed her hands on his arms. She wanted to comfort him. She didn't know how.

"Mobius," she breathed.

He watched her, his look raw and vulnerable, waiting. Something about his face just then, the expectant need in his gaze, triggered an equal need in her. She leaned closer, lifted her head, and, her heart dancing a crazed jig in her chest, pressed her lips to his.

He stood stiffly at first. Then, when she lifted her mouth ever so slightly, he let out a soft groan, wrapped his arms around her, and pulled her tight against his chest. His mouth captured hers, and he kissed her hard and deep and with a passion both unknown to Aurora and yet strangely familiar.

Her hands traveled up his arms, reveling in the hardness beneath his clothing and the muscles bunching under his skin. The feel of his lips on hers, his body against hers, made her legs weak and her flesh tingle with desire. Heat flared at the apex of her thighs and spread up her spine. Her blood rushed through her veins with dizzying speed.

Mobius's mouth moved to her ear. He pressed kisses there, then over her neck. His large hands roved her lower back, then moved down to her buttocks. He cupped them in his hands, rubbed circles over her plump behind, and pulled her hips closer to his.

His hardened shaft pulsed against her belly, and her body responded with a flood of wetness between her legs. They ended up on the bed, with her half atop him, although she had no idea how that had happened.

Her senses were filled with Mobius: his scent, clean and slightly spicy; his hair, thick and silky as she twined her fingers in it and guided his lips back to hers.

His tongue slipped between her lips and danced with hers, deepening the intimacy of the embrace. She sank into him, let her limbs and her torso relax over his as though they were merging. It felt as if they *were* merging. Like the harmonization they'd shared, only sexier, more urgent. Her breasts became heavy and weighted. Her nipples pressed against the soft robe she wore, making her even more aware of her as-yet-untouched flesh. She wanted to feel his hands on her bare skin.

Mobius shifted, his lips trailed over her throat, and his tongue teased the hollow there. Cool air brushed the skin of her legs and thighs and made the goose bumps already erupting double in number. Her robe had become twisted up around her waist. Mobius took advantage of the access. His hand closed over her thigh and stroked her softly, making her ache to have his hand move higher and touch her in a much more intimate place.

His fingers traveled ever so slowly over her waist, her stomach, making her abdominal muscles bunch and tense in anticipation. Her breath became labored and ragged as her excitement built.

Goddess, she wanted him. The couple of encounters she'd had with her ex-boyfriend had been rushed, amateurish, and had left her unfulfilled. Mobius created a need in her like nothing she'd ever experienced. His mouth claimed hers again. The kiss was hard and fierce. His fingers cupped one of her breasts. Her nipple sprang to life in his palm, and he lightly squeezed the engorged nub between thumb and forefinger. She gasped and squirmed, wanting more. Much more.

Mobius lifted his head, making ready to trail kisses elsewhere. "Mobius," she breathed. She wanted to tell him that she needed more, but the words died in her throat.

His amber gaze had turned to liquid gold. He stared at her with blazing desire. He let out a ragged breath, then sat up and moved away from her.

"What am I doing?" he murmured to himself. His hands fisted, and he rubbed them over his eyes before standing.

"What's wrong?" Aurora asked, slowly rising to a sitting position and straightening her robe. She touched her fingers to her lips. They felt swollen. They tingled for more kisses.

"I should not have started this."

She frowned. "You didn't start it. I did."

"Be that as it may, I should have ended it quickly. Gods don't have sex."

His abrupt withdrawal from her stung. Embarrassed, she reacted without thinking. "Don't, or can't?"

Mobius raised his eyebrows at the insinuation. "Are you suggesting I cannot perform?"

She recalled the hardness of his erection pressed against her belly as they lay on the bed locked in hot kisses and frank desire. It was a ridiculous insult. And he knew it just as well as she did.

She sighed. "I'm sorry. That was stupid." She brushed her mussed hair from her eyes. "So, why don't you have sex?"

"It is a waste of our energy. We harmonize instead to build energy, share it, and strengthen our power.

Humans are entirely too quick to share their bodies with each other. They don't realize how they merge in the act of lovemaking. Each lover leaves an imprint in one's aura. Sometimes, that is not a good thing."

"Huh. I never thought of it like that before."

"Most don't."

"Well, I'm still glad I'm half-human."

"Oh?"

"Yeah. Because I don't have to avoid sex. I mean, it's clear you gods experience desire. It must be horribly frustrating to have to stifle your passion."

Mobius clearly had no idea how to respond to this. He simply stared at her for a moment, then turned toward the couch.

"You really should rest now. I will stay nearby and keep an eye on you. Just to be sure you do not experience any other ill effects from the Violet Fire treatment."

Realizing she had been dismissed, Aurora settled back into the plump cushions of the bed. She didn't voice the thought that popped into her mind: obviously, Mobius had given in to passion once. Then again, he'd probably say that was different. It was for his mission.

She wasn't sure why she should care if he didn't want to break his no-sex-for-gods vow for her. Why should he? *I'm just part of another mission for him. And not one that includes making a baby. That's a good thing, isn't it?*

Axiom drove north on Interstate 75, heading toward what, he did not know. Wayne sat next to him, and Thumper occupied the backseat. Humidity hung on the night air. It was exceedingly warm, even at ten o'clock in the evening. A waxing moon peeked from beneath the few clouds in the otherwise-clear sky, and the scent of orange blossoms wafted through the open car windows.

The tranquil scenery and peaceful ambience belied their purpose that night. They were out for much more than just an evening drive.

They'd been driving for hours, heading wherever Wayne picked up the stench of the Umbrae. A couple of times, he had thought he had a solid fix on them, but then the connection had been broken like a severed telephone cord, ending the metaphysical conversation. Axiom hoped they were on track now.

"We're going the right way," Wayne murmured as though reading Axiom's thoughts. "I can feel 'em real strong here. Turn right off the next exit."

Axiom obeyed, and soon they were headed east.

Florida evergreens and poplar trees lined the road, the only things to be seen for miles. The road narrowed to two lanes, twisty and full of curves, then gave way to steep hills. Axiom was surprised to see something other than completely flat terrain. As they reached the crest of another hill, Wayne's spine stiffened.

"Stop. Stop here. Pull over," Wayne said, his raspy voice full of excitement. Axiom pulled to the side of the road and put the car in park, then turned off the ignition.

"What is it?"

"Umbrae. And the thicker energy of some Grays."

"Any idea how many?" Thumper asked from the backseat.

"A number of Umbrae. A handful of Grays."

"Since my vision at night is just as good as during the day, I will lead. You two will stay behind me, with Wayne directing us where to go," Axiom instructed. Neither man argued. They would be making the rest of their journey on foot, into the woods, in the dark. The use of their flashlights would have to be kept to a minimum in order to avoid detection.

Minutes later, the three trudged over the uneven and

muddy terrain. The smell of orange blossoms had been left behind. Now only the sharply distinct scent of the evergreen trees permeated the air. Axiom was glad he had worn tennis shoes with his shorts and T-shirt. He wondered how Wayne was faring in his ever-present cowboy boots.

Axiom scanned the area, sensing no movement other than the occasional bird or tiny woodland creature. His keen eyesight allowed him to survey the woods around him with surprising accuracy. Nothing.

"Go left, Ax," Wayne said.

The three turned and moved with slow, precise steps. Only their breathing and the swish and slurp of their shoes in the mud marred the silence. When it seemed they had been walking forever, Axiom stopped in his tracks. He was aware of a new odor. Sulfur. Umbrae.

He glanced at the other two. By the looks on their faces, they had noticed the scent too.

"I'm picking them up straight ahead, Ax," Wayne whispered. "We'll follow ya." Thumper nodded his agreement.

For a moment, Axiom wondered if he had been too hasty in his decision to seek out the Umbrae's lair. Although this particular trip was solely to pinpoint the location of the turned Grays, he knew that if he and his companions were discovered, they would be drawn into a battle. And although he had faith in their ability to defend themselves, their chance of defeating an entire army of Umbrae and Grays without Aurora and Mobius and the rest of the coven to assist was not good.

Thumper must have been thinking the same thing, because he grabbed Axiom's arm, and his mouth twisted with concern. "We know where to find them now. Maybe we should wait and come back with the whole group later." Fear tinged his whisper.

Axiom thought about this suggestion for a moment,

then shook his head. "We need to know how the Grays are being turned and just how many of them there are. Since I am able to move more quickly, perhaps you two should wait here."

Wayne let out a snort. "No way, Ax. You may need us."

"He's right," Thumper agreed.

Axiom turned at this, and continued forward. He followed the rotten-egg odor to an opening in the trees. Ahead, the terrain changed, shifting upward. As he moved closer, Axiom realized a hill sat in front of him. At first it appeared they had reached a dead end. Then, he looked deeper. A hole in the side of the hill had been covered by some type of magical illusion. Any passerby who happened upon this hill would not see the entrance.

He stepped closer, held his hand up to the entrance, and his palm buzzed with an electrical current. Witchcraft had not built this facade. But what? There was something familiar about the feel of the magic.

He walked through the portal with Wayne and Thumper close on his heels. Up ahead, dim light shone and flickered over the cave walls. Torches of some kind. The three approached with stealth. By the time they rounded the corner, they could hear voices. Lots of voices. Axiom pressed himself against the wall. The other two followed suit until shadows hid them.

Axiom stood closest to the opening of the main chamber. He craned his neck slightly to gain a better view. At least five Finders stood, all clothed in black pants, black shirts, black shoes. He wondered how they stood the heat in the place. No breeze moved inside the cave, and sweat trickled down Axiom's forehead and over his chest.

In the other corner congregated several beings he recognized as Gray Gods. Three males. One female. All with the distinct silver eyes and strong bodies of Balancers. Unfortunately, they were no longer contributing to any type of balance between the forces of good and evil.

No, they had clearly been consumed by the dark; all that was good in them had long since departed. He could read the truth in their energy fields, which were thick with the taint of the Umbrae.

The distinct odor of the Umbrae pierced the air, so strong he expected to see a number of them mixing with the Finders and the Grays. As soon as he had this thought, the air shimmered near the Grays. A space seemed to open in the air and two scaly, greenish gray hands reached through, long nails trailing sparks. Out stepped the most disgusting Umbra Axiom had ever laid eyes upon.

Chapter Fifteen

The thing stood at least seven feet tall, its body composed of a squirming mass of smaller Umbrae. The stench coming from the thing was almost unbearable.

"Bring me a fresh Gray," the thing commanded. Two of the Grays nodded and disappeared farther into the recesses of the cave. They returned moments later with an inert blonde-haired female Gray. They rolled her in on a wheeled metal table. The mammoth Umbra hovered over her, red beady eyes located in the center of its chest, mouth with razor-sharp teeth open and twisted in a sneer. He bent and sniffed her.

"Hmmm, she has been kept nicely. It is time to reanimate her and make her one of us." The thing's voice came out a hoarse, ragged whisper.

The other Grays and the few Finders in the room all murmured their encouragement.

Reanimate? The Umbrae had figured out how to keep the Grays alive while suspending them in an inactive state. Obviously, they had not figured out how to reanimate them and turn them until recently, or they would have used the knowledge against the coven and Aurora long ago. For that matter, they would have utilized the turned Grays against mankind centuries ago. Back when the first Grays had been banished.

What had changed to make this possible now?

The Umbra motioned to one of the other Grays.

"Come, it is time." The Gray God, a black-haired male of broad shoulders and impressive height, approached the table. He sprang atop it with the telltale speed of a god. He leaned forward, fit his form snugly over the unconscious female, and closed his eyes.

His body began to undulate and grind against the female. Their individual aura fields flared and expanded, then merged as shades of crimson, orange, yellow, blue, and more swirled between them.

A harmonization. One Gray was reanimating the other with a harmonization. Sharing his power, his life force.

Rage built inside of Axiom. His stomach burned with anger. Who had reanimated the first Gray? It had to have been a god. A god was helping the Umbrae.

A few minutes later, the male lifted himself from the female. He departed the table, and the woman sat up.

"Where am I? What's happening?" she asked, rubbing her hands over her eyes.

The Gray who had reanimated her placed one hand on her shoulder. "You are on Earth. You were banished here centuries ago from the Light Realm."

She frowned. "I don't understand. How is it that I still exist?"

"The Umbrae."

For the first time, the woman noticed the disgusting creature standing to the side watching the exchange. Her body tensed, and her fists clenched as she readied for battle. The dark-haired Gray held one hand up in protest.

"No, sister. This is Nilram. He is the one who leads the Umbrae. The Umbrae saved us. They are no longer our enemies."

The female's eyes widened. "How is that possible?"

"When those in the Light Realm would have left us here to perish, the Umbrae took us in. They kept us safe until such time as we could thrive again. They gave us new life."

The Gray Goddess's face twisted as the male's words sank in. "Were all of us saved, then? Many friends were cast out alongside me."

The male shook his head, sorrow etched into the turn of his mouth and the lines in his brow. "No. They saved as many of us as they could, but many more are gone."

The female's eyes filled with tears. Axiom's throat constricted, and he experienced her anguish as his own. The injustice of what had occurred to the cast-out Grays stung as though the tragedy had happened yesterday. The male Gray leaned close to the female as though he knew his next words would upset her still more.

"There are only two ways for you to continue to live. You can assume human form, but your powers will be muted and you will die in three months' time when your temporary body deteriorates in the atmosphere of this place. . . ."

"Or?" she prodded.

"Or, you can merge with the Umbrae and live here as a god indefinitely."

The goddess recoiled and jumped from the table. She shot a quick glance at the Umbra standing next to her, disgust evident on her beautiful face. "There must be another way."

"There is not."

"I do not think I can do it."

"You can. Many of us have."

The other Grays in the cave stepped forward to offer their encouragement. After another minute or two of convincing, the female nodded her acquiescence, and then Nilram cloaked her smaller frame in his own, engulfing her with his massive presence.

Nilram groaned and twitched, and the goddess in his dark embrace caught her breath and cried out in pain. Her head fell backward. Her eyes rolled shut. Her body shifted and jerked for several minutes, then went still.

The other Grays caught her beneath the arms as Nilram released her. She coughed and sputtered a few times, then shook her head as though to clear it and stood straight.

Her eyes no longer held a hint of silver light. Instead, blackness saturated them. The sign of the turned.

"It is done," Nilram said.

"What is next?" one of the Finders asked. "What can I do to assist you?"

"Ah," Nilram murmured, his misshapen mouth even more distorted as he attempted a smile. "Rhakma has already seen to the next step."

"Tell us, Master," the Finder pleaded.

"You would not understand," one of the Grays responded. He appeared annoyed at the Finder's questions. "Finders do not know of the silver cords. Only gods do."

Axiom's entire body went as numb as if he had been doused with ice-cold water. He turned to Wayne and motioned toward the entrance to the cave. It seemed eons before the three of them made their way just as slowly and quietly out of the cave as they had entered it.

Once they were safely out of earshot of anyone in the cave, Thumper took in Axiom's face and said, "Something's wrong. Even more wrong than that really, really gross thing they called Nilram."

"What's up, Ax?" Wayne asked.

"Let us return to the car. I need to contact Laurell. The Umbrae are going after the silver cords."

Realization dawned on Thumper's face. "Fuck. I thought that's what that thing said. But how would they know how to do it?"

Axiom's jaw clenched, and though he attempted to restrain his fury, he knew it was evident in his every movement. "Rhakma."

Chapter Sixteen

Aurora woke to find Mobius gone from his chambers. She clothed herself with a formfitting gown of soft burgundy, choosing silk for the material. She added spaghetti straps and purposely created a skirt that stopped above her knees so that her legs would show. She took her hair down, letting it sweep over her shoulders in a shining cascade, and then stained her lips ruby red.

Why was she getting all gussied up? *I'm just practicing my manifesting abilities. I'm not really trying to impress anyone.*

Self-delusion, she decided, could be a good thing. *Especially if it keeps me from making a fool of myself over Mobius.* She had no business harboring a romantic interest in him anyway. But she wanted him. And why couldn't she have a physical relationship with an attractive male? Love was out of the question, but sex was another thing altogether. And Goddess knew it was high time she experienced real passion.

Mobius had made clear his intentions toward her, or lack thereof. She would have to accept his decision. But she could also make him regret it.

Besides, something told her there was more to his rejection than just not wanting to step outside the lines of expected god behavior. Maybe her time spent honing her intuition with Dawna was finally starting to pay off.

Aurora waited a few more minutes for Mobius to return. When he didn't, she decided to go exploring. He'd promised to show her more of the Light Realm. Now that she'd completed the Violet Fire treatment, the two of them would no doubt return to Earth soon.

Ever since she'd heard about the Light Realm, she'd wanted to visit it and learn the secrets of the gods. And she'd longed to meet others like herself. Balancer gods.

It's now or never.

She wandered out of Mobius's chambers and found herself in a hallway. Everything was white here, devoid of color. So far, each room she'd visited had been the same, save for Mobius's chambers. And that was only because she'd decided to do some decorating. As she continued down the hall, she came to an intersection. Which way to go? She shrugged and turned right.

Numerous doors lined this hallway. She picked one on the left and glanced around, expecting someone to stop her from entering. Her heart sped. She felt a bit like a naughty kid as she stepped through the doorway into another nondescript room. Although the room itself didn't have much to offer, in the center of it was something very interesting.

Silence surrounded her. It was so darn quiet in the Light Realm. Although she enjoyed peace and quiet as much as the next person, she thought the silence would become oppressive eventually.

How did anyone get anything done with all that quiet? Aurora was used to the bustle around Graves Manor. At any given time various members of the coven were about, spending time with each other, joking, laughing, and enjoying themselves. And when Aurora wasn't there with them, she was off on a Field Trip with her colleagues. Not much time for boring solitude.

A pool of liquid, silver and translucent, swirled several feet above the floor. Vaporous clouds twisted through the base, forming a whirlpool. Aurora stepped closer and peered over the edge of the mass.

"I see you have found the peering pool," a deep voice said from behind her.

Startled, she twirled around. A tall, broad-shouldered man stood in the doorway. He had thick blond hair and deep-set eyes. He crossed the room, his royal blue robe swaying with his movements.

"Who are you?" she asked.

He presented her with a crooked smile. "Reetori."

Up close, she noted his silver eyes. "You're a Balancer," she murmured.

He nodded.

"I hoped I'd get to meet a Balancer or two while I was here."

"Ah, yes. Well, I hope I live up to your expectations, Aurora," Reetori said.

"You know me?"

"We all know of the Earth Balancer."

Embarrassed at her notoriety, she turned back to the pool. "Tell me, how does this thing work?"

"The peering pool is how we view Earth. You think of whom or what you would like to see, and the pool will show you what is happening right at this moment."

"So you can see anyone, at any time, whenever you wish?"

Reetori shook his head. "Not exactly. After a viewing, it takes time for the pool to recharge. Would you like to try it?"

"Can I?"

"Of course. Just gaze into the pool and think about the person or thing you wish to see right now."

She did as instructed and wondered what her mother was up to at the moment. The cloudy matter in the pool parted, and a scene presented itself. Her mother stood in the kitchen of Graves Manor, peeling potatoes and singing to herself. A classic. "What's Love Got to Do with It?" Tina Turner. Her mother's voice left something to be desired. She really couldn't carry a tune. Aurora smiled.

The phone next to Laurell rang. Laurell dried her hands and picked it up.

"Hey, handsome," she said into the phone. It had to be Axiom on the other end of the line. Whatever Axiom said, though, made Laurell's face go pale and her eyes widen.

"Oh my Goddess. Hillary is with them now. I'll go check right away. Get home fast."

She hung up the phone and made a dash for the stairs. Aurora's heartbeat sped. Someone was in danger. Who? Her mother reached the top of the stairs and turned right. *Oh no. Please no.* A moment later, Laurell reached for the door handle of the room where Aurora's and Mobius's bodies lay.

At that same moment, Aurora's shoulder began to burn, the tattoo firing up its warning. *Danger. The Gray.* She sensed him move close behind her.

She twirled around, fists raised, and landed a blow on Reetori's chin that sent him sailing across the room. He didn't stay down long, though. He was up and on her in seconds.

His arm arched, and he jabbed a fist into her side that sent her sprawling on her back, momentarily stunned. Reetori stood over her. His silver eyes turned to onyx.

"I think that is enough for our lesson today, don't you, Earth Balancer?"

"What the hell are you doing?" she gasped, not bothering to hide her confusion. Or her anger. She pulled herself into a sitting position and stood slowly. Why did her ribs hurt so terribly where he'd punched her? It was a solid blow, but she shouldn't be experiencing the pain so acutely.

"I am putting an end to something that should never have begun."

Her eyes narrowed. "You mean me?"

"Of course I mean you."

Aurora shook her head. She failed to see his logic. "I'm one of you. A Gray. Are you planning to do yourself in, too?"

She took a few steps backward, keeping her distance from him.

"No, you are half-mortal." He sighed. "An abomination, really. Mixing gods with humans."

Aurora lifted her chin in defiance, but the insult stung. All her life she'd been different from everyone else. She'd hoped to feel at home in the Light Realm. Especially with the other Grays. *But I don't fit in here any more than I do on Earth.*

Her next words came out before she could think them through. "Strange. Isn't that what the Light Gods originally called you Grays? An abomination? Right before they cast you out of the Light Realm to die on Earth?"

His expression became wild, and his mouth lifted in a snarl. Nope. Definitely wasn't a good idea to bait him. He came at her hard, and she dove to the right, narrowly avoiding his attack. She wasn't moving as quickly as usual. What was wrong with her? Then she remembered. Mobius had mentioned they would be weakened for a while after the Violet Fire cleansing.

Shit. She had to get out of this room and away from this Gray gone wild. She wouldn't be able to fight him without her full powers. Clearly, he wasn't one of the good guys anymore.

She scrambled toward the door, her slipper-clad feet sliding on the quartz crystal floor. She immediately willed some high-tread Nikes onto her feet.

She made it to the door, but before she could step through, massive hands grabbed her around the waist and hauled her to the far side of the room. Reetori slammed her to the floor, knocking the air from her lungs, and climbed atop her, pressing his huge frame against her body.

"Hmmmm," he murmured, his gaze sweeping her from head to toe. "You are an attractive specimen. I will give you that. I wonder if I should harmonize with you before I kill you."

He held her around the throat and his other hand cupped one of her breasts so hard she winced. He pressed his groin deep into hers in an unmistakable threat. Panic surged.

"Or maybe you would prefer I take you as humans do?"

Chapter Seventeen

"You will return to Earth soon?" Willow asked. She sat across from Mobius on a rose-quartz crystal slab in her private quarters.

Mobius nodded. "I must. Although I'm still perplexed by my need to sleep while I've been here. I hope it is not indicative of the worsening conditions on Earth."

Willow sighed. "Of course that's what it is, Mobius. Other gods are being affected—why not you? But try not to be alarmed. It's possible it was a onetime occurrence. A symptom alleviated by your treatment."

"I am sure you are right."

Willow's gaze pierced his as though she was trying to read his mind. She shifted with obvious discomfort. Mobius sensed a change in topic he would not much like.

"What are you going to do about the girl?"

"What girl?"

"Don't be coy with me. Aurora."

"I am going to protect her and the coven and help them destroy this new threat on Earth."

"What are you going to do about your feelings for her? I have seen the way you look at her. You are enamored."

No. He did not like the turn of conversation at all. *Why can't Willow leave this subject alone?*

"It makes no difference what I do or do not feel for her. I have no intention of forming any bond with her beyond friendship."

Liar. You want much more from Aurora. He pushed this thought aside. It mattered little what he wanted.

"You think she's Meri," Willow murmured.

Mobius's jaw clenched. "I *know* she's Meri."

Willow's brows rose above her beautiful lavender eyes. "What if you are wrong?"

Mobius rose to his feet, his limbs restless with agitation. "Let us go now to the Hall of Records and prove this matter once and for all."

Willow shook her head. "You know you cannot. No god is allowed to view the Akashic records of those humans he was personally involved with. It's the same reason you weren't allowed to be part of Meri's re-visioning. Why are you so convinced Aurora is Meri?"

"I just know it to be true. When I saw her from the Light Realm, I saw Meri's soul in her eyes. And when I met her in the flesh, I—I felt the connection with my whole being." Mobius paused, gathering his thoughts. "There are some things the heart simply knows."

Willow strode toward him, reached his side, and offered him a soothing hand on his shoulder. "My friend, that is my concern. If it is your heart guiding you in this mission, it could prove your downfall and the downfall of the Council. You must stay focused. You cannot afford to be sidetracked."

Mobius tugged away from her. He knew she was right, but her words stung. He was a god. He could control his heart, his emotions, certainly his libido.

"It's not too late to send someone else in your stead," Willow offered.

The very thought made Mobius's insides twist. "No. No one else. I will see this mission through."

Willow's full pink lips pursed. She peered at him thoughtfully, her gaze focused on the space surrounding his head.

Mobius's own eyes narrowed. "You're reading my aura."

She tilted her head to one side. "So?"

"So, why do I get the distinct impression you're questioning my motives?"

"Because right now your aura is sparking with a determination that has nothing to do with aiding the Council and everything to do with your very human feelings for one half-mortal woman."

Before he could respond, Aurora's voice, frantic and full of fear, broke into his mind. *Mobius, help me. He's trying to kill me.*

His breath caught. *Where are you?*

The peering pool.

"What is it?" Willow grabbed his shoulder, her face filled with concern.

"Aurora is in danger. Come with me. And bring restraints."

Mobius and Willow reached the peering pool in mere moments. What they found there filled Mobius with a rage such as he'd never known.

A Gray God sat astride Aurora. He had one hand around her throat and the other on her thigh. Her gown had been ripped up the side and the Gray was rubbing himself against her in a lewd manner.

Mobius threw himself against the Gray. He locked one arm around the Gray's neck and tore him off of Aurora. The Gray fought him, twisted out of his grip, and backed away.

How easily the Gray had been able to escape him. *My full powers aren't back yet,* Mobius thought. He growled in frustration and leapt toward the Gray again, who bared his teeth and grinned with demented glee.

"You can't fight me, Director. Your powers are weak," he taunted.

"A temporary situation, I can assure you," Mobius bit out.

"Mine, however, are in tip-top shape," Willow said, coming up behind Reetori, her expression hard as steel. Before Reetori even realized her intention, she'd grabbed his arms, pulled them behind his back, and slapped restraints on his wrists.

He roared and twisted to face her, but not before she'd hooked the restraints to the collar she'd placed around his neck. With a wave of her hand, the device flared to life in a flash of light, and Reetori was paralyzed. He stood stock-still, the veins popping in his neck, his gaze murderous.

Willow circled the Gray, inspecting him. "He's been infected."

"It's more than that," Aurora said from the far side of the room. Mobius rushed to her side and helped her to her feet.

"Are you alright? Did he hurt you?" Mobius's jaw tensed, and a new rage built at the thought of the Gray putting his hands on Aurora's intimate places. She was his. No one should touch her but him. At that moment, he didn't care that he had no right to feel so possessive of her.

"No, no, you got here in time. I'm okay," she assured him. Her eyes narrowed. "How did you know I was in trouble?"

"You telepathed me."

"I did?"

"Did you not?"

"I—I merely thought of you," she murmured, confusion flickering across her lovely features.

"That is all it takes here. Gods often use telepathy to communicate."

"I didn't know," she said. "Cool."

He smiled and touched her face. "You really are alright."

She nodded and he instinctively pulled her against

him and wrapped his arms around her. She rested her head against his chest. He sighed his pleasure. She was well.

"What did you mean?" Willow asked Aurora, crossing the room to where the two stood.

"Huh?" Aurora blinked and lifted her head.

"You said it was more than that. What did you mean?" Willow pressed.

"The Gray. He showed me how to look in the peering pool and he . . . he tried to stop me from seeing something that was happening to us—to me and Mobius."

Willow's brow knit. "To you and Mobius?"

"I think our bodies back on Earth may be in danger. Reetori must be connected somehow."

Mobius glanced at Willow, and he could tell by the look on her face she was thinking the same thing as he. "Interrogate him. I will make a visit to the Astral Plane."

"Why the Astral Plane?" Aurora asked.

"It is the only place the Umbrae could have accessed the silver cords."

Aurora's eyes widened. "You think our cords are damaged? I thought that couldn't happen."

Mobius and Willow exchanged glances. "Only a god would know how to find the imprints of our cords."

Aurora glanced at Reetori, who struggled against his magical bonds. "Reetori?"

"No. Imprint locations are known only to members of the Council," Willow said.

Mobius's expression turned grim. "A Council member aiding the Umbrae?"

Willow's jaw set and she escorted Reetori away to be questioned.

* * *

Aurora paced Mobius's chambers, waiting for the flame-haired god's return. It seemed she was doing a lot of this lately—pacing Mobius's quarters while she waited for him to come back to her. She frowned.

Willow and a couple other members of the Council had gone to interrogate Reetori. She felt helpless—something she didn't like much. She was used to being the powerful one, the one to take control and see things done. Playing the role of protected female grated against her nerves.

She had just given up wearing a pointless trail across the floor and sunk into the couch, when she experienced a bizarre popping sensation in her midsection. A moment later, nausea overwhelmed her, and she had to lean back into the cushions to alleviate a wave of vertigo.

Her entire body began to shake. She placed trembling hands at her sides and pushed, trying to sit up. It was no use. Her body wouldn't budge.

Something's wrong with me. Something is very wrong.

Laurell and Fiona stood over the bed where Aurora's and Mobius's lifeless bodies lay. Laurell watched in horror as first Aurora's, then Mobius's body tensed and all their muscles clenched. Then they relaxed again, but their breathing became labored. They sucked in deep, harsh, fast breaths over and over again.

Laurell stepped inside the crystal circle and pressed a damp cloth to Aurora's forehead. On the opposite side of the bed, Hillary did the same for Mobius.

"What's happening to them?" Laurell murmured.

Hillary's warm brown eyes narrowed with worry. "I suspect it's what Axiom said. Someone's been messing with their silver cords."

"Can this kill them?" Laurell asked.

Hillary sighed. "Let's not go there. We'll figure out some way to help them."

Tears pricked Laurell's eyes as she watched her daughter's ragged breathing. "I hope you're right, Hill."

Chapter Eighteen

Some protection deity I am turning out to be.

Mobius made his way to the Astral Plane and back, then conducted an emergency meeting with the Council to share his findings. By the time he had done this and returned to his quarters, he found Aurora in a near-panicked state.

She lay on the couch, not moving. For the second time in the space of mere hours, worry over Aurora's well-being racked Mobius and filled him with a sense of failure. "Aurora, what is wrong?"

Her face, normally a creamy shade of petal pink, seemed to grow whiter by the moment. Her usually luscious red lips held little more color than the skin surrounding them.

"I don't know," she finally managed to get out. "I had this terrible pain in my middle and then I felt so weak. I had to lie down."

He sat beside her and ran his hands over her face and her belly, frantic to read her energy field. It was as he'd thought. "You're reacting to being separated from your silver cord. My visit to the Astral Plane confirmed that the cords have been severed. In a little while, your goddess half will take over and you will feel well again," he reassured her.

"Well enough to return home?"

He gritted his teeth, frustrated with the knowledge

that neither of them would be returning to Earth anytime soon. "No. Without the silver cords to guide us
back to our bodies, we cannot return."

At this news, she sat up abruptly. "What? Are you
saying I'm trapped in the Light Realm forever?"

He could sense her anxiety, which threatened to turn
to hysteria. He touched her face, hoping to soothe her.
"Not forever. Just until we find a solution."

"How do you know we'll find a solution?" She raised
her eyebrows with skepticism. "How can you be sure?"

"Because we in the Light Realm always find a solution."

Aurora groaned. "The old 'good conquers evil' thing,
huh?" She buried her face in her hands. "I hope it's really that simple." Her words came out muffled.

He trailed one hand over her spine, rubbing her back
in what he hoped was a reassuring manner. Her body
started to tremble, and she let out a soft little sob.
Another sob followed. Mobius's stomach clenched, and
he lifted her head, though she fought him at first, reluc-
tant to share her private pain.

"What is it? What can I do?"

She wiped at her eyes, her frustration at her outburst
clear. "Nothing. I shouldn't be crying. I'm not normally
a weepy person. It's just, so much has happened today,
and I think it's taking its toll on me."

Mobius wanted nothing more than to banish her sorrow and dispel any anguish that tried taking hold of her.
Instinctively, he pulled her into his arms and held her
fast, one arm around her shoulders, the other stroking
her silky hair. She struggled against him for a moment,
but quickly relented, allowing herself to be held. Hot
tears fell through the V-neck of his robe and seared his
chest.

"I can't seem to stop crying," she muttered.

"This is nothing to be ashamed of," he assured her.

After going through the Violet Fire, being attacked by the Gray, and suffering through the trauma of losing her silver cord, she had every right to be upset. She had so much pride. So much of her identity was wrapped up in being powerful and indestructible. Meri had been the same way. Only, she'd longed to be as powerful as a god. She'd never felt worthy of the mission, despite her prowess with witchcraft.

"I hate this. I hate feeling so out of control," Aurora said, her voice clearer now, less tearful. She hiccupped a few times and sniffled, then raised her head.

Mobius pushed her tangled hair from her face and peered into her luminous slate-colored eyes. Even with her tearstained cheeks and her reddened nose, she was breathtaking. She reminded him of all the beautiful dark goddesses he'd had the pleasure of crossing paths with at one time or another—Morrigan, Cerridwen, Sekhmet.

She was an intoxicating creature, this one. The courage and power of a goddess and the fragility and tenderness of a mortal. Perfect in every way. *Ah Meri, you've become everything you ever hoped to be.*

"You do not have to play the role of the powerful Earth Balancer with me. I do not expect you to be infallible. I do not expect you to be anyone but who you are."

The way she looked at him then, with a mixture of gratitude and desire, made his insides quiver like a warrior off to his first battle.

"All these things you don't expect of me . . . What *do* you expect of me, Mobius?" Her words came out breathy and laced with an unmistakable invitation.

He had no answer for her. It didn't seem she really wanted one. Her hand reached out and splayed across his chest, stroked the smooth skin there, then touched the pulse in his neck that now beat erratically.

His gaze went to her lips. Her tongue peeked out and

left them wet and shiny. Mobius's shaft hardened in response.

Source, but he wanted to kiss her. And much more. He wanted to hold her and touch her in places both soft and intimate, and watch her face as he brought her to ecstasy. And it was clear she desired him, too. At the moment, however, he wished she did not. She was making it infinitely more difficult for him to keep his own libido in check.

"Aurora," he murmured in warning as she leaned close to him and lifted her head. He was keenly aware of the weight of her breasts against his chest, her hips fitting into his.

"What?" She raised her eyebrows. "Are you going to tell me again that gods don't have sex?" Her eyes narrowed. "Or are you going to tell me the real reason you won't make love to me, even though it's clear you want to?"

Mobius sucked in a deep breath. There were many reasons he could not make love to Aurora. Which reason was she after?

Her words were flippant, but there was vulnerability in her eyes that made it clear his response was more important than she wanted him to know. He couldn't tell her about their past life together. Doing so would open the door to all sorts of questions: How could he have left her and returned to the Light Realm? How could he have failed to protect and keep her safe? How could his duty to the Council have meant more to him than she? Questions like that were better left unasked and unanswered. She would not forgive him. He couldn't even forgive himself.

She cleared her throat, waiting for an answer.

"Things aren't as simple as you may think," he said.

"They can be as complicated or as easy as we make them," she responded. She pressed her mouth to his in a brief but searing kiss. Her scent drifted over him, sweetness and spice. Delicious. It made him wonder if she would taste as luscious as she smelled.

I must stop such thoughts. It was bad enough he had let things go as far as they had the last time they had been intimate.

Mobius closed his eyes briefly, and then opened them, at a loss as to what to say. She watched him, her look expectant.

"I made a promise to your father," he said, thinking it the most straightforward of his reasons to avoid making love to Aurora and hoping it would answer her question. But the way her jaw clenched told him he'd said the wrong thing.

Aurora couldn't believe her ears. Her father had told Mobius he couldn't have sex with her? Growing up, she'd rarely had reason to take issue with her parents' views. Arguments had been scarce. But at that moment, she was furious with her father's interference in her private life.

How dare he! I'm not a child!

She might have started her flirtation with Mobius this night as a distraction from the upset of the day and a way to make him regret his earlier rejection of her. Hell. There were probably lots of reasons she wanted to make love with Mobius right now, despite her resolution that getting involved with any man could only lead to disappointment. But she didn't relish indulging in self-analysis.

She knew only that Axiom's decree that she not sleep with Mobius and Mobius's agreement with Axiom's directive made her stomach burn and her pulse race with something other than desire. Mobius wanted her. It was obvious. And she wanted him. She'd be damned if she'd let her father keep her, a grown woman, from getting what she wanted.

Mobius was fighting his lust. But she could break his hold on his self-control. She took a deep breath. *Get brave, girl. You can do this.*

She willed her robe away and stood stark naked before Mobius.

"My father doesn't make my decisions for me."

Chapter Nineteen

Mobius stared at the sight before him, struck utterly speechless. In fact, he couldn't even think, let alone form words. The woman who stood in front of him was quite definitely the most exquisite creature he had ever laid eyes upon.

Slender ankles and shapely legs led to creamy thighs and full hips. Her belly had just the right amount of womanly flesh, and a sparkling pentagram pierced her navel and dangled, pointing the way to the triangle of close-cropped dark hair beneath. Her breasts were full, and the darker flesh of the areolae seemed to circle their erect peaks like beacons, guiding him closer.

"Touch me," Aurora whispered. "You know you want to." She lifted her chin and dared him to resist her demand. A raw, exposed look flashed in her eyes.

He tried—oh, how he tried—to remain rooted to the spot. He tried not to move toward her, not to touch that smooth skin. He would not be able to put a stop to this if he touched her now. His fists clenched, his jaw tensed, and it was all he could do to tear his gaze away from Aurora's body.

He focused on the floor . . . anything but her. He just needed a moment or two to collect himself. Surely this was more than any male, mortal or god, should be expected to stand.

He sensed her gliding closer to him. Her hands rested lightly on his arms.

"Mobius," she whispered. "I know you're trying to fight this, but you don't have to be the big, strong god with me. I don't expect you to be infallible." She repeated his own words back to him. And they struck a chord inside of Mobius, and made his gaze fly up to meet hers.

With a groan of surrender, he twined his hands in her hair and pulled her against his chest, his lips claiming hers in a kiss that was anything but tentative. His mouth consumed hers, his tongue sliding out to tease the curves of her lips, begging for entrance. She sighed and readily opened to him.

He caressed her shoulders and back, delighting in the goose bumps that broke out over her flesh. He trailed his fingers over the sun and moon on her shoulder, his lips following to kiss the smiling representations of the God and Goddess.

He reached for her plump bottom and cupped her there, pulling her tightly against him. She moaned in response, and her hips did a quick gyration against his. His erection became almost painful in response, and he forced himself not to haul her to the bed, throw her down, and take her immediately. No—he would not rush this if he could help it. He had ached for her far too long to hurry.

A moment later, cool air brushed his skin, and he realized his clothes had disappeared. He pulled back from the kiss, eyebrows raised. *He* hadn't willed away his clothing.

Aurora's eyes twinkled with mischievousness, and he knew his nudity was her doing. She grinned and glided away from him toward the bed. He followed, and as he moved, her gaze swept his naked body with a lust she didn't attempt to hide.

Aurora took in Mobius's body with frank appreciation. He had damn sexy legs, something she hadn't noticed before. Had he ever worn shorts around her? She didn't think so. His body was lean and taut, the muscles thick and defined on his thighs, stomach, chest, and arms. He was large, but not in an overdeveloped, shot-up-on-steroids kind of way. His smooth, hairless chest led to six-pack abs and a thatch of trim reddish hair. And between his legs, his cock stood at attention, beautiful and ready for her. Just looking at him caused moisture to pool between her thighs and created an ache deep inside her sex.

Standing in front of the bed, eyes hooded, crimson waves cascading over his shoulders, and naked flesh bared, he certainly looked the part of a god. A *sex god*.

Aurora's heart beat faster as she lowered herself to the bed, the satin sheets cool against her back. Mobius followed suit. He slid next to her and placed one of his thighs between hers, propping himself on his elbow. He kissed her softly at first, while his free hand explored her body.

She closed her eyes, reveling in sweet anticipation as he drew circles around each of her breasts. He lifted his head and kissed a trail down her neck. He teased her nipples first with fingers, then with tongue and lips. He suckled her softly, then harder, and she arched her back as wave after wave of pleasure washed over her.

By the time his hand reached the apex of her thighs, she was more than ready for him to touch her there. Her legs fell open and she instinctively lifted her hips. *Please, please touch me*. She didn't think she could bear much more of this exquisite torture.

Mobius's fingers slid over her mound and drifted between the lips of her sex. He found the hard little nub he sought and rubbed it first very lightly, then with more pressure. Aurora moaned in response.

He wanted to taste her in the most intimate of ways. He shifted his body so that his head hovered over her sex. In doing so, he had given Aurora access to his erection, and she soon made use of this position. Her small hand clenched around his cock, sending the air whooshing from his lungs. It had been so long since he'd been touched like this. She tugged and stroked, and heat welled up and threatened to spill over.

"Wait," he muttered, pulling her hand away. "Not yet."

She gave him a small pout, but the pout quickly gave way when his tongue dashed out and tickled the sensitive button of flesh at her entrance. He teased her with light brushes. She grabbed his head and pulled him toward her, making clear her need for his mouth to claim her more deeply. He was happy to oblige. He suckled her there as he had her nipples. She bucked beneath him, her cries of pleasure almost enough to push him over the edge.

He couldn't take any more. He had to have her, had to be inside of her. She was so wet. So ready for him. He lifted himself, poised himself between her legs, and made ready to enter her. But first, he waited for her to open her eyes, waited for her to lift her hips in acceptance, and for her breathy "Please."

Then he was inside her, thrusting, watching her face as her mouth formed a little O, then melted into a smile of pleasure. She moved with him, met him halfway until their bodies danced in perfect synchronicity, as though they were old lovers, having met each other in this place of delight many, many times before.

And of course, he thought, *we have.*

He reached between their bodies, tilted his body to the side, and lifted himself just enough to rub her little pearl in time with his thrusts. Her moans grew more intense, louder, and she reached her peak just seconds before Mobius gave in to an orgasm that rocked him to the core.

Afterward, he spooned her. He held her close and

buried his face in the crook of her neck, breathing her in. His chest tightened with both contentment and sorrow and a joy he had absolutely no right to feel.

Aurora. Meri. How she made him ache to turn back time, to unwind what had been wrought so very long ago. But many lifetimes had been lived since then.

And although he was a god, there were some things not even a god could control.

Aurora lay in Mobius's arms dazed with wonderment. *So that's what it's supposed to be like. That's what passion feels like.* Mobius. Even his name caused her heart to flutter; it filled her with sensations she couldn't even begin to decipher.

When they made love, it was as though he knew exactly what she wanted, what she needed, and when she needed it. He touched her with an odd familiarity that made her both comfortable and afraid.

She could relax in his company in a way she couldn't with anyone else. He said she didn't need to be the Earth Balancer with him, and she believed him. There was so much she still didn't know about him. But right now, in the afterglow of their passion, she had a sudden urge to throw her "no men" resolution out the window and learn more.

Much more.

Axiom, Wayne, and Thumper arrived at Graves Manor to find the place a flurry of activity. All members of the coven, except for Reese and Fiona, were on the scene. Wayne and Thumper disappeared outside to do a perimeter sweep and to be certain nothing and no one had breached the protection circle around the property.

Laurell barely looked up from her *Book of Shadows* as she worked on a new spell that she hoped might help Aurora and Mobius. Dawna sat cross-legged in the library, trying to meditate to see if she could get any information psychically about how to fix the severed silver cords. Her pet squirrel, Reba, perched on Dawna's shoulder and leaned against her ear as though she might whisper the answer to her.

Lynn waved hello as they came in, then quickly returned to thumbing through crystal books for inspiration. Hillary was upstairs preparing to perform Reiki healing on Aurora and Mobius.

As she flipped the pages of her book with one hand, the fingernails on Laurell's other hand took a beating. She always chewed her fingernails when nervous or stressed.

Axiom approached his wife and pulled her into his arms, hoping his hug would calm her nerves.

"Am I ever glad to see you," Laurell murmured against his chest. "I couldn't bear it if you were hurt, too."

"Aurora will be okay," he reassured her.

"How do you know? It looks so awful. Have you seen her?"

He shook his head. "Not really. I peeked in the room and saw Hillary about to do a Reiki healing, so I decided to let them have some privacy."

She lifted her head, displaying swollen eyes. She'd been crying. "Well, we can lend our energy to the healing. Come up with me."

She tugged his hand and ascended the stairs, pulling him behind her. The bedroom smelled woodsy and clean. Tendrils of smoke drifted from a sage herb stick that Hillary waved over the bed.

Hillary murmured the ancient Reiki symbols, "Dai Ko Myo, Sei He Ki, Cho Ku Rei." As she uttered the words, she drew the symbols in the air, and Axiom could see the shapes sparkle with white light as they floated around the bed.

The two seemingly comatose bodies on the bed shook and sputtered. They arched and relaxed repeatedly. Their skin was wan and waxy. Seeing his daughter in such a state filled Axiom with horror. No wonder Laurell was so distraught. His fists clenched as he thought of the god responsible for this situation.

He would make Rhakma regret his actions.

Hillary circled the bed, moving her hands over the bodies in the various positions required for a Reiki healing.

Laurell held her hands out, palms forward, willing her own energy into the act, to lend strength to Hillary's healing. Axiom mirrored her movements, and his palms tingled as power seeped from them into Aurora and Mobius.

After half an hour of ministrations, Aurora's and Mobius's bodies relaxed and stilled, their breathing deep and even. The seizurelike activity ceased. *Thank Source,* Axiom thought.

Hillary stood and ran her fingers over her broad features. She looked tired, as though the healing had drained her. "That should help keep them comfortable, at least for now," she said.

Laurell nodded. "It should at least help stave off any bodily deterioration for a while longer."

Axiom closed his eyes briefly, not wanting to think of what would happen to Aurora if the silver cord could not be repaired and they could not find a way to guide her back to her body. The thoughts pierced his mind anyway. She would be trapped in the Light Realm. Her physical body would die. He would never see his daughter again.

"Thank you for your healing," Axiom said.

"It's not by me, but through me," Hillary said. She would never take credit for her healing abilities. Credit was due the Lord and Lady, God and Goddess, the

Wiccan version of the energy that the gods themselves referred to simply as Source.

Laurell wandered to the bed as Hillary left the room. She touched Aurora's face, her expression pained. "Axiom, tell me we will find a way to save her."

"We *will* find a way," he said.

Chapter Twenty

Mobius watched Aurora sleep. Source, but she was stunning. Her black lashes fanned her cheeks like the wings of a blackbird. Her lips, swollen from his kisses, were relaxed and slightly parted. Her breathing was deep and even, and she appeared utterly at peace. A quiet joy filled him: he knew he'd played a considerable part in her current tranquil state.

He sighed. He couldn't just lie here studying her while she slept. He needed to find out how Reetori's interrogation had gone. With Avina so ill, it would be harder to obtain information.

Avina had the ability to see into other gods' thoughts and therefore usually conducted interrogations. Since she was in no condition to assist them at the moment, he hoped Willow and Helios had been able to get some type of confession out of the Gray God.

Willow, have you information to share regarding Reetori? he telepathed to the golden-haired weather goddess.

Yes. Shall I come to your chamber now?

Mobius glanced at Aurora lying naked next to him. Willow would not approve. *No. I will meet you in yours.* He left the bed slowly, careful not to wake Aurora. He imagined himself wearing a sleek silver robe, and immediately the garment sheathed his body.

A moment later, he stood before Willow's private

quarters. She must have sensed his presence, because she bade him enter even before he could ask.

Willow's chambers looked very much like Mobius's had before Aurora embarked upon her decorating spree. Ivory walls, crystal slabs for furniture, and everything pristine. Willow patted the seat next to her, and he sat.

"Helios was to join us," she said. "But he was called to assist with another Light God showing signs of infection."

"Another?"

"Yes."

"This does not bode well, Willow."

"It gets worse, I'm afraid."

Mobius nodded. "I know. I've been thinking about the Gray, Reetori. The Grays have been integral in keeping the balance here in the Light Realm, and without them the Umbrae would be able to infiltrate. This is the first time we've seen a Gray dwelling in the Light Realm infected by the Umbrae. It concerns me greatly."

Willow's lavender eyes flashed with alarm. "The darkness is rising. We must stop it. At least we know who is behind the silver-cord business."

Mobius tilted his head to the side, his gaze questioning. "Reetori's role is minor," she went on. "He is infected, yes, but he was also in league with Rhakma."

Mobius's gut clenched at the mention of the Light God whose attempts to thwart Axiom's prior mission to Earth had cost two innocents their lives. "Rhakma is imprisoned. What does this have to do with him?"

"Reetori set him free. Now he is in on Earth and in league with the Umbrae."

Mobius bit back a feral growl at this news. Such behavior would not become the Divine Director. The others on the Council looked to him to remain rational and levelheaded.

When he'd calmed somewhat, he said, "It makes sense now. Rhakma would have known that with the increased infiltration of the turned Grays adding to the Umbrae's collective energy, they would affect Aurora greatly. As a member of the Light Realm and former Council member, he would know that we might attempt a Violet Fire cleansing."

"And in case he was not certain whether you two came here for that purpose, he had Reetori to confirm your arrival," Willow added.

"He would have needed some personal artifact from at least one of us to locate the silver cords." He paused and frowned, wondering just what the Umbrae had in their possession. "And he waited until our power was low after the initial cleansing before severing the cords." Mobius stood with clenched fists and paced the room.

"We must find a way to get you two back to your bodies. Aurora's life is in danger," Willow said. She stood and crossed the room. The skirt of her purple robe made a swooshing noise as she walked.

Her usual scent, that of a distant rainstorm and freshly cut grass, followed her. She touched his arm, and his muscles relaxed. Willow had a calming way about her. It was what made her so important to the Council. She often found herself in the position of mediator when Council members disagreed.

"Mobius," she began. "There is a solution to this problem. We will find it."

Mobius replied, "I believe we will." *I just hope it's in time to save Aurora.* He let out a heavy sigh.

Willow circled Mobius until she stood in front of him, gazing into his eyes with a scrutiny that made him uncomfortable. She didn't say anything, just gave him a worried frown.

"What is it?" he asked.

"You still do not look yourself. I am concerned about you," she said.

"What do you mean?"

"Your aura appears a bit cloudier than it was earlier. What have you been doing with yourself for the past hours?"

If Mobius could blush, he probably would have. Instead, he focused on the space above Willow's right shoulder. He would not explain to her that he had made love to Aurora as humans do.

"I am fine," he said without answering her last question.

Willow cleared her throat and shifted from one foot to the other with barely concealed discomfort. What was she up to? She leaned toward him and placed both hands on his chest.

"I have been thinking about your harmonization with Aurora. I wonder if perhaps it was not effective for you because she is half-mortal. Her ability to transfer power may not be as well developed as a full god or"—she paused—"goddess's would be."

Mobius sensed where the conversation was going. It had been many years since Willow had approached him about her interest in harmonizing with him. He had turned her down then, wishing to preserve their friendship and not jeopardize her place on the Council.

She was his second in command, and the rest of the Council would not look favorably upon a personal involvement between them. Since that time, she had not broached the subject again.

"I can guess what you are offering, but the answer is no, Willow," he murmured softly.

Willow's Cupid's bow lips tilted in a wry smile. "I don't think you understand. I offer you a harmonization for purely practical reasons. I am not interested in

my own pleasure. I want to do what I can to help
invigorate your strength."

She glided closer to him, until their bodies touched,
her breasts to his chest, her slender legs brushing his
thighs. She tilted her head, and the golden waves of
her hair shifted to cascade over her shoulders.

"I do not wish to upset you," Mobius said. "I don't
wish for you to feel I am rejecting you, but—"

She placed her index finger on his lips, halting his
words. "Then don't. Let me do this for you. As your
friend for many millennia."

But the way she left her finger on his mouth, softly
stroking the full lower lip, belied her talk of friendship. Mobius placed his hands over hers, planning to
gently remove them.

Before he could, a buzzing sound drifted to his ears,
and he knew they were not alone.

"What the hell?" came Aurora's voice. He turned his
head to see her standing with hands on pink-robed
hips, eyes narrowed with a suspicious gleam.

He let go of Willow's hands and set her away from
him. "You are awake," he said, hoping she would not
get the wrong impression from what she had just wit-
nessed. "Are you feeling well after your rest?"

"Yeah," she quipped. "But apparently not as well as
you."

Aurora couldn't believe her eyes. She'd woken to find
Mobius gone, and after reliving their delicious, mind-
blowing sex, she hadn't been able to stop thinking
about him. Waking up to the empty bed had grated on
her nerves.

*So he doesn't need to sleep. He could have woken
me to say good-bye, at least.* She'd been overcome by
an irrational need to be with him. So she'd decided to
go to him. To find him cozying up to Willow was just

a bit much to swallow. She almost wished she hadn't learned how to teleport in the Light Realm. This was one scene she could have done without witnessing.

She lifted her chin. She would not let him know how much his actions bothered her. *Screw it. It was just sex. It's not like he proposed to me.*

Mobius walked over to her, head tilted to the side, brow furrowed. It was clear he was preparing to defend himself.

"Are there any leads on getting me out of here?" she asked, purposely changing the subject before he could present her with some excuse that would only piss her off more.

"We are exploring options." This from Willow, who did not seem the least bit embarrassed that Aurora had barged in on their embrace.

"Care to share them with me?" Aurora pressed, trying her best to keep the bite out of her voice.

"As yet, I've nothing concrete to share," Willow began. "The Council will be meeting to discuss the situation. Oh, and in the Light Realm, it is customary to ask permission to enter someone's private quarters."

Willow then turned to Mobius, dismissing Aurora as though she were nothing more than a pesky child.

Aurora ground her teeth and teleported back to Mobius's chambers. Damn Mobius. And damn Willow. And damn it all that she was stuck in the Light Realm.

I take it back. I don't want to get away from it all. I don't need a vacation from being the Earth Balancer. At that moment, she longed for nothing more than her return to Earth.

Chapter Twenty-one

"Innocents are dying. We can't stay holed up in this house hiding forever," Wayne said to Axiom as they sat at the kitchen table in Graves Manor. Wayne let out a long, phlegm-choked cough.

"You should consider giving up the cigars, old friend," Axiom said.

"Hell with that. What about the innocents?" Wayne barked.

Axiom pushed away his plate of half-eaten chicken and dumplings. He did not have much of an appetite. Aurora and Mobius's condition worsened by the hour.

To make matters worse, the local news had reported an attack on a nearby New Age center. The owner and two patrons were dead. A security camera had picked up the attackers, a man and a woman who moved with amazing speed and displayed extreme strength.

"The minute we leave the protection circle, we will be surrounded by Finders and Grays. We cannot save anyone if we are unable to get through our own front yard," Axiom said.

Wayne harrumphed. "I haven't picked up any Umbrae or Grays during my perimeter checks."

"You cannot detect Finders."

"Well, I ain't afraid of Finders," Wayne said, tapping his side, where Axiom knew he kept a holstered gun. Wayne was the only member of the coven trained to shoot a firearm, although he rarely had to use his weapon, because of the coven's prowess with elemental magic.

Before Axiom could respond to Wayne, Dawna burst into the room. "There's a pattern," she said.

Axiom's brows rose. "What?"

"The people the Grays are attacking. They all have something in common."

"Explain."

"I was meditating, trying to come up with a plan to help Aurora, and Goddess told me that all of those being attacked are Lightworkers."

Axiom sighed. "Of course. The Umbrae would rather attack those whose light energy shines the brightest."

Dawna nodded. "They can't turn them, so might as well get rid of them. That way they are able to increase the dark energies on the planet faster."

Wayne tilted his hat back just a bit and took a swig of his soda. "Lightworkers. You're talking about ordinary people who don't necessarily even know they are vibrating to a higher frequency. They wouldn't see the attacks coming."

"Some of them know," Dawna said. "But yeah, many don't." She pulled a chair out and sat at the table. "To test the information, I started doing some Internet research on the recent attacks. A number of those attacked appear to be highly devout, spiritual people: a metaphysical minister and a couple of his parishioners, a Buddhist devotee, a Methodist man who funded and runs a local homeless shelter. And that's just a few of them. Even those who didn't have any particular religious affiliation were known for their kind acts and generous natures."

Wayne leapt to his feet. He stuck his hands in his jeans pockets and shifted from one foot to the other with barely restrained frustration. "We can't just sit here."

Axiom tilted his head to Wayne. "Easy, friend. I want

to stop this madness as much as you do, but we must be smart about it."

He fixed his gaze on Dawna. She ran her hand absently through her long black hair and then tapped her lime green fingernails on the tabletop. "Dawna, see if you can ascertain where the Grays will strike next. Perhaps the coven can weave a temporary protection spell around the intended victims."

Dawna nodded. "I'll see what I can do."

"If she can figure out where they're gonna strike next, we can head 'em off," Wayne offered.

"Perhaps," Axiom said. "But I agree with what Laurell said when all this started. We are stronger with Aurora and Mobius at our side. Let's find a way to get them back here before we go looking for trouble."

"You are upset with me," Mobius said, appearing in his chambers what seemed like hours later. Aurora forced away the sheen of involuntary tears and gave him a blank look.

"I couldn't care less what you do in your free time. Though I would have appreciated a little more honesty on your part."

Mobius lifted one eyebrow and tilted his head in question. "I have told no lies."

"No, but you certainly didn't tell me you were intimately involved with Willow. I was embarrassed to walk in on you two."

The scene flashed through her mind again. Willow pressed close to Mobius, Mobius holding her hands in his. She clenched her jaw, annoyed at the ache in her chest. *I am not falling for him. We had mind-blowing sex. That's all.*

Mobius strode across the room. Goddess, he was a sight. All that fiery hair around his shoulders, his amber eyes fierce.

He touched her arm. "Aurora, there is nothing between Willow and me. You misunderstood what you saw. I feel only friendship for her."

"I told you, I don't care what you do or don't feel for Willow. It's none of my business anyway."

She tried to twist away from him, ready to end the conversation. She regretted having said anything at all. But he wouldn't let her ignore him. He placed one hand on her cheek and tugged her chin toward him.

"After what happened between us, I would say it is your business."

She blinked, fascinated by the sudden smoldering in his gaze as he mentioned their lovemaking. A tiny breath of air drifted between them, carrying his scent to her nose. Clean and sweet and full of promise.

Her eyes widened at the implication of his words.

"You are surprised? Did you think I would simply enjoy your body and walk away from you?"

She cleared her throat and tried to ignore her heart's sudden rapid acceleration. "Something like that. I mean, on Earth, people often have sex without being committed."

"Do you engage in this type of behavior?"

"No," she admitted. Casual sex had never been her thing. Not that she'd had a lot of chances for sexual exploration.

"God or man, I do not take such things lightly either."

"So what does this mean? Are you asking to be my boyfriend or something?"

He sighed, removing his hand, which had been softly stroking her cheek. Strange how naked her skin felt at the loss of his touch.

"I'm not certain what it means."

If she'd been looking for a definitive answer, she would have been awfully disappointed.

"What I do know," he continued, "is that you mean much to me. And despite the fact that I have betrayed my promise to your father and have behaved in a manner most unbecoming to a god of the Light Realm by taking advantage of someone I am supposed to be protecting . . . I find it hard to regret what I did."

Well, that got her hackles up. "Uh, as a reminder, I don't need protecting. And I came on to you first, so that's not your fault either."

His eyes flashed with arrogance. "I am a god of the Light Realm. I should be able to resist all temptations, but . . ."

"But?" she prodded.

His stance softened, and he sighed deeply. "I find I am far from immune to your charms."

At his admission, a quiet pleasure spread through her limbs. "Well, you're not half-bad yourself." Then, before she could stop herself, she said, "Even if you don't want to be my boyfriend."

His reluctance to formalize their relationship shouldn't have bothered her, but it did.

"I never said that," Mobius responded. "There are many things I want, but not all of them are possible."

"I don't understand."

"It's complicated."

"So you've said before, but I don't buy it. Explain what you mean."

Mobius groaned his frustration. "Suffice it to say that while I may appear to be a desirable lover now, you might change your mind were you privy to all that I have done in the past."

That got her attention. So Mobius had a big, bad, scary past that he was afraid to share with her. "I might surprise you. You don't really know me that well. How can you be sure how I'll react?"

Mobius peered into her eyes so deeply and with such intensity, it seemed he looked into her very soul. "I do know you. I know you as well as I know myself."

* * *

Evan rapped lightly on the door of the bedroom Dawna and Lynn used when staying at Graves Manor.

He heard a muffled "Come in" and entered the room. He found Dawna seated cross-legged on a colorful floor cushion, cast in shadows, eyes half-closed as she stared into a large, black mirror stationed on a low table a few feet in front of her. She wore an ankle-length violet robe, ceremonial attire that indicated she was engaged in some type of ritual.

On the table, a candle burned. The flame swayed in the slight breeze from the heat register as the furnace cycled on. Nag champa incense released a sweet aroma as tendrils of smoke drifted through the room.

Realizing he'd interrupted a scrying session, he turned to leave, but Dawna spoke without even opening her eyes to see who had come into the room.

"It's okay, Thumper. I'm just about finished. I called on the goddess Antevorta to help with my scrying, and she really came through."

"She's a Roman goddess, right?"

"Mmm. Lately, I've been exploring the Roman pantheon."

Dawna took a deep breath, released the air from her lungs, and pressed her hands into the Namaste pose. "Thank you, Goddess Antevorta, for assisting me this night. Stay if you will. Go if you must. Hail and farewell."

"Hail and farewell," Thumper repeated.

He took a seat next to her on the floor. "So, what did you find out?"

"There's a bit of activity in Madison at the University of Wisconsin. I picked up a group of students there who are targeted. Some type of group related to women's rights."

"When?"

"Tomorrow night."

"A trap to draw us out?"

"Too close to home for it to be a coincidence." She sighed. "That's not all. The Umbrae are also going to attack a metaphysical center in Tampa. A place called Serendipity."

"What is it with the Umbrae and Tampa, anyway?"

Dawna shrugged. "Heck if I know. I wouldn't think Tampa would be a high-traffic area for bad guys. Nothing there but retirees and palm trees."

"But obviously something is attracting them."

"Yup. Maybe they're finally realizing that attacking locals isn't going to draw us out and they're moving on?"

Evan frowned and pushed the glasses that threatened to slide down his nose back into place. "I'm not sure if that's good or bad."

"Ain't nothin' good about any of it," came a familiar gravelly voice. Evan turned to see Wayne standing in the doorway of Dawna's room. The old man sure could move with uncanny stealth when he wanted to.

"I didn't hear you come in," Evan said.

Wayne looked abashed. "Sorry if I made ya jumpy. I'm heading into town for supplies. Anything either of you need?"

Evan raised his eyebrows. "I didn't think it was safe for any of us to leave the protection circle."

"Well we sure as shit can't let ourselves starve," Wayne griped.

"Does anyone else know you're planning to go? Axiom? Hill?" Evan asked.

"Yes."

"Just in case . . ." Dawna stood and crossed the room to a mahogany dresser where a jeweled box rested. She lifted a necklace from the box. Two chunks of crystal, one purple and one pitch-black, dangled from a long silver chain. Between them hung a silver pentacle.

"Wear this," she said, handing the necklace to Wayne. "Lynn charged it with a protection spell. It's not likely to hold up against an onslaught of Grays, but it might help against the occasional Finder."

Wayne took the necklace and touched the tip of his Stetson in his usual gesture of salutation. "Thanks. I'll be back soon."

Chapter Twenty-two

After the Council learned about Reetori's turning, a new but growing panic set in. Willow eyed the gods and goddesses, who sat around the meeting table in various states of anxiety.

Reetori was a Gray, a Balancer for the Light Realm. The Grays and their ability to neutralize the Umbrae's dark energy were integral in keeping the Umbrae from infiltrating the Light Realm. That one of their kind had been turned was a very frightening omen.

The god who appeared most distressed, however, was Mobius. He occupied his usual seat at the head of the table, but appeared oblivious to the chatter around him. His topaz gaze veered off into some distant place.

A momentary flush of embarrassment swept through Willow at her earlier attempt to harmonize with him. She didn't know what had made her bring up that old issue. It had been many years since she'd revealed her feelings to Mobius, and he had made clear then, as he had now, that he had no interest in her beyond friendship.

Seeing him with the Earth Balancer and observing the way he interacted with the beautiful half-mortal had made her envious in a way she couldn't explain. Goddesses did not—should not—desire the love and intimacy experienced by humans. And until recently, she hadn't. But two gods she knew well, Mobius and

Axiom, had fallen for human women and had never been the same since. She wondered, was she missing out?

Helios, a god of war whom all respected and who had been a member of the Council for some time, spoke up amid the chatter of the gods and goddesses. "I believe we may have found a way for Aurora and you to find your way back to your bodies." The rest of the Council quieted as all heads turned to Helios.

This news pulled Mobius from his silent reverie. He blinked and straightened in his seat. "Explain," he said.

"The coven needs to create a light bright enough for your soul selves to see when traveling between realms."

Willow leaned forward, tapping her fingers on the slab of clear quartz that made up the table. "Yes! A beacon to guide you home."

"And the silver cords?" Mobius asked.

"Once you are back in your bodies, the cords will heal themselves."

"But what can be used as a beacon?" Mobius wondered aloud.

"I do not know. We must get the message to the coven. Does Laurell still astral-travel?" Helios asked, his brow raised hopefully.

Mobius shook his head. "No. There has been no reason for a Liaison assignment for some time. And as things stand, there's no way to get word to her to advise her to meet with a newly assigned Liaison on the Astral Plane."

"Well," Willow said, "then one of us needs to go to Earth and deliver the message personally."

Helios nodded his agreement. "But who will go? The Director cannot create another human body."

Mobius frowned. "No. And even if I could return right now, I would not. I am needed here with the Earth Balancer. After her experience with Reetori, it is clear she requires protecting."

Willow observed this comment with interest. She didn't bother to point out that any one of the members of the Council was powerful enough to protect Aurora.

She rose from the table, smoothed her hands over her robe, and said, "I will be the one to go."

Mobius found Aurora where he had left her. In his chambers. When he'd left for the meeting, he had asked her to remain there until his return. The defiant tilt of her chin had concerned him. He'd been afraid she would venture out again on her own to explore. Fortunately, she had obeyed—something he knew she did not do easily.

She rested on the sofa, petal pink robe tucked up and around her legs and feet. Her eyes were closed, and her long black lashes fanned her cheeks. She sighed in her sleep, plump lips parting just slightly as though she waited for a lover's kiss. Source, how he longed to press his mouth to hers!

Her earlier questioning as to the nature of their relationship had caught him off guard. Their lovemaking had opened up a chasm inside of him that he'd tried desperately to close. He did not want to examine the private agony that he had grown used to pushing back into the recesses of his mind.

He'd been tempted to tell her about their past-life connection, but held back. It would serve no purpose.

If she knew the truth about me, that I left her, that my abandonment contributed to her demise, she would despise me. He couldn't bear to see a look of betrayal in her slate-colored eyes. He had seen that look once before. The day he'd left Earth, and Meri, behind. Her face haunted him still.

Mobius perched on the couch next to Aurora. He trailed one finger over the smooth line of her cheek, admiring the softness of her skin. She stirred slightly, and he pulled his hand away.

"No," she murmured in her sleep. "Oh—the baby!" Her words came out on a strangled moan. Her face scrunched up in dismay.

Mobius touched her shoulder again, intending to wake her. "Aurora," he said.

Her hands flew to her face and covered her eyes for a moment, before fluttering back to her side, as she struggled to push away the dream that had taken hold of her.

"Aurora," Mobius said, gently shaking her. "Wake up."

"Stop! Oh Goddess no, not the baby!" Her voice reached a high-pitched wail, and she suddenly jerked upright, eyes popping open, wild with fear, chest heaving.

Her entire body shook. Instinctively, he embraced her. He cradled her against him, and her curves melded into the hard lines of his chest.

After long moments, Aurora spoke. "I was dreaming."

"Yes."

"About a baby with red hair. A little boy. He was—he was my baby. Only, I know that can't be."

Mobius's spine stiffened. She could only be referring to one child. *It's truer than you think.*

"Sometimes dreams can be so vivid they seem real," he murmured past the lump in his throat. A memory flashed. A child's cry as the Umbrae attacked and destroyed his bright but tiny light.

"This was more than that. You were there too," she said before disengaging from him and sitting back on the couch.

He studied her closely and noted the genuine disquiet in her gaze and the way her body still shook slightly. "What exactly did you dream?"

"The baby was killed. He was only hours old. I had nursed him and laid him down to sleep. I went to change.

I was so weak after the delivery. When I returned, he was dead. And—" She glanced up at Mobius, eyes narrowed. "And you were there, holding him. You were sobbing, staring at the baby. . . ."

Pain clamped down on Mobius's chest with a viselike grip. He did not want to relive that scene. He had already replayed it enough in his mind in the time since the child's death. The Umbrae had attacked. He'd been overcome, unable to destroy them all before they claimed the child's life. Decades had passed before he could close his eyes without envisioning the haunting image of the baby's slack body and wan features. He could not afford to return to that place of unbearable pain.

Aurora was recalling their past life together. Something had triggered her memories—but what?

"How long have you been having these dreams?"

The question seemed to throw her off balance. She chewed her bottom lip and did not meet his gaze. "This is the first time I've dreamed about anything that is so obviously from your life with Meri. Why is it happening?"

"I don't know," he said. His mind raced with possibilities. "Perhaps it has to do with our harmonization."

She nodded. "Hmm. So I've sort of picked up some of your memories?"

"It is the best explanation I can think of," he said. It was not a lie. He could not imagine why she would suddenly be having a past-life recall. And in truth, a harmonization really could cause her to experience some of his memories. At least, he thought it could. There was no precedent for gods and humans harmonizing. There was no way to know what might come of such an exchange. He struggled to keep his expression blank lest she realize there was more to her dream than he was willing to reveal.

Her gaze softened, and she lifted her hand to his face.

"Mobius, I'm so sorry. Seeing that baby and your anguish made me realize all that you went through. Goddess, how awful for you."

He shifted uncomfortably, unused to someone looking at him with such compassion and sympathy. He was a god. The Divine Director. Others viewed him only with respect and admiration. He did not display emotions such as sorrow and regret. They were signs of weakness.

Aurora touched his face with a gentleness that moved him. He glanced away, suddenly overcome by an emotion he didn't want to face.

"Uh-uh," she said. "Look at me."

Her words compelled him to obey. He faced her again, and her silver gaze penetrated him. He could see his heart, his soul, the entire universe reflected in those striking eyes of hers. Did she see the same in his?

"You don't have to be the big, strong god with me. You offered me that assurance once, and I gave it back to you. I still mean it. Talk to me."

Her words, an echo of his own, reached a place inside of him he had not known existed. A secret place of sorrow and despair where a deep need to be something other than an invincible god resided.

She leaned forward and pressed her lips to his forehead in a gesture both tender and sweet. That simple exchange elicited an undeniable and fierce desire inside him.

"Aurora, you are making me crazy with need for you," he confessed.

"Is that such a bad thing?" Her mouth lifted in a teasing smile.

"It could be," he muttered, his voice husky. "Right now, all I know is how much I wish to kiss you."

Her tongue slipped out and wet her lips. He didn't miss the invitation.

"Then kiss me."

He needed no further encouragement. He cupped her cheek with one hand and pulled her lips to his, kissing her with an almost desperate fervor. Their mouths collided and parted and met again in a heated dance. He couldn't get enough of her. Her mouth tasted sweet. Her body, melting and pliant against his, made his pulse race and his cock immediately harden and throb.

She sighed and took his hand, then boldly placed it on her breast. He plucked her nipple between thumb and forefinger. Her sharp intake of breath pleased him. The fabric of her robe suddenly became an irritant to him. He needed to be skin to skin with her. He willed away the garment, and she started in surprise as the cool air hit her burning flesh.

"You are naughty," she murmured, but her heavy-lidded gaze made clear she didn't mind his taking the lead.

"You are exquisite," he responded, his gaze traveling from her luscious breasts and their erect, pink peaks to her ample hips and the thatch of dark hair between them. She sank back into the couch and he willed himself naked, then reclined beside her.

He trailed his fingers over her breasts, running circles over and over every inch of them until only her nipples were left untouched. Then, when she thought she'd die if he didn't touch their aroused tips, he lightly pinched each nipple between thumb and forefinger.

He followed the action with his lips and tongue. She arched into a pleasure that shot straight to her core. Moisture seeped between her thighs in response. She ached to feel his fingers there as well. As though reading her thoughts, he obliged.

His hand moved between her legs, and she eagerly parted her thighs and lifted her hips, begging for him to put his fingers inside. He dipped first one, then two fingers into her, making her feel deliciously full. He moved them in and out of her while continuing to suckle her breasts.

Waves of pleasure pounded through her, leaving a dizzying surge of increased desire in their wake.

Mobius lifted his head and watched her. His eyes darkened to the shade of deep, smoky quartz. The way he looked at her made Aurora feel like the most beautiful woman in the world—made her feel bold, carefree, and desirable.

"Lie down," she commanded. Mobius's hand stilled, and he raised his eyebrows in question. "It's my turn to explore you," she told him.

His harsh intake of breath let her know how her words affected him. That, and the erection bucking against her thigh. He didn't argue. They shifted positions until it was he who lay on his back and she who reclined against him. She brushed her breasts teasingly across his chest, and he groaned in response.

She claimed his mouth with her own, ate at his lips with tongue and teeth, first gently, then with more aggression. His arms circled her waist and stroked her buttocks. She shivered with delight, but broke their kiss and shook her head.

"Nope. It's not about me. Yet."

She slid down his body, admiring the solid lines of his smooth chest, his taut stomach, and the length and girth of his cock as it strained toward her, a tiny tear dripping from its tip.

She grasped his erection with one hand and dipped her head, taking him in her mouth with one deep swallow. He tasted salty, sweet, and all man. His groans of ecstasy drove her own as she continued her ministrations, tasting him, lapping at him, suckling him.

"Stop," he gasped out. "I can't hold off."

She lifted her head just a little and released him only long enough to say, "Then don't."

His cry of release and the way his huge body shook with it made her ache even more for him. Her thighs were slick with her need.

After Mobius came back to himself, he peered at the voluptuous goddess poised between his legs and let out a deep sigh. "Ah, my lovely. Now how will I pleasure you?"

"I don't have much experience, but I've read about lots of different ways and positions I'd like to try." With a naughty gleam in her eye, she slid up his body, lifting her legs until she was poised above his mouth, her core open and presented to him.

"Are you game?" she asked, her voice soft and breathy.

He didn't answer her. His response was clear as his hands clamped down on her thighs and he claimed her with his mouth.

Bright colors, like fireworks, sparked through her and she thought she'd explode from the delicious sensations.

Yes, she thought, *boyfriend or not, I will enjoy this time with Mobius. I will enjoy his body. And, oh!*—she gasped as his tongue darted inside her—*he will enjoy mine.*

Chapter Twenty-three

Evan stood on the back porch of Graves Manor and stared at the moon. The scent of lilacs wafted on a slight, cool breeze. Besides the moon, only the porch light gleamed to illuminate the night. It would be Beltane soon.

Normally, he attended a large festival in Mount Horeb, Wisconsin, where pagans from all over traveled to worship deity and celebrate the changing of the seasons together. He had hoped to attend and maybe even meet a nice Wiccan girl, someone he could trust with the secret of his membership in Hidden Circle Coven.

All the members of the coven had to be careful whom they trusted; it wasn't safe to divulge information about their private lives. Dawna and Lynn had each other, as did Reese and Fiona. Those couples didn't have to worry about the perils of dating. Hillary, though single, said she had no interest in dating. She'd had a bad marriage with an abusive husband, and her experience had left her unwilling to try again.

And Wayne was notorious for wining and dining women and then letting them down easy, without getting too close. Strangely, none of the women seemed to mind. The cantankerous old goat had a way with the ladies.

Evan sighed. He, on the other hand, had gone way

too long without someone special in his life. He was only thirty-one years old, and he was leading a celibate life. Definitely not by choice.

He wiped the sweat from his brow and began to return to the house when movement to the left of the porch caught his eye. A figure strode purposefully across the lawn. Evan's spine stiffened. Had a Finder somehow breached the protection circle?

As the invader drew closer, he realized it was a woman. A woman with long, blonde hair, wearing a white robe. Before he could formulate a thought, let alone call for help, the sliding glass door behind him opened and closed, and he turned to see Axiom.

"Fiona has come up with a spell to protect the metaphysical center Dawna says the Grays will next attack. We need you to—" Axiom's words died as he stared over Evan's shoulder.

"Willow!" Axiom called, hurrying past Evan and striding across the lawn to the woman. When he reached her, he pulled her into a hug.

The two exchanged words Evan couldn't make out, then ascended the steps to the porch.

They paused in front of Evan. The woman eyed him from head to toe and seemed to study him as if he were a science experiment. She was drop-dead gorgeous with shoulder-length blonde hair and eyes such a startling shade of pale purple, he had to look twice to be sure he hadn't imagined their unusual hue. She had high cheekbones and Cupid's bow lips. Her presence made his stomach do a crazed jig.

"This is Thumper," Axiom said.

"Uh . . . Evan. You can call me Evan," Evan said, holding out his hand to the woman. She tilted her head to the side and stared at his hand with a blank expression.

"That's how humans greet each other," Axiom explained.

"Oh! Yes, I remember that now," she said, taking his hand. A jolt of electricity ran through Evan at her touch. "I'm Willow."

Her eyes locked with his, and he had to force himself to break away and glance at Axiom. "How did she get inside the circle?"

"She is a goddess of the Light Realm, sent to give us a message. Let us go inside and inform the others."

And with that, Axiom led the woman inside the house, Evan trailing behind.

Axiom immediately called a meeting. Once the coven members had been introduced to Willow, they all settled down to discuss their individual ideas for getting Aurora and Mobius back into their bodies. Everyone was present save Wayne, who Evan assumed had gone to perform one of his perimeter checks.

"We need to establish a signal for Aurora and Mobius to pick up during astral travel. Something to guide them back to their bodies," Willow explained.

"But what?" Dawna wondered aloud, twining one finger through her black hair.

"It will need to be something that pulls in the highest vibration of energy, so that its electric current is strong enough for them to discern," Willow said.

Lynn, who had been quiet up until then, perked up. Her robin's egg blue eyes crinkled at the corners as she grinned, the only evidence of fiftysomething years in an otherwise-smooth face.

"Phenacite and moldavite," she said.

"What-ite?" Evan asked, wondering if she was speaking another language.

Dawna smacked one hand to her forehead. "They're crystals. Sheesh. Why didn't we think of this sooner?"

"Excellent," Willow said. "Do you have enough of these crystals to construct a device to fit over both of them? A pyramid shape would be best."

Lynn shook her head. "Um, no. Those are two of the most expensive crystals around. I do have boxes of clear quartz, though, which I'd intended to use to build a sculpture. We can use them as the base and as an amplifier for the center stones."

"Good," Axiom said. "Let us get to work."

"Just one problem, though," Lynn said.

"What's that?" Axiom asked, already pacing the room in obvious agitation at the idea of yet another roadblock in the way of getting his daughter back.

"I don't carry all those stones around with me. They're at my house."

Hillary stood. "I'll go."

Axiom shook his head. "Too risky. We cannot afford to lose our acting High Priestess. Especially with Fiona and Reese out of the country. We do not know how many Finders or Umbrae, or Grays for that matter, may be lying in wait."

"It's true," Evan offered. "They're probably hoping we'll split up. We're easier to defeat if separated."

Willow sighed. "This is obvious. I am in god form. They are not expecting me, nor will they be able to overcome me easily."

Axiom nodded. "Who will escort her there?"

"I will," Dawna offered.

Lynn clasped her girlfriend's hand and shook her head vehemently. "Not without me, you won't."

Axiom's brow furrowed. "We cannot risk you both."

Willow turned to Evan, and her gaze washed over him in frank assessment. "Do you know where to find the crystals?" she asked him.

"Well, yeah, I know where Dawna and Lynn live."

Satisfied, Willow rose from the table, smoothing the shiny material of her robe. "Then it is settled. Evan will take me there."

The fact that she'd referred to him by his given name

sent a shiver of pleasure through Evan. He didn't know why. It wasn't a big deal, really. After all, he'd asked her to do so.

Axiom eyed Evan. "Are you in agreement, Thumper?"

"Absolutely."

An hour later, Laurell, who had been getting some much-needed and hard-to-come-by rest, came charging down the stairs, hazel eyes wild with panic.

"Aurora's dying!"

Aurora lay back on the bed and stretched languidly after what seemed like hours of lovemaking. She was naked and, for once, didn't care. Mobius had explored, touched, and tasted just about every inch of her, and after his continual praise of her beauty and his lust-filled murmurings of adoration, she was starting to believe him. Maybe she really was sexy.

Mobius lifted himself to recline on one elbow, his flame-colored hair trailing over his shoulders and chest, drawing her eyes to the sculpted contours of his bare flesh. He shifted, and his splayed legs displayed another part of him that was equally hard. Mobius definitely did not have any problem being naked.

"How long have we been here?"

"Here, as in the Light Realm?"

"Yeah. Time doesn't pass the same here as it does on Earth, right?"

"That's correct," Mobius agreed.

"So, how long have we been here in Earth time?"

"A few days," he said.

"What's happening to our bodies right now?" She sat up, suddenly anxious. "What will happen if we don't find a way back?"

Mobius pulled himself upright. He tenderly fingered a loose tendril of hair that rested on her cheek. "You know the answer already."

She smoothed her brow with both hands and tried to ignore the slight tremble in her fingers. She'd never really experienced fear before, and didn't like the feeling at all. She pushed the emotion away and instead gave in to the frustration that had been eating her up. Frustration that, strangely, made her smile.

"You find our being trapped here amusing?"

She groaned. "Hardly. I was just thinking it's funny how a few days ago, I'd have given anything for some time away from being the Earth Balancer. I wanted nothing more than a vacation from my life."

"And today?" he prodded.

"I can't think of anything but getting back there to fight. I can't stand being stuck here, unable to help. Let's do something. Something to take my mind off of things until Willow returns."

His mouth curved into a devilish grin.

If she hadn't already moved way past embarrassment, her face would have turned pink at the innuendo she read behind that not-so-innocent smile of his. "I don't know how you have any more energy left!"

"If I were in my human form, I would tire more easily," he said. He leaned forward and pressed a quick, soft kiss to her lips. "Hmmmmm." He thought a minute, then opened his palms, and a sketch pad and charcoals appeared.

Aurora smiled, touched by the gesture. "Thank you. That's really sweet. Maybe I'll do a sketch of you."

His eyes sparkled his pleasure at the idea that she found him worthy of being the subject of her art. Really, she just wanted some time to study him without interruption and without being worried she was going to look like some besotted kid.

"Do you wish to sketch now?" he asked.

"Later. Right now, I want to see more of the Light

Realm. Can we explore?" she asked, feeling a sudden excitement at what she might learn from the place.

Mobius rose and willed himself into an indigo-colored robe that made his hair look an even deeper shade of crimson and his eyes a more robust hue of pale golden brown.

"Come. You asked me about the re-visioning device previously. I will provide a demonstration."

Aurora perked up at this offer. She imagined herself into a black gown. Everyone else in the Light Realm seemed to like robes. She liked to dress up, too, but really—robes? She much preferred the idea of a sexy, slinky gown. This one had a plunging neckline and hugged her body in places she hoped Mobius would appreciate.

His gaze heated and told her that the outfit was having the desired effect. Moments later, they teleported into the re-visioning room. A man lay on a table in the middle of the room. Across the screen, scenes from his life played in vivid color. A fair-haired god tended to the man. His hands moved through the air over the prone man's head, changing the pictures on the screen as if he were pushing the fast-forward or rewind button on a VCR.

The god nodded to Mobius and went about his business as though they weren't there.

"This man recently transitioned."

"Transitioned?"

"From Earth. He died."

"Oh. And you're looking at his memories?"

"It's not that *we* are viewing his memories so much as that *he* is viewing them. To some extent, he is reliving them through this process. It's how humans determine which aspects of their lives they may wish to repeat and do differently."

"Oh, right. So they—um, we see our past life and all

the things we did right or wrong. And then we decide if we want to come back for a do-over, right?"

"That's one way of describing the process."

"So how do I see one of my past lives?" she asked.

Mobius's jaw tensed. "You don't."

"Why not?"

"No one is allowed to participate in his or her own re-visioning, except between lives."

"Oh." Was it just her or did the mere mention of her seeing a past life make Mobius jumpy? "Are you sure you couldn't make just one little exception?" *After all, it's not every day a girl gets a chance to see her past lives so vividly.* This would be way better than the one past-life-regression class she'd taken. She'd gotten only a vague sensation of foreboding, a glimpse of a large cauldron full of herbs, and the distant cry of a child during that regression attempt. She'd been sorely disappointed.

He tugged her toward him in a possessive gesture, and she willingly melted against him. He pressed a kiss to her neck. *He's trying to distract me. Why?*

"Do you like to swim?" he asked.

"Love it," she said.

"Good. Then you will enjoy the crystal springs."

"Do I have to wear a swimsuit?" she asked, giving him a teasing wink.

"I should hope not."

Now that sounded promising.

Chapter Twenty-four

Willow swept through the kitchen of Graves Manor and left behind the flurry of activity there. The members of the coven were sketching plans for a pyramid-shaped structure of quartz crystals with the phenacite and moldavite taking center stage at the top of the triangle.

Evan had dubbed their creation the "homing beacon," apparently after some television program he enjoyed watching that had long since been canceled. Not that Willow knew much about television or its programs, but Evan had explained this to her with a sheepish smile that was rather endearing, and then looked embarrassed that he had admitted to watching and enjoying this particular program.

She found Evan in the upstairs bedroom where Aurora and Mobius lay. He stood at the foot of the bed, face twisted with worry, hands bunched in his jeans pockets. She observed from the doorway, careful not to make her presence known just yet. She'd sensed his interest in her from the moment he first saw her. One of her god powers included being able to read the emotions of those around her.

It wasn't telepathy, but it had served her on more than one occasion in the Light Realm when she had assisted Avina with an interrogation or needed to assess the best approach to take when dealing with one of the other gods or goddesses.

She read guilt in Evan's aura. She wondered what he fretted over. She studied him, assessing his features. He was tall, about six feet, if she had to guess. His frame was solid but compact, what humans would call a tennis-player build. Thick, dark brown hair curled just over his collar. Earlier, she'd noticed wide-set pale green eyes behind his wire-rimmed glasses. His jaw was square, and he had a small cleft in his chin. He was an attractive man.

"I should have said something." Evan's softly spoken words tugged Willow from her appraisal. Realizing he'd sensed her presence, she crossed the room to where he stood.

"About what?" she asked.

"I noticed something sort of weird a couple nights ago. But I thought I'd imagined it and didn't tell anyone."

"What did you see?"

Evan gestured toward the figures on the bed. "This."

Aurora's and Mobius's bodies jerked and spasmed. Their skin was pale and pasty looking, and dark hollows shadowed their eyes.

Willow put a reassuring hand on Evan's shoulder. He stiffened at the touch, but did not move away. "There was nothing you could have done to prevent this."

"How do you know?"

She lifted one brow and gave a wry grin. "I am a goddess of the Light Realm."

He let out a deep breath, clearly relieved. "Well, I can't argue with that, can I?" The sardonic ring to his words contained a tinge of humor.

She smiled. "It is generally best if people do not argue with me."

He sighed. "So when do we head out to Lynn's house?"

"We should go now. As Laurell said, we are running out of time." Willow glanced back at the bed and the two who lay there. Mobius would weather this set-back well. The Earth Balancer, however, would die if they did not make haste. She was too important to all of them, the gods and goddesses included, to let that happen.

They left the room and headed down the stairs. Hillary met them halfway, eyes flashing with purpose. "While you two get the crystals, we're going to go ahead and perform a protection spell for the places the Umbrae are going to attack next."

Willow nodded. "An excellent plan. Do you need something from us before we leave?"

Hillary shook her head. "No, no. I was actually looking for Wayne." She eyed Evan. "You seen him?"

"He went for supplies."

Hillary's jaw dropped. "What? No one was supposed to leave the protection circle, and certainly not alone."

"He said you knew," Evan blurted out, his expression turning to one of panic.

"Shit," Hillary swore, sweeping back down the stairs. "I've gotta let Axiom and Laurell know."

"Uh, Hill?"

She halted and turned back to Evan with a quizzical look.

"I think I know where he went."

Evan and Willow arrived at Lynn and Dawna's home around two o'clock in the morning. The small Craftsman-style house was cloaked in shadows cast by a nearby streetlight. Dome-shaped solar-powered lights lined the pebbled walkway through the yard and led to the front door. Evan moved slowly, Willow trailing behind. He climbed the steps to the front porch and took the key from his jeans pocket. Every nerve in his body was on high alert for signs of Finders or Umbrae or, worse yet . . . Grays.

He entered the house, careful not to trip over the jade Fu dogs he knew rested inside, facing the door as though to protect the home from any would-be intruders.

He fingered the crystal talisman that circled his neck. It was similar to the one Dawna had given to Wayne. By the look of things so far, he had nothing to worry about. No Finders or other unsavory sorts in sight.

"She keeps most of her crystals in her meditation room," Evan said. He led Willow down the hallway to the room in question. The scent of old nag champa incense filled the space. Yup. They were in the right place.

He flipped the light on and quickly located the phenacite and moldavite in a jeweled box. "I don't see any containers of clear quartz in here. They must be in the gar—" He pivoted to face Willow and his words were cut off as soft lips pressed against his, and a supple body melted into him.

His initial shock quickly gave way to desire, as those compelling lips plundered his. She was tall, the tip of her head level with his nose. Her slender body had just the right amount of curves in all the right places. She smelled like the air after a fresh rain. Her mouth tasted like sun-kissed peaches.

She continued to press herself against him, and he finally regained enough of his senses to kiss her back, taking control of the situation and gently probing her lips with his tongue. She sighed and opened to him, and he deepened their kiss. His blood raged through his veins until all he could hear was the roar of it in his ears.

Goddess, she turned him on. He'd been too long without a woman in his life. His cock hardened and bucked, creating a painful lack of space in his jeans. Willow's hands twined in his hair, continuing to tug his face to hers.

It seemed as if the kiss would never end. He sure hoped it wouldn't. Until the distinct sound of a gun cocking penetrated the fog in his brain. His spine stiffened, and he abruptly broke the embrace and set Willow away from him.

A brown-haired woman stood in the hallway, dressed in black from head to toe, arms outstretched with her weapon. Behind her, an ebony-skinned man towered. Evan could make out the dark pools of his eyes even in the dim light from the table lamp. Shit. A Gray.

Axiom pulled his Honda up next to Wayne's beat-up Ford pickup truck and sighed with relief. He had been circling the vast University of Wisconsin campus for hours, looking for a sign of Wayne or his vehicle. He had started to think Thumper and Dawna had been wrong about where Wayne might have gone. He had hoped they *were* wrong. Finding Wayne's truck had been a stroke of luck. Good or bad? He did not know.

"Thank Source," he murmured as he climbed out of his car. He glanced around the area. The campus, at least this part of it, was quiet. Only the chirp of crickets marred the silence. No students milled about. The streetlights illuminated clumps of trees and stretches of lawn. Where was Wayne? He walked toward the nearest building, noting the slow burn of a half-smoked cigar stomped into the gravel parking lot. He bent and picked up the cigar. Wayne's brand. He was not far away.

Evan barely had time to react to the intruders before the Finder took aim. He had never been very good at elemental magic and usually relied on his own specially blended concoctions to blast Finders out of the picture. He always carried a couple vials of the potions with him, but either one could do some serious damage to Dawna and Lynn's home. He needed to get out of the house.

He hurled his body at the Finder, knocking her off her feet. Immediately, the woman started throwing punches, which Evan did his best to evade. Damn, but she was strong.

All Finders were. Once evil took over, they inherited an uncanny ability to push themselves beyond the normal abilities of humans. Finders possessed extreme strength and an ability to withstand pain. They became little more than robots, puppets directed by the Umbrae. Evan wondered how their bodies ached and protested from the abuse after Aurora reclaimed them and they came out of their Umbrae-induced comas.

The Finder was able to twist out of Evan's grasp and got off a shot from her gun. The bullet narrowly missed him and made impact with a three-foot amethyst cathedral. Evan cringed. That was going to piss Lynn off. At least Dawna's talisman was doing its job.

The woman took aim again. Evan managed to mutter a few phrases of one of the coven's oft-used chants to call the element of air. He only hoped it worked.

"Element of air, the breath in my lungs, your powerful force from my will now comes." He sucked in air, then blew out through his mouth.

A gust of wind formed and surrounded the Finder, holding her back. He paused, pleased with his handiwork. Not bad. Not bad at all.

He glanced at Willow and saw she was engaged in battle with the Gray but clearly holding her own against him. Reassured, he raced out the front door.

He released the wind tunnel that held the Finder and, sure enough, the woman was hot on his heels in a matter of seconds. With the Finder safely out of range of the house, Evan lifted a vial of green liquid from his pocket and tossed it at the woman's feet. The resulting blast caused the ground to quake and knocked the Finder off her feet. He grinned. Earth element had always been his favorite. She let out a yelp and landed flat on her back, gasping, the breath knocked from her lungs.

Evan took advantage of the Finder's position to wrestle the gun from her hands. He pointed it at her and ordered, "Don't move."

The Finder's black eyes narrowed, and she spat at him. "You haven't won, witch."

"Haven't I?" he mocked, cocking the gun. Not that he knew how to use a gun, but this one seemed pretty simple.

"You won't kill me. Harm none. Isn't that your code of ethics?" the Finder sneered, tossing her hair over one shoulder in defiance.

Evan tilted his head to one side. "I wouldn't kill you now, while my life isn't in any immediate danger. But just give me a reason to call it self-defense."

A loud crash reverberated through the night. Evan pivoted toward the house. Willow was in trouble. A second later he lost his footing and found himself lying on his back, staring up at the stars. The face of the Finder loomed over him.

"You really should pay better attention," she said.

Despite the fall, he had not dropped the gun. He pointed the weapon at the Finder.

"No matter," he murmured. "I still have this."

The Finder rolled her eyes. "I dare you."

More movement in the house. A thud followed by a groan. He needed to get in there and help Willow. He pointed the gun at the Finder's leg and fired one shot. The bullet grazed her thigh.

"Fuck!" she shrieked before turning tail and hobbling off down the road. He watched her until she faded into the darkness. Huh. He'd never seen a Finder run away before. Maybe she was a new recruit.

He glanced around. Good thing Lynn and Dawna's house was so secluded. The nearest neighbor was half a mile away. With luck, no one had heard the gunshots. Or the blast from the potion.

Evan scrambled to his feet and sprinted back to the house. Heart thudding so hard he feared it might break out of his chest, he swept into the living room. Finding no one there, he crossed to the kitchen area.

The Gray lay on the floor, dazed, ebony eyes narrowed in frustration. He struggled to pull himself up as Willow directed wave after wave of current into him. The energy sparked golden as it zigzagged into the Gray. His lips curled and he snarled. His massive body bucked and reared as he fought the energy.

Clearly, Willow could hold her own. He'd worried for nothing.

"That looks like lightning," Evan said.

Willow flashed him a half smile. "It *is* lightning."

Evan's brows rose. "You can harness lightning? You'll have to teach me that trick."

"I'm a weather deity," she said, as though this explained everything.

"Cool, but what do we do with him?"

Willow's brows knitted in concentration. Her jaw clenched, and she focused intently on the Gray. The current surrounded him more fully and sparked and sizzled as she amped up the energy. The Gray's eyes widened in realization.

"Fuck you," he hissed just moments before his body turned to one giant golden flame. A second later, with a strange popping noise, the Gray disappeared entirely.

Smoke tinged the air, and the linoleum wore a black outline in the shape of the Gray's body—but he was gone.

"Did you kill him?"

A grim expression took over her fine features. "Yes."

Evan didn't bother to hide his shock. "I don't understand. We weren't in any imminent danger. I mean, you had him. You . . ." He didn't know how to finish the sentence.

Willow tilted her head and flashed him a withering look. "What would you have had me do? Let him go? As long as the turned Grays live, the darkness eating this planet continues to grow like the fungus it is."

Acid burned Evan's stomach. "It just goes against everything I believe in."

"Your coven has never had to kill?"

"Only in self-defense or when we had to protect an innocent."

"I see." She eyed him thoughtfully. "Then consider this killing one that will protect many innocents. Does that make you feel better?"

"Not really, no. I still think we could have found another way to deal with him."

Willow spun fully around until she faced him head-on. She closed the few feet between them until they stood eye to eye. Her words came out harsh and ominous.

"Like it or not, we're in the middle of a war, Evan. As in any war, there will be casualties. It pains me to take any life, but this is the reality of our situation. Earth and the Light Realm are in grave danger. There will likely be many things we will have to do in the days to come that we will not like. But for the good of all of mankind and of *my* kind, we cannot afford to hesitate. It's us or them."

Evan didn't miss the fear behind Willow's words. He moved to take her into an embrace, wanting to soothe her, though he realized he had no pretty speeches to give and no promises to make. He could offer nothing but his presence. For what it was worth.

She stepped back before he could hold her, and her spine stiffened. "Let's get the crystals and return to Graves Manor before the Umbrae send more of their minions to stop us."

Chapter Twenty-Five

After minutes of searching, Axiom noticed a sign on one of the doors leading into the brick building:

TONIGHT: WOMEN'S CIRCLE: EMPOWERMENT THROUGH THE GODDESS 7 P.M.–9 P.M.

Ah. He had a feeling he was in the right place. He glanced at his watch. Almost eleven o'clock. The meeting had been over for hours.

He grabbed the door handle and stepped inside an auditorium, replete with theater-style seating for at least a hundred. The room smelled stale, as though it had not been aired out in a while. The main lights had been turned off. A stage dominated the far side of the space, dim backlighting providing the only illumination. At first, he thought the room was empty. Then, a scuffling sound drifted to his ears, followed by a grunt and a female voice whimpering in fear. The sounds came from the stage.

In moments, he reached the stage, moving with the superhuman speed of a Gray. Not for the first time, gratitude washed over him. He had been allowed to keep his powers when he had become human. He could thank Mobius for that. He leapt onto the stage and quickly found the source of the noise.

Two women in their early twenties sat on the floor,

holding each other, eyes round with terror. They whimpered, and their bodies trembled as they watched what was unfolding before them.

A dark-haired man, a Finder, lay on the floor, apparently unconscious. Wayne stood a few feet away from the inert man, an Umbra's thin, talon-tipped hands wrapped around his throat as he struggled to fight off the vile, scaly creature.

Wayne grunted and used one hand to attempt to break the Umbra's grip; with the other, he fired a jolt of ruby red current at the thing. The Umbra hissed and jerked, but did not budge.

Axiom rushed to his friend and wrapped his hands around the Umbra's neck. He hated to touch the creature, but did not wish to utilize elemental magic. Not with Wayne in such close range. He might miss and hit Wayne instead.

Axiom's hands slid on cool, slimy flesh. He fought back the bile in his throat. The scent of rotten eggs combined with the disgusting texture of the Umbra's skin threatened to make him lose his dinner.

Finally, he got a good grip on the thing. Utilizing all of his considerable strength, he pried the Umbra off of Wayne. Wayne fell to the floor, gasping for breath, but not before he managed to send another blast of fire energy toward the Umbra. The Umbra squealed in pain; this time, it had apparently had enough. It quickly tore a hole in the air and pulled itself through. The hole closed up and the creature disappeared.

Axiom held a hand out to Wayne. Wayne took it, still gasping for breath. After a coughing fit, the color started to return to his face.

"What happened?" Axiom demanded.

"A women's circle was just letting out. Apparently it had gone later than expected. A group of Wiccans and New Agers. They were doing some kind of ritual to heal the planet." He motioned toward the two women still cowering in the corner. "Those two were the only ones still here when I arrived."

"And a Finder attacked?"

"Yeah. Then an Umbra."

"I suppose I do not need to tell you coming here was a bad idea," Axiom said, not bothering to hide the disapproval in his tone.

Wayne shrugged, managing to look at least a little ashamed. "I know. But I had ta do it."

"Why take such a risk?"

Wayne rubbed his hands over his face. At first, he did not meet Axiom's pointed gaze, but after a moment, he took a deep breath, clearly resigned. "I'm dying of lung cancer."

Of all the things Wayne could have said, this was the last Axiom expected to hear. His chest tightened.

"You are serious?"

"Hell, yeah. You think I'd joke about something like that?"

"No. I know you would not. It was wishful thinking."

"I s'pose I wanted to do somethin' good while I could. Make a difference," Wayne explained.

Axiom sighed heavily. "You make a difference every day by being part of Hidden Circle and fighting the Umbrae."

Wayne looked sheepish. "Yeah, well, maybe I wanted more immediate action. I don't know. I just couldn't stand sittin' around waitin' for something to happen." He gestured toward the two students, who stood and crept toward the door. "We should probably do something about them, though."

Axiom swallowed the lump in his throat. They would talk more about this once they returned to Graves Manor. Perhaps Wayne's assessment of his illness was incorrect. He refused to believe his friend was really dying. He turned to the two girls, prepared to wipe the memory of the Umbrae, the Finder, and the battle from their minds. He walked toward them, hands raised to indicate he was unarmed.

"I will not hurt you. You are safe now," he said.

One of the girls, a tiny blonde with a short shaggy haircut, stifled a sob, and her eyes went wide as she looked over Axiom's shoulder. Axiom's body grew rigid as his senses registered danger. He spun around to see Wayne striding toward him, oblivious to the figure that rose behind him, arm outstretched, gun cocked and aimed.

"Wayne!" Axiom hollered. He sprinted toward the Finder. Wayne turned, pulling his own weapon from its holster.

Axiom covered the space between himself and the Finder faster than any human could have. And yet, it was not quick enough. The shot rang out with a deafening blast just as Axiom pulled the Finder into a choke hold.

As if in slow motion, he watched in horror as the bullet made impact with Wayne midchest. Wayne's gaze met his and he slid to the ground. One of the students let out a shrill shriek.

A rage unlike anything Axiom had ever experienced bubbled below his skin, swam through his blood, and arced through his body. His arm tightened around the Finder's neck.

"No!" he roared. Wayne made a gurgling noise, then fell silent. Axiom forgot for a moment about his superhuman strength. He forgot his vow to harm no humans. In that moment, all he could see, touch, and taste was pure undiluted fury. He squeezed the Finder's neck until he heard a sickening crunch. He tossed the now-limp Finder to one side and knelt at Wayne's side, touched his neck, and found no pulse.

Tears choked him. He forced himself to push them away and focus on the matter at hand. The two students were creeping toward the door.

He rose and strode toward them.

"You're doing a bang-up job of distracting me from the fact I may never make it back to Earth," Aurora murmured with a flippancy she didn't feel.

They stood in a room that looked just like every other space in the Light Realm. White walls and ceiling, pale translucent light that emanated from thin air. However, in the center of this room an S-shaped pool sparkled with cerulean blue water. Fountains flowed at each end of the pool, sending swirling ripples through it.

Chunks of quartz crystal in varying shapes and sizes, from palm sized to as big as a compact car, surrounded the space. Some of them dipped into the sides of the pool and morphed into benches where bathers could sit beneath the inviting water. The briefest hint of roses and citrus drifted through the air as though the water had been scented with essential oils.

Mobius trailed his fingers over her arms, eliciting goose bumps. "I know you're worried, but Willow is resourceful. She will help the coven get you home."

She sighed. The mention of Willow still irked her. "Let's not talk about Willow."

He dipped his head and pressed his mouth to hers in a short but sweet kiss. "I told you, you have nothing to worry about."

"I know," she reluctantly agreed. "It's just a female thing."

"A female thing?" he moved closer to her and touched her breast, lightly pinching her nipple between thumb and forefinger. "Like this is a female thing?"

Her breath caught at the sensation that shot from her

breast to between her thighs. She gave him a small smile. "You're funny," she said.

He grinned, his straight white teeth flashing between full lips. "I try."

She cocked her head to the side, assessing him anew. "You know, I thought all gods and goddesses were stiff and ultraserious like my dad. I mean, you can't even get the guy to speak in contractions! But you're different."

Mobius's eyes crinkled at the corners, and he let out a chuckle. "I'm much older than your father. And I've been to Earth before. The speech patterns of humans rub off."

"I can see that. It hasn't worked for Dad, though." She raised one eyebrow. "Not that you're down with the current slang or anything." Her words were purposely teasing.

"Slang?"

"Yeah. You know—jargon. The way young people speak."

He gave her a blank look.

"Never mind. Let's swim."

She quickly did away with her gown and descended the steps to the pool, not missing the way Mobius's gaze darkened with desire as he, too, got naked and submerged himself in the water. He approached her from behind. His big hands circled her waist. Just that simple touch jolted her and made her want to spin around and seduce him with mouth and hands and parts of her body that should still have been tired and sore from their latest round of lovemaking.

She wasn't tired, though. She wanted more of him. She lifted his hand to her mouth and suckled his index finger briefly, just long enough to hear his harsh intake of breath. Then she dove beneath the water and swam away.

Hmmmm. She'd never had a boyfriend around long enough to practice her feminine wiles on him. *Teasing can be fun,* she thought, knowing Mobius would come after her. And of course, he did. The liquid sliding over her body felt delicious. She'd never swum naked in public before. Not that this was actually a public place, but she most definitely wasn't alone.

She surfaced near a massive chunk of amethyst and grabbed onto a corner of its sleek form, waiting for Mobius to reach her. His head emerged from the water, followed by broad shoulders and gleaming, massive chest. He flipped his head back, pushing his wet hair from his face. Drops of liquid trailed down his cheeks and over his chest.

Goddess, he's beautiful. He made her feel so comfortable, so free. She could be herself with him.

How did he manage to do that, despite the fact he didn't want a relationship? How had she allowed herself to become so enamored of him? *Was* she enamored? She liked him. A lot. That was certain. She sensed they were kindred spirits. Both of them wanted to be able to be themselves, to be more—and less—than god and goddess. Together, they could let their guard down.

When she thought about it, each of them was the only possible choice of partner for the other. Perfect complements. *Does he see it too?*

Mobius shifted closer to her. He swept one arm around her waist. "What were you thinking just then?"

She shook her head. "Nothing."

"Come now. Tell me the truth."

She swallowed and thought about fibbing, but for some reason, she just couldn't lie to the man. He looked at her as if he knew every inch of her soul, as if he could see right into her heart of hearts. Would he know if she lied? Yes. She believed he would.

"I was thinking about how much I can be myself with you. I've never been able to let my guard down with anyone before."

There. That wasn't too much of a confession. Nothing she would be embarrassed about later.

Mobius's gaze turned tender. He lightly fingered a lock of her damp hair. "I am glad I make you feel this way. I too am enjoying your company."

That was it? He enjoyed her company? *What more did I expect? A declaration of love? Stop it,* she told herself. *Stop getting yourself worked up.* She had made her decision to pursue this thing with Mobius without knowing where it would go, assuming it would go nowhere. No point getting all melodramatic now.

She sidled closer to him, rubbed her body along the hard lines of his, and willed all thoughts away as she stood on tiptoe and pressed her mouth to his lips. When she kissed or touched Mobius, all other thoughts had an uncanny way of falling by the wayside.

Chapter Twenty-six

Axiom pulled into Graves Manor with two bodies in his car. One belonged to the Finder he had killed. The other belonged to his best friend. Laurell came barreling down the drive the moment he pulled up. She'd been waiting for his return. He put the car in park, switched the ignition off, and stepped from the vehicle with a heavy heart.

The moment Laurell saw his face, her own features twisted with worry and she rushed to his side. She ran her fingers over his arms, torso, and face. "What is it? Are you hurt?"

He shook his head. "No. I am fine."

"You don't look well. You look like you just lost your best friend."

At the grimace her words elicited from Axiom, her eyes rounded. "Where's Wayne?"

Axiom gestured to the backseat of the car, where he'd gingerly placed his friend's lifeless form, careful to keep his ever-present cowboy hat on his head, as he knew Wayne would have wanted.

Laurell yanked open the car door and let out a gasp. "Oh God!" She stared at the man lying lifeless on the seat. "Oh no. Axiom, no."

Axiom pulled her into his arms and hugged her tight, needing solace just as much as she. He felt cowardly for soaking up some of his wife's strength, but he thought he might just topple over from the weight of the grief pressing down on him.

Laurell lifted her tear-filled gaze and searched Axiom's face for answers. "What happened?"

"A Finder killed him."

"At the university?"

Axiom nodded. "And then I killed the Finder."

Laurell's back arched in surprise. She opened her mouth to speak, but must have read the anguish in his face, the raw pain, and decided against it.

"We will need to tell the others." She glanced at the car. "And we'll need to have a proper ceremony for Wayne." She choked back a sob, took a deep, steadying breath, and shook her head as though to clear it. "We also need to dispose of the Finder's body."

The sound of wheels crushing gravel intruded upon the otherwise-quiet night. Thumper's hybrid Toyota rolled up the drive. Thumper and Willow emerged, boxes in hand.

"We've got the crystals," Thumper said. "Let's get Aurora and Mobius back here. Things seem to be going from bad to worse."

Laurell ran one hand through her hair. "You don't know the half of it."

"Stay with me," she said.

"The child is dead. The mission is a failure," he replied.

"Stay with me anyway."

"I belong in the Light Realm. I am needed there."

"You're needed here. I need you."

"I must find a way to defeat the Umbrae."

"You don't owe anything more to the Grays. You can't fix the past. We can make a future together. I know you love me."

"I do love you."

"But it's not enough, is it?"

Aurora slept fitfully. The dreams invaded again. She experienced the anguish of losing her lover, her beloved. That was what he'd called her. His *beloved*. Then, he'd left. How could he? How could he call her his beloved and then part from her?

She'd wanted to die from the pain of his departure. A piece of her soul had been torn out and sent away with him when he'd gone. Then, they had come for her. Those disgusting demons that had killed her child, snuffed his little life out before it had had a chance to begin.

She'd fought them with the witchcraft taught to her by her mother, powerful magic passed down through the generations. But all the power she possessed wasn't enough. There had been too many of them. Her last thoughts as the Umbrae choked the life out of her were of Mobius. *Mobius, come back to me. My heart. My love. My beloved.*

Aurora sat up, gasping for air. Her blood pounded in her ears, and her chest ached as though concrete blocks pressed down on her sternum. Her eyes popped open to see Mobius's reassuring face peering down at her. His amber gaze was filled with concern. He touched her cheek.

"You were dreaming," he murmured.

"It was a nightmare." She pressed her eyelids shut, then opened them again in an attempt to clear away the last vestiges of the dream.

"Do you wish to share your dream?"

"I think we should avoid future harmonizations," she murmured, flashing him a wry smile and trying for a nonchalance she didn't feel.

Understanding dawned. "You dreamed of Meri and me again."

She nodded. "You left her." Her words were free of judgment, simply a statement of fact.

"I did. And I've regretted that decision ever since."

"But you did it because of the Grays. Why?"

"Before I'd accepted my first mission to Earth, I'd proposed that the Grays be allowed to remain in the Light Realm. I'd met with much opposition and needed to return to see that my proposal was acted upon." His face clouded with an old shame. "I was among those who first banished them to the Earth plane."

Aurora trailed one hand over his neck and chest, stroking him to lend comfort. "My father said you were also the first supporter of the Grays. And of him. If you hadn't fought for the rights of the Grays, the Council might never have discovered their ability to neutralize the Umbrae. Dad told me how you fought for him to have a place on the Council."

Mobius took a deep, ragged breath. "It wasn't enough to make up for what I did. And now, having left Meri behind, I have yet another wrong to make right."

"The Umbrae killed her. It wasn't your fault."

"If I had stayed, she would have lived."

"Maybe. Maybe not. From what I know of the Umbrae, they are pretty resourceful. If they saw her as a threat, they would have found a way to get rid of her."

Mobius stared intently at her, his gaze searching. "You would forgive me so easily, would you? After all that I have done?"

Aurora shrugged. "It's not my place to give or withhold forgiveness. I'm not Meri."

"And if you were?"

The way he clenched his jaw and the stiffness of his spine made it clear to her just how important her answer was to him. She leaned toward him and gave him the softest of kisses, hoping he would sense and soak up the tenderness and empathy that welled inside of her.

"Mobius, if I were Meri, I'd forgive you. And I'm sure wherever she is now, she's already done so. You've got to stop beating yourself up over the past. You can't change it."

His lips curled into an affection-filled half smile. He didn't respond to her comment. Instead, he gathered her closer to him and pressed kisses on her forehead, her nose, her cheeks, and her neck.

She giggled. "What did I do to deserve all these kisses?"

"Just being you is enough."

Aurora snuggled closer to Mobius, enjoying his attention. Her mind turned, as it usually did when he was around, to thoughts of lovemaking. Before she could act upon those intentions, however, a strange pulling sensation sprang up in her midsection.

"What the heck?" she murmured.

Mobius grew still. "I feel it too."

The feeling grew stronger, as though someone were tugging at her stomach. "What is it?"

"I'd say the coven has found a way to direct us back to our silver cords. We need to prepare for astral travel."

The sound of wind rushing through a tunnel filled her ears. She was floating. Then falling. Then landing with an abrupt whoosh that stole her breath. She felt her soul self settle into her body. She was back! She sensed her hands, arms, and legs. Her limbs tingled, but she couldn't move them. Panic surged. She was in her body but couldn't move.

Then her mother's reassuring voice whispered over her. "Aurora, stay calm. Give your body a chance to adjust to your return. Breathe."

She did as told. She sucked in a deep breath and let it out. A moment later she tried to move her hand again. Relief flooded her as her fingers wiggled. She flexed her toes. Her eyelids fluttered open. The bedroom at Graves Manor and then Laurell's soft features swam into view. Her mother's favorite scent, spicy amber oil, drifted to her nostrils. The smell of home. She really had made it back. Thank Goddess.

She sat up slowly, biting back nausea as the room tilted off center and then righted itself again. Beside her, Mobius stirred, and moments later he, too, sat up. He climbed off the bed and stood as though unaffected by the harsh reentry into his body. At least, Aurora assumed his reentry had been just as harsh as hers had been.

He saw her watching him, and as though he read her thoughts, he said, "I have astral-traveled many times before. I'm not as affected as you must be."

Aurora glanced up, and for the first time, she noticed the pyramid-shaped crystal structure covering the bed. "What is that?" she asked no one in particular.

Lynn stepped forward. "Thumper calls it the homing beacon. It's what guided you back to your silver cords and to your bodies."

It was then that Aurora realized the whole coven was crowded into the room, all eyes on her. Laurell pulled her into a tight hug, squeezing just a bit too hard.

"Mom, easy. I'm okay."

Laurell pushed a lock of hair from Aurora's eyes and smoothed her hand over her cheek as she'd done when Aurora was a child. "I know. I'm just happy to see you back in one piece."

Axiom appeared at her side and pressed a glass of water into her hands. The cool liquid slid easily down her throat, crisp and refreshing.

She glanced around the room. Everyone was there. Hillary, Thumper, Dawna, and Lynn, and the one being she could have done without, the Goddess Willow. She was so happy to be back, though, she decided to let that slide.

She frowned. "Where's Wayne?"

She didn't miss the look that passed between Laurell and Axiom.

"What is it? What's wrong?"

Her father bent and placed his hand on her shoulder. "Wayne's dead, Aurie."

Chapter Twenty-seven

Shock froze Aurora's limbs. She shook her head vehemently. "No way. Not possible."

Her mother's tear-filled gaze spoke volumes. "Oh, Aurie. I'm so sorry. It's true."

Aurora stood, ignoring the trembling of her limbs. "How did he die?"

"A Finder shot him," Thumper explained.

Rage spiked through her, and she immediately tensed, ready to wreak havoc on the Finder. "Where is this Finder?"

"Dead," Axiom said, his face grim.

"At least that's something," she murmured past the lump in her throat. She couldn't believe it. *Wayne's gone.*

Memories flashed. Wayne holding her on his lap when she was very small, making her giggle by wiggling his dentures. Wayne instructing her how to hone her empathic skills. Wayne looking out for her. Throwing himself in harm's way more than once when a Finder or an Umbra attacked her. She would sorely miss his cantankerous but sweet ways.

Her vision swam behind the moisture that veiled her eyes. Her insides ached and twisted, and at that moment, had a Finder appeared before her, she would happily have wrung the life from his or her neck. Wiccan Rede be damned.

Mobius moved to her side. She glanced at him, expecting, waiting for him to pull her into an embrace and lend comfort. He raised his arms as though to do so, then glanced at her father and lowered them to his sides. He shifted from one foot to the other, clearly confused as to how to proceed. *Oh, right. He promised Dad he wouldn't touch me.*

She stifled a hysterical laugh. It seemed so silly now, the whole don't-touch-my-daughter thing. A man was dead. A good man who had been her friend her entire life. And she wanted to lash out at something or someone.

Mobius seemed a good target.

"What's the matter?" she hissed. "Afraid to touch me now that my dad is watching?"

Mobius's jaw dropped. He glanced from her to Axiom and back again. "Aurora, we should talk about this—"

"Oh, now you want to talk? You were pretty happy doing everything but talking when we were in the Light Realm. Now, what? It's back to business as usual? You want me to pretend nothing happened, right?"

Axiom's eyes darkened, and his jaw clenched. "What does she mean, Mobius?"

Aurora spun around to face her father. "You know exactly what I mean. And how dare you try to decide for me whom I can and can't sleep with. I'm an adult, in case you haven't noticed!"

Axiom took a step toward Mobius, hands fisted. "I told you that if you laid a hand on my daughter, I'd—"

"You'd what?" Aurora demanded, standing on tiptoe until she was in her dad's face. "You're going to beat him up?" She let out a sharp laugh. "Great. Just great. That makes a hell of a lot of sense."

Mobius seemed to finally come out of his state of indecision. He tugged her into his arms and hugged her close. She didn't fight him. She pressed her face into his chest and breathed in his clean, spicy scent. A scent she was quickly coming to love. *Love? Did I really just use that word?* Good Goddess, she needed to have her head examined! She couldn't start thinking things like *love* and *Mobius* in the same sentence.

Her spine went rigid, and she disengaged herself from the embrace. "You know what? Screw you both." She glared at Axiom. "Screw you for interfering in my love life." Her gaze pinned Mobius next. "And screw you for not standing up to my dad when he interfered."

She stalked out of the room, leaving both Mobius and Axiom with mouths agape. Once in her bedroom with the door safely shut behind her, Aurora dropped to her bed and melted into a puddle of tears. She wasn't even really that mad at Mobius for not standing up to Axiom. Nor was she all that angry at Axiom for trying to protect his daughter. He'd acted no differently from most loving fathers.

She didn't know why she'd suddenly been overwhelmed by such fury that she'd needed to take it out on them. She grabbed a pillow, cradled it to her chest, and stifled a sob in its soft surface. Or maybe she did know. Wayne was dead, and there was no Finder or Umbra or Gray on which to take out her anger. There was only the memory of a man she'd loved like an uncle, and a tormenting ache in her heart that made her want to howl her suffering.

And Mobius. Mobius, who didn't want to be her boyfriend. Mobius, who made her insides quiver, set her body on fire, and made her heart lurch with hope whenever he was near. *What a mess. What a fine mess.* She was falling for him. No use denying it to herself. Just another painful truth to add to the rest.

She burrowed into the bed and let the tears fall freely. She rarely cried. Other than her one disastrous experience with that sorry excuse for a boyfriend, she'd really had little reason to shed tears. And she didn't like to lose control or display weakness. The Earth Balancer should be strong, in charge, and have her act together.

Right then, though, it felt good to take a break from that role. She didn't care if her tears made her fallible. Human. She was *half*-human, after all.

The coven dispersed and left Axiom and Mobius to talk. Mobius sensed their curious eyes on his back as they filed out one by one. Laurell paused at her husband's side, her face scrunched in concern.

"Husband, don't do anything foolish," she counseled.

"I would not think of it," Axiom said. She let out a derisive snort in response but left the room.

Once they were alone, Axiom eyed Mobius with contempt. "You did not keep your word. A god who does not keep his word is not honorable."

The words made Mobius cringe. "I am sorry, old friend."

Axiom shook his head. "Sorry cannot fix this error. I demand to know your intentions."

Mobius's eyebrows rose. "My intentions?"

Axiom's silver eyes flashed with warning. He almost growled his next words. "Do you intend to continue to use my daughter for your sexual pleasure? Is that what she is to you? A body to relieve the desires of your human form?"

Mobius's skin heated. "Is that what you think of me?" He couldn't keep the indignation from his voice.

"What should I think of you? After you lied to me?"

"I am still the same Mobius as I was. I am a god of the Light Realm and your friend. You must know I would not abuse Aurora in such a manner."

Axiom's lips curled into a sneer. "I know no such thing. I know only that I read affection for you in my daughter's eyes, and I smell trouble ahead for her should she give her heart to you."

Mobius sucked in a deep breath and took a moment to center himself. He glanced around the small bedroom, vaguely registered the flowered wallpaper, the hardwood floors, the dim lighting from a bedside lamp, and the faint smell of lilac from a lit candle.

An innocuous enough space to be sure. Certainly not the type of place where gods ought to get into a fistfight.

He eyed Axiom's taut stance, his clenched fists, and the dark intent in his eyes. The man was ready to pounce. He did not wish to fight his friend.

"Axiom, I respect Aurora. She is much more than just some woman to satisfy my sexual desire. You must believe that."

Axiom tilted his head to one side. "Do you love her?"

The question made Mobius's heart thud so loudly, he wondered that his eardrums didn't burst. Love her? *Of course I love her.* He'd loved her from the moment he'd met her so long ago. He'd loved her as Meri. He loved her now as Aurora. Nothing and no one could change the way he felt about her.

"Yes."

Axiom frowned. "I can see the truth in your eyes. Yet I wonder how this love has come about so quickly? You barely know her."

"I've known her for a century."

Axiom's eyes narrowed with suspicion. "How could this be?"

Mobius sighed loudly. *Should I tell him? Will he believe me? Will he think I've lost my mind?* Either way, he had to explain himself. "I believe Aurora to be Meri reincarnated."

Axiom's jaw dropped. "You mean the woman from your mission? The one you refuse to talk about—

although the pain of her loss is obvious to anyone who dares to look close enough?"

"Yes." Mobius flinched. He'd no idea his pain was that obvious.

"You confirmed this with the Hall of Records?" Skepticism laced Axiom's words.

"You know I cannot."

"Then what makes you so certain Aurora is Meri?"

Mobius cringed inwardly. Willow had asked him this question as well. And she'd been dubious about his answer. *Because I know. In my soul, I feel it.*

"I just know," he said.

Axiom sighed. "Forgive me if I find your evidence to be less than satisfactory."

"You are not the first to doubt me."

Axiom raised one eyebrow. "And if you are wrong?"

"I'm not."

Axiom ran one hand over his eyes. "I am weary, Mobius. This has been a day full of difficult emotions, and I do not wish to fight you."

That was a relief. "I don't want to fight you either."

"I know my daughter well. And despite her earlier outburst, she feels for you. I ask only that if your plan is to return to the Light Realm and leave her here pining after you . . ." His words trailed off.

"What are you asking me to do?"

Axiom let out a strangled, frustrated groan. "Break it off now. Before she becomes even more attached to you. You will only cause her greater pain later."

Mobius couldn't argue with him. He had caused her pain in the past. As Meri. He didn't know what the future would bring or what would happen between him and Aurora. He did know, however, that he would not lie to Axiom or give him any further false assurances.

"I can't make any promises. I am sorry."

A pulse ticced in Axiom's neck. He looked as though

he might just hit Mobius after all. Instead, he moved close to Mobius, so close they stood eye to eye.

There was no mistaking the message in his hard, slate-colored gaze. "Watch yourself, friend. I would tread lightly if I were you."

Then, he stalked past Mobius and out the door.

Aurora found her father brooding in the library hours later. She'd attempted to nap a bit, cried more than a bit, and decided that since she wasn't yet ready to confront Mobius, she'd deal with her father first.

Her father unfolded himself from his chair when Aurora entered the room. Worry lines creased his forehead as he studied her. She could imagine how she looked. She hadn't bothered to wash her face or comb her hair after her less-than-restful nap, and the tears had left their mark. Her eyes burned as though they'd been rubbed in sand.

She crossed the room and stopped in front of him, lifting her head to meet his wary gaze.

"You are still angry with me," he said.

Her eyes narrowed. "Shouldn't I be?"

He sighed. "I probably should not have interfered—"

"Probably?"

"I should not have interfered," he corrected himself.

"You're right. You shouldn't have."

"I was worried you would get hurt," he said. "I wanted to protect you." The earnest expression on his face and obvious contrition in his voice melted away the last remnants of her irritation.

After all that she'd been through in the past few days, including learning of Wayne's death, her father being overprotective was the least of her worries. It was silly to stay mad at him.

"It's okay," she said. "I probably overreacted. It's just that so much has happened recently."

"And for the first time in your life, you have felt as though you had no control over your destiny?" he prodded.

She frowned. "How do you know that?"

He let out a soft chuckle. "You are so much like your mother."

She flashed him a wry grin. "Yeah, but that's a good thing."

"A very good thing."

His gaze turned serious again. "I know you love him, Aurora."

His words rang in the room and seemed to echo off the wood-paneled walls and hardwood floors.

She swallowed and shrugged. "Perhaps."

He tilted his head to the side. "It is alright to admit it."

She bit her lip. *I should have known my own father would be able to tell how I feel about Mobius.* He always could read her easily.

"I'm afraid to say it out loud," she said.

"That makes it more real," he agreed.

"Yes."

He offered her a reassuring smile, and his straight white teeth flashed. "One thing I have learned in my time on Earth—you cannot avoid love. Once it has found you, it will not let go. Fighting against your feelings is futile." Aurora knew he referred to her mother, and to his own mission to Earth, which had resulted in his falling in love with Laurell and giving up his god form to become human and stay with her.

"Thanks, Dad." She knew he wasn't giving her and Mobius his blessing. Not exactly. But he was starting to soften.

Axiom gave her a quick, hard hug and resumed his seat in the wingback chair.

She noticed he had no reading material, no drink in hand, nothing to occupy him in this room. "Dad?"

"Hmm?" He was staring out the window into the night as though he'd already forgotten she was there. The dim light from the table lamp cast shadows over his face and made his square jaw and full mouth appear even more pronounced.

"What are you doing in here, exactly?"

He tore his gaze from the night sky and sighed. "Thinking about Wayne."

Sorrow engulfed her, and she felt her father's pain, a thick and heavy burden on his heart. "Do you want to talk about what happened?"

He cleared his throat. "Wayne died. A Finder died. There is nothing more to tell." His eyes slid from hers quickly, though, and she sensed there was a lot he wasn't saying.

"I'm not buying it, Dad. What are you afraid to tell me?"

"I already answered your question."

She leaned forward and squeezed his shoulder. "Let me be here for you. Like you just were for me."

His gaze pierced her, and she could sense his inner struggle. Finally, he sighed loudly and drew a deep, ragged breath. "I killed the Finder."

She shrugged. "So? I'm sure you had no choice."

He shook his head. "No. But not for the reason you think. I did not kill in self-defense or to protect another. It happened in a fit of rage."

Aurora's lips pursed and her brow furrowed in confusion. Realization came slowly, but when it did, her father's brooding manner suddenly made sense.

"I see. And now you hate yourself."

He tilted his head to the side. "I am not proud of my actions." His jaw clenched. "It was as though I was a Gray God again. I suddenly could not control my shadow side. My rage spilled over, and the next thing I knew, the Finder was dead."

Aurora crouched low and placed her hands over her father's. "Dad, you're human now. Humans have a dark side too, you know. You reacted to the sight of your friend being killed."

He blinked. "Does that make it right?"

She didn't have an answer for him. She had a feeling they would all be tested in the days, weeks, and months to come.

"Oh, Dad," she murmured, wrapping her arms around his neck and hugging him. "I love you." It was all she could offer him. She didn't have the answers he needed. *Does anyone?* she wondered.

Chapter Twenty-eight

The next evening there was a full moon. Aurora found the rest of the coven congregating on the back porch, clad in their ritual attire of cloaks in various colors and fabrics. Aurora had slept most of the day away. She'd been overcome with a fatigue unlike any she'd ever known. Laurell came in to check on her a couple of times, forcing her to eat and remarking that she was worried Aurora was depressed.

Aurora had reassured her mother she was fine, but in truth, she wasn't so sure she *was* okay. She didn't know if it was the stress her body had been through while awaiting her return to Earth or receiving the news about Wayne or what, but she didn't feel like herself.

She yawned, shook the cobwebs from her mind, and approached Hillary. "Someone should have woken me. I almost missed the ritual."

A sympathetic smile creased Hillary's broad features, though the smile didn't quite reach her eyes. No one was smiling much since Wayne died.

"We would have woken you before we started. Dawna is still gathering some supplies. You need your rest," she said.

Hillary wore a long black robe with spiderwebs woven into the fabric to symbolize the goddess she felt such an affinity for, Ariadne. The hood surrounded her face like a picture frame, making her striking dark eyes stand out even more. She looked beautiful. And every bit a High Priestess.

While Fiona and Reese were away, the rest of the coven had been taking turns leading ritual. Next to the High Priestess and High Priest, Hillary had been a practicing witch for longer than anyone else in the group. She had also known Wayne longer than any of them. It seemed fitting she should lead the night's ritual.

Aurora glanced at the coven members, all of whom were adorned in robes and cloaks. She had an urge to get into her own ritual attire. She was underdressed.

They'd buried Wayne on the property in the Graves family graveyard. Hidden Circle Coven was his family; he had no living relatives. Laurell had thought it fitting that he should be buried there.

Axiom had explained to the coven Wayne's reason for taking off on his own to fight Umbrae, but it had not made his death any easier. Dawna had been quick to point out that people survived cancer all the time. If anyone had been stubborn enough to kick the disease, it would have been Wayne. Soon after, Dawna had found the protection talisman she'd given to Wayne on his dresser. He had purposely not worn it the night he died.

"Why would he do that?" Aurora had asked, horrified at what she already knew to be the answer.

"He believed he was dying. He wanted to go out in battle," Lynn had murmured.

"That sounds like something Wayne would do," Thumper had agreed.

Aurora sighed now, blinking back tears. Tonight, they would perform a ritual for Wayne, to bid him a safe and happy passage to the Summerland.

Tomorrow, they would plan their attack on Rhakma, the Umbrae, and the Grays. Wayne's death made it clear they couldn't delay confronting their enemies any longer. And now that Aurora and Mobius were back, the coven was better prepared to fight. Even Willow had offered to hang around a bit longer. Of course, she could only remain on Earth in god form for a couple more days.

"Go change. You have time," Hillary said, breaking into Aurora's thoughts.

"I'll be right back." Aurora hurried into the house and up the stairs. Once in her room, she donned a red dress and a crimson cloak made of sheer fabric with tiny pentagrams embroidered over it. Wayne had loved the color red. He would have approved.

Besides, it was almost Beltane. Red was the color associated with the holiday, the hue of passion and love, fresh roses and ripe apples, things that represented growth and fertility. Beltane was also Wayne's favorite holiday. It wasn't unusual for him to bring a lady friend to Beltane celebrations and disappear halfway through the festivities.

She smiled at his love of life.

Aurora sighed and turned to head back outside. Before she could, however, Mobius appeared in the doorway. He wore black slacks and a shirt of the same color. Moisture clung to his hair from a recent shower, and the flame-colored locks looked even brighter against the dark backdrop.

The scent of soap traveled to her nose. She cleared her throat, realizing she was staring. *Why does he have to be so damn good-looking?*

"What do you want?" she asked, unable to bear the silence.

He stepped into the room and crossed the distance between them. He lifted his hand to her cheek and stroked her skin lightly. "You look beautiful," he said.

"Thanks."

"I wish you were dressed up for a happier occasion."

"Me too."

His hand trailed over her face, then to her shoulder, where he rubbed light circles. Just that brief touch made goose bumps break out over her skin. The room heated with the unmistakable combustion of their sexual chemistry.

She wanted to kiss him. She wanted to be naked with him and to forget all about death and loss and grief. She found herself leaning into him, her lips parting in invitation. He moved closer as though to press his lips to hers. Instead, he kissed her forehead. Racked with disappointment, she twisted away from him. He tugged at her hand, and she tilted her head to him, though she purposely avoided his gaze.

"We should talk," he said.

"Three words no one wants to hear," she muttered with sarcasm.

"I don't understand."

She shrugged out of his grip. "Never mind. We'll talk after the ritual." *He probably wants to tell me it's over.* Her heart lurched at the thought, but she forced herself to lift her chin and keep her spine straight. She wouldn't let him know how much the idea of having a breakup talk upset her. *Of course, we'd actually have had to be together in order to break up.*

Mobius hesitated, his mouth open to say something more, but he decided against it. "After ritual then."

The ritual was beautiful. Lit tiki torches created a circle on the back lawn of Graves Manor. The coven filed in deasil, moving clockwise one by one until each had taken a place around the circle. After Hillary anointed the group with a sweet-scented almond oil, Dawna cast circle.

Laurell invoked the elements. "We call air, element of the East, and ask that you keep the memory of our friend alive in our hearts. We call fire, element of the

South, to keep the candle lit and the fire burning for our friend as a beacon for his crossing to the Summerland. We call water, the element of the West, in order to give voice to our emotions, so that our tears may fall freely and cleanse our grief. We call earth, element of the North, to keep us strong in the face of our loss."

Thumper spoke next, raising his hands to the heavens. As he spoke, Aurora could have sworn the stars dotting the night sky twinkled a bit brighter. "I invoke thee, Lord and Lady, God and Goddess. In particular, on this night, I ask Cerridwen, Celtic goddess of death and rebirth, to preside over this ritual in honor of our friend and fellow witch, Wayne. Guide him to his place in the Summerland and help bring him peace as he embarks upon a new journey and a new beginning. I ask the god Borvo to be with us this night, in order to lend his powers of healing to all those who have loved Wayne and who grieve for him now."

Lynn stepped forward then, holding a withered rose in her hand. "For death and rebirth are all one. And although our hearts are heavy, we also experience joy for Wayne because we know he will return when the season is right." She tore the petals from the rose and lifted her palm, letting them be taken by the gentle breeze.

"For as we die . . ." Laurell began.

"So shall we be born anew," Axiom finished. He held his hand aloft and the tiny seeds he'd carried in his palm were picked up by the wind and carried away.

Hillary took center stage again. "Let's take this moment to think of our friend, our brother in the Craft, Wayne. Each one of us will present a memory of Wayne to share with the group. I'm passing a stick of burning sage around the circle. As you hold the sage, present your memory of Wayne, and when you are finished, blow softly on the sage and send your intent into the smoke that Wayne's passage be swift and his rest be free of illusion and full of peace until the time comes for him to rejoin us here on Earth."

One by one, the coven members shared stories of their time with Wayne. Some of the stories made the group laugh. Some brought additional tears. When the time came for Aurora to say her piece, she had a lump in her throat the size of a Buick. She cleared her throat and glanced at her mother, who smiled her encouragement.

"In all the time I knew Wayne, I never saw him without that damn cowboy hat on his head." This brought chuckles of agreement from the coven. Aurora had been told no one besides Axiom had seen him without the hat. And that was only while preparing him for burial. He'd been buried in the hat as well. And Axiom wasn't telling what he'd seen when the hat came off.

Aurora continued. "I don't know if he was hiding a Mohawk or a shiny bald head or a third eye or what, under there." Her lips curled wryly. "But I do know that behind that gruff exterior of his was a heart as big as the state of Wisconsin. And he would have done anything for any one of us. He risked his life for me more than once. I, for one, am forever indebted to him." She blew on the sage stick Hillary handed to her.

"Until we meet again, my friend," Aurora murmured. The sweet herb filled her nostrils, and tendrils of smoke drifted in a spiral higher and higher until they blended with the night.

Rhakma entered the dank, dark cave and found only a few Finders and a couple of Grays milling about. The Umbrae came and went according to their master's bidding. Most of the Finders had housing in town, apartments and homes they shared, financed by whichever Finder's bank account and credit hadn't been completely obliterated yet.

The turned Grays were living among the Finders, taking refuge where they could.

The cave was as dark as usual, the few torches providing only marginal lighting. The foul odor of the Umbrae and the stench of the Finders' sweat was almost too disgusting to bear. A couple of Grays sat in a corner and stared listlessly into the darkness. They had a catatonic look about them that made Rhakma wonder if they were ill. Not that he cared.

"You," he directed to a female Finder with short blonde hair and circles under her eyes. "Where is Nilram?"

She shrugged. "He was here for a little while earlier. He left something for you, though." She pointed to a metal table. Rhakma did his best to ignore her odor: sweat and urine and a crude attempt to cover the scent with sickeningly sweet perfume.

A small wooden box sat on the table. Rhakma opened it to find the lock of ebony hair he needed. Good. Nilram had gotten his message and left Aurora's hair for him as requested. Now, he just needed the witch.

Footsteps mucking through mud and the beam of a flashlight bobbing indicated his guest had arrived.

"Damn, it stinks in here!" came an agitated female voice from the opening of the cave. A tall, heavyset woman with short hair died bright orange stepped into view. Her ample body was covered with tattoos and piercings. She wore a T-shirt that said "Hex You."

He'd found her hustling people out of cash by giving them fake psychic readings and removing nonexistent curses. She had no intuitive ability. She liked to think of herself as a witch, though she had none of the power or the tedious moral code of a true witch.

What she did have, however, was some knowledge of spell casting. Certainly enough to help with the spell against the Earth Balancer, who according to his source in the Light Realm had found a way back to Earth despite his best efforts to thwart her return.

The woman, who called herself Kali after the Hindu goddess of destruction, glared at him with hands fisted on wide hips. "You could have warned me I'd be walking through swampland to get here."

Rhakma offered a false smile. "My apologies. I am glad you made it safe and sound."

She grunted. "Yeah, well, no thanks to you. I tripped twice out there on some rocks, and I'm pretty sure I hurt my back again. Which is probably going to mess up my Workers' Comp claim."

He stepped forward and handed her a wad of cash. "Here is the money I promised."

She grabbed the money from his hand, her mouth pulled into a wide, greedy grin. "All five hundred?"

He nodded. "It's all there."

"Where's the hair?"

"Here." He pointed to the box on the table. She hurried over and dumped the contents of her bag onto the table. She noticed the Grays as she did so. "What's wrong with them? Are they high?"

Rhakma nodded. It seemed as good an explanation as any. "Very."

Kali shrugged and went to work on her spell. Fifteen minutes later, she'd finished. Five minutes after that, Rhakma grabbed the witch from behind and twisted her neck until it snapped. Better not to leave any loose ends. He would not want the Earth Balancer's coven to trace the spell back to the witch and therefore to him.

He stared at her lifeless body, head cocked to one side. "I've met Kali," he murmured. "She is a fierce and powerful goddess. You are not fit to wear her name."

Chapter Twenty-nine

Evan found Willow reclining in a lawn chair on the back patio, her head tilted back and face turned to the sky. Her golden hair shimmered beneath the porch light, and the silver, close-fitting robe she wore sparkled like diamonds. She appeared every bit the goddess. Just her profile, small straight nose, and pouty lips took his breath away.

The breeze washed over him, refreshingly cool. He smelled rain in the air, though no hint of cloud marred the otherwise-perfect night sky.

His heart raged against his ribs with such ferocity he almost turned back, but, sweating palms and all, he forced himself to approach her. After all, she was the one who had come on to him.

"Stargazing?"

"Something like that." She didn't turn to face him. She just kept staring off into space.

He pulled a chair next to hers. "Mind if I join you?"

Her gaze swept over him with only mild interest. That stung. "If it pleases you."

He plopped into his chair and cleared his throat. "How long will you be staying here?"

She shrugged. "A couple more days. After that, I would have to take human form to survive here."

"What keeps you here for a couple more days?" A quiet hope flared inside of him.

"I sense a final battle drawing near. I might be needed."

"Oh." *So much for her wanting my body,* he thought. Obviously, he'd misunderstood her intentions. Their exchange at Lynn's house had been some kind of strange fluke. Or maybe all goddesses ran hot and cold. It wasn't as if he'd had much experience with such beings.

Hell, it had been a long time since he'd been intimate with any woman, let alone a goddess.

Feeling foolish, he started to rise, but she stopped him with a hand on his knee. Her touched burned even through his blue jeans.

"Why are you leaving?" she asked.

"I thought you might want to be alone."

"No. I am enjoying your company."

"So, you want me to stay?"

"Yes. If it pleases you."

He smiled. "It does."

She returned his smile, pearly white teeth flashing even in the dim light. Was there any part of her that wasn't perfect? He doubted it.

"So, tell me what it's like in the Light Realm. What do gods and goddesses do in their spare time?"

She blinked. "Spare time?"

"Yeah. You know, for fun."

"Fun. Hmmmm." She pondered his question for a moment, her brow crinkled in concentration. "We help humans transition from one lifetime to the next, we do what we can to protect Earth from evil . . ."

"And?"

"And we study the ancient texts to strengthen our powers." This last comment came out a little hesitantly. She clearly didn't know how to answer him.

"That all sounds like work. What do you do for pure enjoyment?"

She bit her lip. Then, her eyes lit. "Sometimes I swim in the crystal springs."

"Ah! That's something, at least."

"Yes. It is quite enjoyable."

Silence ensued. Willow studied her fingers. Evan studied Willow. *Think of something to say. Make conversation,* he commanded himself.

"Why did you kiss me?" he blurted out. The words were spoken before he could stop them. Ah, hell. It was what he'd been wondering all night. Might as well ask the question and get everything out in the open.

Willow tilted her head in consideration. "I kissed you because I was curious."

That was certainly not the response he'd expected. "Curious about what?"

"I wanted to understand why Axiom and Mobius are so drawn to mate with humans."

Evan's lips twisted wryly. "And what did you decide?"

"I enjoyed our kiss. I especially liked it when you pulled me tightly against you and I could feel the hardness of your sex against my own."

Evan's blood heated at her words. The frankness of her talk both confused and excited him. He'd never met anyone like her. No woman had ever spoken so openly to him.

"I'm . . . um . . . glad that you liked it." He pushed his glasses back to the bridge of his nose and wiped moisture from his brow.

More silence. She stared at him with such intensity, he shifted in his chair and wondered if he had something on his face.

"As much as I enjoyed our earlier encounter . . . ," she began, tossing her hair over one shoulder and leaning close to him. Her stunning eyes sparked with mischievousness. "I fear I do not have the whole picture yet."

Evan's mouth parted, but he couldn't speak. She was

coming on to him again. He hadn't been flirted with in a while, but he knew feminine wiles when he saw them.

"No?" He finally managed to eke out that one word on a whisper.

"No. So, Evan, do you think you might like to make love with me tonight?"

Evan didn't hesitate. He grabbed her hand and rose quickly, pulling her to her feet. "Absofuckinglutely."

Mobius rapped his knuckles three times on Aurora's door. It was late. He'd purposely waited until the rest of the group had settled and the house was quiet before going to her room. He'd wanted to avoid the curious stares of the rest of the coven.

"Come in," came Aurora's voice. He entered the room and shut the door behind him. She was perched on her bed, still wearing her red dress. Her black hair cascaded around her shoulders and shone like silk in the reduced light from the bedside lamp. A red candle burned in the corner of the room on a little altar and scented the air with apples and spice.

She noted Mobius's gaze. "I'm burning it for Wayne," she said. "Apple pie was his favorite."

His throat tightened as sorrow claimed her features. He crossed the room and sat on the bed beside her. He noted the moisture in her eyes and wanted to wipe away her pain. His palms itched to touch her, but when he raised his hand to her face, she shrank back.

"You said you wanted to talk," she said. "So talk, but don't expect me to cry and beg you not to break up with me. I don't really care what you do."

Confusion spiraled through him. "Is that what you thought I came to say to you? That I don't want to be with you?"

"Isn't it?"

"Of course not. How could you think that, after the

time we have spent together? Isn't obvious in the way I touch you? The way I kiss you?"

Her breath caught at his words. This time, when his fingers trailed her face, she did not move away. She turned in to his touch.

"What are you saying?" she asked, a mixture of hope and trepidation filling her silver eyes.

"I'm saying that I love you, Aurora. I do not know what that means for our future, but I know that it means I want to figure out a way for us to be together."

It was the truth. He didn't know how their relationship would work, he didn't know how the battle with the Umbrae would end, and he didn't see that he could abandon his place on the Council to become human.

He just didn't have the answers. But he knew he could not imagine his future without her.

Tears filled her eyes. He didn't know if it was joy or more grief that caused this. He leaned in and kissed her forehead, her nose, her cheeks, willing the tears away.

"I don't know what to say," she murmured. "I mean, you hardly know me. I hardly know you."

It didn't matter to him that she didn't profess her love for him too. He knew she loved him; he could read it in her eyes, feel it in the way she touched him.

"In my soul, I've known you forever," he said.

Aurora clutched his shirt, her eyes darkening. "Mobius, I'm tired. I'm tired of fighting and darkness and death. Make love to me. Let me taste life."

Her words came out breathy and strained. Mobius wrapped her in his arms and eased her back onto the bed. He ran one hand over her cheek and traced her lips with the tip of his finger. She opened her mouth and her tongue teased the tip of his finger; then she sucked his finger in. Her mouth was hot and wet against his skin. His breath caught, and his cock hardened in response.

She released his finger, and he claimed her mouth. He

devoured her lips with a kiss. His tongue danced with hers, each stroke, each mesh of lips and teeth becoming more aggressive than the next.

There was a quiet desperation in the way she responded to him, in the way her body undulated and her hands grabbed at his clothes.

He'd intended to take her slowly, to let their passion reach a slow burn, but she wouldn't allow a leisurely seduction. Her small but able hands undid his shirt, and she broke their kiss long enough to help him yank the garment over his head. Next, nimble fingers unbuttoned his pants, and they, along with his boxers, joined the shirt on the floor, a pool of black fabric against the brown of the hardwood floor.

Her hand closed around his erection. His pulse sped, and it took all his self-control not to buck against her hand and beg for her to increase the friction. Source, how she tested him! How easily she made him lose control.

"I'm naked and you are not," Mobius whispered in between kisses and licks over her neck, her shoulders, and her décolletage.

"You're right," she responded, a naughty gleam in her eye.

"This is not fair," he said. He ached to feel her bare flesh against his own. He slid the straps of her gown over her shoulders and tugged her out of the dress in one fell swoop. He ran his hands over her breasts, her waist and hips, relishing her soft curves and satin skin. Goose bumps dotted her arms, and she shuddered at his touch.

Mobius painted first one breast, then the other, with his tongue, lapping at each taut peak until she squirmed beneath his mouth and grabbed his head, pulling at him for a deeper intimacy. He suckled the erect nubs, then nipped lightly with his teeth.

"Oh," she breathed. "More."

He lifted his head. "You want more?"

She gazed at him through heavy-lidded eyes. "Yes."

He suckled and licked his way down her belly. When he reached the triangle of soft ebony curls at the apex of her thighs, he blew lightly on her sex. Her legs fell open in acquiescence, and she lifted her hips toward his mouth. Her head twisted from side to side, and her face flushed. Her lips parted as her breath came out in little pants.

Knowing that he was the cause of her excitement only made Mobius more crazy with desire.

Lust raged through his veins hot as forest fire, but it was nothing compared to the absolute and irrevocable love he had for her.

"Taste me," she commanded.

His arousal grew fiercer at her boldness. The soft sheets of her bed were agony as they teased the heat of his erection. He needed to have her wet, open, and ready beneath him. But first things first.

He let the tip of his tongue dip into her sweet valley with quick, shallow strokes. She moaned and tried to grab his head, but he circled her wrists with his hands and held them down. He would tease and torment her. He wanted to make her crazy with desire.

Aurora writhed and squirmed beneath the delicious onslaught of Mobius's tongue. As he changed the pace and switched from teasing her with his tongue to suckling her with his whole mouth, the heat surging in her blood turned into an inferno. Her sex was on fire. Moisture trickled down her thighs. Mobius lapped and suckled her with an intensity that made her head spin.

She didn't want to climax yet. She wanted him, the whole wonderful long, hard length of him, inside her when she touched ecstasy.

She grabbed at his head, twined her fingers through his thick hair, and tugged. "Mobius, please."

He lifted his head. His amber eyes were deep and smoky colored, the hard angles of his face soft with passion. "What is it you wish of me, my beloved?"

My beloved. The endearment reached through the haze of her passion and warmed her insides even more. Made her need for him to take her fully still more intense.

"I need you inside of me," she breathed.

He slid up the length of her body, hard planes brushing against pliable curves. His chest against her chest, a tantalizing taste of the deeper joining to come. He prepared to enter her. She shook her head.

His eyebrows rose in question.

She twisted beneath him until her back was to his chest and she could feel the length of his body pressed along hers. "This way. I want you in me as far as you can go."

The thought that he would take her this way, that he would join with her as deeply as possible, made her wild with longing. She needed to be taken fully. She needed to make this real.

He loved her? Then let the truth of his declaration be ground into her with each thrust. One sinewy arm slid beneath her, palm splayed across her chest. The other cupped her mound as seeking fingers flicked the engorged pearl at the tip of her entrance.

He pushed inside her with one thrust and filled her to her core. His erection throbbed, and her inner muscles spasmed in response.

"Is this what you wanted?" he whispered in her ear.

"More," she rasped. "I want more."

He moved in and out, and with each entry and withdrawal pressure built inside her like a mounting storm threatening to break loose. The ache between her legs grew in intensity. Each flick of his finger between her legs in time with each plunge of his cock brought her closer to her peak.

"I can't hold off much longer," Mobius murmured, his voice strained. "Come for me."

A moment later, her world exploded into a million pieces, and she cried out her pleasure as Mobius roared his own release. Afterward, he turned her to face him and cradled her in his arms. She snuggled close.

This is home, she thought. Her eyes welled with inexplicable tears. For the first time, she had someone in her life who made her feel safe, who seemed to see deep inside her, and who didn't expect her to be anyone but herself. An aching sensation spread through her chest and constricted her throat. That dark, empty space in her heart was suddenly bathed in sunlight and the gentle breeze of hope.

He loves me. And despite herself, she loved him.

The realization made her catch her breath. A moment later, she released the breath slowly, evenly, and with resignation. She wasn't going to hide. It was too late to slam the door on her feelings and pretend she was only interested in a physical relationship.

Completely satiated, she felt sleep pulling at her. She fought the exhaustion and opened her eyes. Mobius's lids were shut, his jaw slack, his lashes dark shadows over his cheeks. His hair tumbled around his face, red flames against tawny skin, mussed from her hands raking through the silky strands.

"Mobius," she whispered, her heart like a Ping-Pong ball against her ribs. "I love you." It was the truth, no matter how unbelievable to her, no matter that it made no sense. She knew in her bones that the depth of feeling she had for Mobius was the real deal.

He hugged her hard and kissed her forehead. "Ah, my beloved, my Meri. I love you too."

That one sentence filled her veins with ice. And the glimmer of joy that had settled inside her at Mobius's admission of love quickly flickered out like a candle flame extinguished by an unexpected gust of wind.

Chapter Thirty

"Get out," Aurora cried, jumping up in bed and pushing at Mobius's chest.

Half-asleep, Mobius moved slowly, his eyes taking a moment to focus. Aurora's face scrunched, and she shoved his chest again with frenzied, frenetic movements.

"What's wrong?" he asked, trying to grab the hands that continued to pummel his shoulders and torso. She was fast, though—he couldn't quite get hold of her. When her fists landed, it didn't tickle; she had the strength of a goddess, after all.

She ignored his question. Instead, her eyes sparked with fury, and she shoved him hard. So hard that he toppled backward off the bed and landed on the floor.

"What the . . . ?" He scrambled to his feet.

"Here. Take your clothes," she hissed. She tossed his shirt and pants at his feet.

He held his hands up in surrender. "Wait a minute. Tell me what's wrong and I will leave." What had gotten into her?

"You don't know?" she snapped. "You make love to me, you tell me you love me, and all the while you're thinking of another woman." Moisture welled in her eyes.

It took several moments for Mobius to realize what she referred to.

"You mean Meri," he murmured. Contrition lanced him. He had not meant to refer to Meri. Half-asleep and 100 percent spent, he had experienced the same surge of love and adoration and pure contentedness he'd always felt after making love with Meri. Meri. Aurora. They were one and the same. Only, Aurora didn't understand that, and now she thought he was in love with a ghost from the past.

"Yes, I mean Meri," she said. "You're still in love with her. How can I compete with a dead woman?"

"You don't understand," he said.

"I think I do," she retorted, her chin lifted in defiance, her back ramrod straight. He recognized this stance: she feigned indifference and a tough-girl facade whenever she hurt most inside. His stomach clenched. *I am the one causing her pain, and that is not acceptable.*

"Let me explain," he pleaded, hands splayed in a gesture of surrender.

She sighed loudly. "Will you leave my room without having your say?"

"No," he said.

"Fine. But put your pants on first." She glanced at his crotch. Heat flooded her face. "Your nudity is distracting."

He slid into his pants and sat next to her on the bed, noting with frustration her quick shuffle away from him as she put a foot of space and a pillow between them.

He didn't bother to point out that if he wanted to touch her, no pillow would stop him. She hugged the sheets to her chest tightly, hiding her own nakedness. The unspoken message behind her actions made his chest ache.

A wave of possessiveness washed over him, and he longed to yank her hands from the sheets and press her bare body against his again.

How was it that mere moments ago they were melted

together as one, and now a chasm existed between them that seemed a mile wide?

"You fear I am still in love with Meri and therefore cannot really love you."

She nodded.

"It's true. I do still love Meri. I love her as much today as I did then. It is as if no time has passed since our parting. That is how strong my love is," he said, emotion making his words thick.

She watched him warily, and her shoulders slumped. He scooted closer to her and put his hands on her shoulders, wanting to offer comfort. She stiffened, but didn't pull away.

"But Aurora," he continued, "my loving Meri does not diminish my feelings for you. I believe that you and Meri are one and the same person."

Confusion tinged her features. "I don't understand."

"You are Meri reincarnated." Now that he'd finally spoken the words, a weight lifted from Mobius's shoulders. It seemed he had been guarding this secret forever. It was a relief to tell Aurora his belief about their past-life connection.

Besides, it no longed seemed necessary to hide the information from Aurora. Hadn't she already said that if she were Meri, she would forgive him for leaving as he did?

Silence greeted his announcement. Long moments ticked by while he awaited Aurora's reply. Wariness touched her face.

"You seriously believe that, don't you?" she asked finally.

"Yes. I do."

"Do you have any proof?"

"I know it in my heart, Aurora. And you know it, too."

"Do I? How do you figure that?" she quipped, scrambling from the bed and crossing to her dresser. She found a T-shirt and shorts and pulled on the clothing with quick, jerky movements.

Mobius bit back his exasperation and tried to keep his voice calm and cajoling, though he wasn't certain he succeeded.

"You said you have been having dreams of me and of Meri. I believe you are remembering our past life together."

Hands on her hips, she tilted her head and gave him a pointed look. "You said the harmonization could be making me pick up your memories."

He cleared his throat. He had said that. "Yes, I know, but—"

"Can you honestly say it's not possible that the reason I had the dreams is due to the harmonization?"

He could not lie. "I do not know of any god who has harmonized with a human before. I do not know what type of reaction it would cause."

She nodded. "Have you confirmed this in any other way?"

His jaw clenched. "No. There is no way for me to be certain."

"Well, then, that's that." She brushed her hands together as though she were dusting her palms. "You should leave my room now."

Mobius grimaced at the dismissal. He glided closer to her and raised his hand to her cheek, letting his knuckles caress her face. "Aurora, you must believe me. I love you."

She flinched and took a step backward. His heart sank at her retreat.

"No. It's not me you love. It's some warped idea of who you think I am." Her eyes glistened with tears. "I thought you were different. I thought I could be myself with you. You're just like everyone else. You only care for me because of who you think I am or who you want me to be."

His jaw hardened. *It's not true. I know you. I know you better than you know yourself.* "You have this all wrong."

"I was wrong, alright. I was wrong to fall for you." She swallowed hard and wiped at her eyes. "But I won't make the same mistake again."

He lifted his palm to her and held out one graceful yellow tulip that had suddenly appeared in it—a last effort to touch her. She blinked, clearly still impressed by his ability to create matter from nothing.

She took the tulip with a grudging expression. "How the heck do you know yellow tulips are my favorite?"

He offered her a half smile. "They were Meri's favorite, too."

She scowled and flung open the door, waving her arm toward the hallway. "Get out."

Willow sank into Evan's kisses with fervor. She scooted farther from the edge of his bed and pressed her body close to his. The heat from his skin seeped through her gown and made her own flesh tingle. His hands roved her body, touching her face, her breasts, her hips, then moved back to her breasts, where her nipples waited, erect and ready.

His mouth trailed her ear and her neck, and then he kissed his way down the neckline of her gown. Her breathing became heavier, matching his labored rhythm. She rubbed her hands over his shoulders; they were surprisingly taut and muscular, something she hadn't noticed during their last intimate encounter. His stomach muscles bunched beneath her hands as she lightly dusted them with her fingers.

His mouth closed over her breast, hot and wet through her gown. Spirals of pleasure shot through her limbs as the silky fabric of her garment became saturated. Her nipple responded as though his tongue teased bare flesh.

So this is what it feels like, she thought. Pleasurable. Not as pleasurable as harmonization, however. Then again, she realized she had not yet experienced the gamut of human lovemaking. She knew there was more to come. She was just about ready to demand he get on with it, when his hands circled her back, and he lifted his head.

His pale green gaze met hers, seeming to search her face for something. His hands fumbled at her back and then over her hips.

He smiled sheepishly. "Sorry, it's been a while. How do I get you out of this thing?" He gestured toward her gown.

Suddenly, his aura flared with shades of pink and red. She read emotions in his energy field. He was experiencing extreme attraction to her. Some might say he was feeling—how did humans phrase it?—*a crush.*

She also detected nervousness and vulnerability. A realization hit her. Their mating would mean much more to Evan than it would to her. When she refused to engage in further relations with him and returned to the Light Realm, he would be hurt. She frowned. Perhaps he was not the right choice of human for her sexual experimentation.

"Evan, I have changed my mind," she said, pushing at his chest.

He sat up, confusion flickering across his handsome face. "Did I do something wrong?"

She shook her head. "No. I just realized it would not be right for me to use you in this manner."

He fumbled on the bedside table for his glasses, which he'd discarded there earlier. He slipped them back on his face and regarded her with a mixture of surprise and confusion. "Use me?"

"Yes. For sex. I would be using you and your body, and that would not be right."

His mouth curved wryly, and amusement twinkled in his eyes. "Please, use me. Use my body."

She was not fooled. He might not realize it at this moment, but having sex with her would only cause him pain in the long run.

She stood from the bed and brushed her hands over her clothes, smoothing the wrinkles.

Evan rose. "Willow . . ." His voice trailed off. He sighed loudly, at a loss for words. Disappointment tinged his features.

"I am sorry, Evan." She touched his cheek with her hand. "You should know, however, that I found your kisses and your touches very arousing."

"Uh, thanks," he murmured.

And with that, she swept out the door and down the hall.

Chapter Thirty-one

"This protection spell should do the trick," Lynn said, scribbling the spell into the coven's *Book of Shadows* the next morning.

Laurell glanced over Lynn's shoulder and scanned the document. "We should perform the ritual tonight. Dawna didn't have a time frame on when to expect the attack. We probably shouldn't wait."

Aurora came around the corner and entered the kitchen just in time to witness this exchange. A number of supplies crowded the countertop: candles, an athame, a minicauldron, and representations of all the elements, including salt for earth, a red candle for fire, spring water for—what else?—water, and incense to represent air. In the middle of the supplies sat a silver, engraved pentacle.

The aroma of freshly baked blueberry muffins drifted to Aurora's nose and made her stomach growl. She grabbed one of the muffins from a plate sitting on the counter.

"Who are we protecting?" she asked. She took a bite of the muffin and swallowed. Delicious.

"A metaphysical center that Dawna had a vision about," Lynn answered, pushing a chunk of her spiky blonde hair out of her eyes.

"The Umbrae plan to attack this center?"

Lynn nodded. "From what we can tell, yes."

"Why there?"

Laurell answered this time. "We aren't exactly sure, except that all the people they've been targeting appear to be Lightworkers."

"At first we thought they were just picking on local folks to lure us out of our protection circle, but now we realize there is something more going on," Lynn finished.

"Tampa isn't local," Aurora murmured more to herself than to her mother or Lynn.

"No, it's not," Laurell agreed. "But it's where the Umbrae seem to have set up some sort of headquarters."

"Why Tampa?" Aurora asked.

"We don't know the answer to that," Lynn said. "We think there is a large amount of light energy in that area. You know, possibly a heavy population of Lightworkers."

Aurora nodded. "Well, let's get the protection spell done then. Might as well do what we can to help out."

"Yes. Let's," Lynn agreed. She paused and tilted her head to the side. "You know, someone should probably go to the metaphysical center and warn the pastor of the church there."

"What are we going to say? Earth is a battleground between good and evil forces, and we're pretty sure your church and its members are in the middle of the war zone? Oh, and you're being targeted by foul-smelling demons? And by the way, we did a protection spell for you, so that should help ward them off for at least a little while?" Laurell's sarcasm was tinged with wry humor, but her point was made.

"Mom's right, Lynn. We can't just go announce ourselves to the pastor. He or she will think we're nuts."

Lynn shrugged. "Maybe. Maybe not. New Age sorts are typically pretty open-minded."

Aurora glanced at the muffin in her hand. Her stomach turned, and nausea kicked in. She set the muffin on the counter. She sighed and went to the sink to get a glass of water, hit by an immediate and extreme thirst. She filled a cup and gulped its contents down in a few swallows, then set her glass in the sink.

A wave of dizziness came over her suddenly and then disappeared just as quickly. She returned to the table on unsteady feet and sat.

Her mother gave her a quizzical look. "You okay, Aurie?"

Aurora rubbed her eyes and yawned. "Yeah. I'm just tired." She hadn't slept well at all. After she'd kicked Mobius out of her room, she'd lain awake for hours replaying the time they'd spent together over the past days.

Their conversations, the rare but heart-stopping appearance of his dazzling smile, their life-altering love-making . . . All of these moments had flashed through her mind and sliced painfully through her heart.

The part of her that had opened up to Mobius, that tiny corner of her soul she kept just for herself, had closed back up again, tight as a fist.

Aurora pushed these thoughts from her mind and struggled to focus her energy. Her mother still stared at her suspiciously.

"We should perform the ritual. The sooner the better," Lynn said, pulling Laurell's attention from Aurora.

"Okay. I'll see if any of the others want to help. The more energy being lent to the spell, the better," Laurell said, standing.

"I'll help," Aurora offered.

Aurora didn't miss the worried glances Laurell and Lynn exchanged.

"Not a good idea, Aurie," Laurell said. "You've been through a lot, and you still don't look well. Please go rest some more."

Aurora started to argue, but another bout of vertigo hit, and instead she nodded her agreement. Five minutes later, she was back in bed, preparing to drift off to sleep.

A couple minutes after that, Willow and Mobius appeared in her doorway.

Aurora blinked one eye open and sighed at the sight of the god who had broken her heart and the goddess who wanted him for herself. "I'm almost afraid to ask."

"Her aura is somewhat murky," Willow announced after peering at Aurora for what seemed like hours.

"Any idea what is causing the problem?" Mobius asked.

"I am not certain. It appears to be of a minor nature."

"A slow energy drain of some kind?"

"Yes. The question, however, is what is the source of the attack?"

"That's it!" Aurora cried, sitting upright in bed and pushing her covers aside. "Will you two quit talking about me like I'm not here?"

Mobius tilted his head to one side. "My apologies."

Aurora noticed that his face was drawn, and he had dark smudges beneath his eyes. *He didn't get any sleep last night, either. Good.*

Willow didn't offer any apologies. She simply continued to stare at Aurora, chin in hand, brow furrowed in concentration.

"Why exactly are you two here?" Aurora asked. She smoothed her hand over her hair and hoped that in her very brief period of rest, she'd avoided bed head. *Not that I should care what I look like. Mobius and I are history.*

"Your mother said you didn't look well," Mobius answered. "I informed her of Willow's ability to read energy."

"And now you think I'm under attack again?"

"So it would seem."

"Who is trying to get to me now?" Aurora sighed. This business of being psychically attacked was getting old. A few weeks ago, the Umbrae were too busy steering clear of her to even attempt such a thing. Now with the Grays and Rhakma on their side, they were growing bold. And she didn't like it one bit.

Willow ended her inspection. "I am not certain who is the culprit this time." She turned to Mobius. "Frankly, I am perplexed as to why she is not more resilient after the Violet Fire cleansing. She should not be so easy to attack psychically."

Mobius nodded his agreement. "Any suggestions?"

"Hello! You're doing it again," Aurora protested. "I'm sitting right here."

Willow ignored her. "The good news is that the force behind the attack isn't very strong. She may kick it on her own. But you might consider performing additional harmonizations with her. That may help strengthen her for now. At least until we can determine the source."

At the suggestion of another harmonization with Mobius, Aurora's spine stiffened. She did not want to be in such close proximity to him anytime soon. She needed to keep her distance from him so she could get her head, and her heart, together.

No doubt Mobius sensed her unease. He gave her a wary glance. "I'm not certain Aurora is interested in further harmonizations with me."

Willow's curious gaze fluttered from Mobius to Aurora and back again. "Oh? Lovers' quarrel?"

Heat flooded Aurora's cheeks. "None of your damn business."

Willow's perfectly arched eyebrows rose. "Would you prefer to harmonize with me?"

Mobius smiled as though this were the greatest idea ever. "That is an excellent solution!" he exclaimed.

Aurora's eyes widened as disbelief spiraled through her. "It is?"

"Of course. Willow is a goddess. She is just as capable of performing harmonizations as I am."

"Um. That's just sort of weird."

"Why? A harmonization does not have to be sexual in nature. Humans turn it that way, but a god can keep the energy exchange quite neutral."

Gods turn it that way, too, Aurora thought, but kept the words to herself. Mobius certainly had to assume some of the blame for their previous harmonization taking a lusty turn. It couldn't have been just *her* desire making the process steamy.

Strictly platonic exchange or not, she had no desire to cozy up to Willow. The goddess might have good intentions, but for some reason, maybe an irrational one, she seemed like the enemy to Aurora. *Maybe enemy is too strong a word. Maybe more like a rival. Although she doesn't know it yet, she's already won.*

"If I absolutely have to harmonize, I'll do it with Mobius." Her narrowed gaze warned him not to read too much into her agreement. "As long as we keep things strictly platonic."

A pulse ticced at his temple. "Of course."

Chapter Thirty-two

Mobius sat on the back porch of Graves Manor sipping on the vile brew Axiom so enjoyed, scotch. Thumper had been enjoying the same liquid on the back porch when Mobius had arrived, and had practically insisted Mobius partake as well.

He had mumbled something about *weird-ass, can't-make-up-their-minds women* and convinced Mobius it would be impolite to let him drink alone. Of course, mere moments after Mobius had agreed and settled beside him with his own glass of scotch, Thumper had said he didn't feel well and wandered back into the house on unsteady feet.

Mobius had then begun to reflect on Aurora's sudden dismissal of him the night before. She believed he was in love with a ghost and that his feelings for her hinged upon his belief that she was Meri.

Coming so close to having Meri's love back in his life, only to have it ripped away again, made him ache inside. He hadn't slept a wink and had stayed up most of the night searching for a way to convince Aurora it was safe to love him. He scowled. In order for him to do that, he would have to convince her she was Meri.

"You and the Earth Balancer have had a parting of ways? Perhaps sleeping with her was a bad idea." Willow's voice broke Mobius's silent reverie. He glanced over his shoulder to see her striding across the deck, golden hair shimmering under the late-afternoon sun. Her white and bronze gown made a swooshing sound as she walked.

He gave her a pointed look.

She sat in the lawn chair beside him. "What? You did not think I was aware of the intimacy of your relationship with Aurora? I knew when you were in the Light Realm that you had been doing more than just harmonizing with her."

He frowned. "I didn't speak of it."

"Your confession wasn't necessary. The way she reacted when she saw us together in my quarters made the situation obvious. Human women are so predictable with their jealousy." She sighed and relaxed back into her chair.

He ran his fingers through his hair in agitation. "I have made a mess of things. Axiom is barely speaking to me, and Aurora wants nothing to do with me."

Aurora snorted. "Axiom I can understand. What happened with Aurora?"

Mobius sighed. He wasn't sure he wanted to talk about the situation. Then again, he often turned to Willow for advice in the Light Realm when dealing with important issues. Perhaps she could shed some light on this matter.

"I told her that she is Meri. She doesn't believe me and thinks my interest in her is solely due to my belief in our past-life connection."

Willow arched one eyebrow. "Isn't it?"

Mobius scowled, but decided to let the comment go. "I need to convince Aurora that she is Meri." *If I can do that, perhaps she will understand we belong to each other.* But how could he make her believe him? He peered at Willow, an idea dawning.

"What?" she asked. "Why are you looking at me like that?"

"I need you to do me a favor," he said.

She eyed him dubiously. "What sort of favor?"

"I need you to visit the Hall of Records and confirm that Aurora is Meri."

Willow's pale purple eyes flashed with unease. "No one is supposed to review another's Akashic records. That task is limited to humans who are between lives, and they are only allowed to see their own records."

"I'm aware of the rules. Just this once, let's bend them a little?"

She frowned. "If you're so willing to bend the rules, why don't you do it yourself?"

"I would not get past Moira." Moira was the goddess in charge of keeping the Akashic records safe, and she protected the Hall of Records.

"True."

"You and Moira, however, are close. Perhaps she owes you a favor? Just as you owe me?" He hated to remind Willow of the one time he had bent the rules for her. During Axiom's mission to Earth, there had been a security breach. Before they'd realized Rhakma was the culprit, they'd needed to interrogate the gods and goddesses.

Avina, the goddess of justice, had been asked to perform a mind sweep of all the gods. After confessing to Mobius that she had more-than-friendly feelings toward him, Willow had asked that the results of her interrogation not be released to the rest of the Council. Mobius had reluctantly agreed.

Now, Willow pursed her lips, her distaste evident as she soaked in Mobius's words. She flipped her hair over one shoulder. Her movement surrounded him with the aroma of a summer storm, earthy and slightly metallic.

"You know once I return, I can't come back again in god form."

"I realize this, yes."

"I could return, I suppose, in human form. That would allow me a few months' time here." She frowned. "But then I would be no more powerful than you and would not add much to your battle."

Mobius smiled. "Even in human form, you are a force to be reckoned with, Willow. However, you do have a point. And truly, I think you should be back in the Light Realm, leading the Council in my absence."

"Fine," she finally said. "But then we are, as they say, even. Yes?"

He nodded.

"Suppose that I do determine Aurora is Meri. Why do you think that Aurora will believe me? I can sense her distrust of me."

"She believes you want me for yourself. And if that were true, the last thing you would admit is that Aurora and I are soul mates, linked together in a past life and bound to reunite." Mobius knew that Willow did have some interest in him, but he also knew the goddess had the utmost integrity. He trusted her to bring back the truth from the Hall of Records.

"And what if I determine she is not Meri?"

"You won't."

That night, Mobius appeared once again at Aurora's bedroom door. She let him in with knots in her stomach.

"I'm here to harmonize with you," he said, his voice low so as not to wake the rest of the household.

She glanced at the clock. "It's after midnight. I thought you'd be here earlier." They hadn't actually confirmed a time to meet, but she had assumed it would be sooner. She'd been sitting in nervous anticipation for almost two hours. She didn't like being nervous. It wasn't her style. Damn him for always having such an effect on her.

"I was telling your parents what transpired in the

Light Realm during our trip." His expression turned grim. "Tomorrow, the coven will meet to formulate our plan of attack against Rhakma and the Grays."

They needed to eliminate Rhakma and as many of the Grays as possible in order to bring light and dark energy back into balance.

"Right now, though," Mobius continued, "we need to get you as strong as possible."

She grimaced. "I'm tired of feeling weak. I don't understand why the Violet Fire didn't protect me better. I thought it was supposed to make me even stronger."

Mobius sighed. "It is. Perhaps we underestimated the strength of the dark energy on Earth right now and its pull on your shadow side."

She didn't like the sound of that.

"Well, let's get this over with," she said with a matter-of-factness she didn't feel. She'd insisted that they keep their harmonization platonic, but the truth was, she didn't know if she'd be able to stop herself from taking it to the next level. She seemed to have very little control of her body when Mobius was around.

If I can control my heart, I can control my body, she thought. *And control it I will.*

Mobius stepped close and placed both of his large hands on her shoulders. Her skin beneath tingled and throbbed.

If only he didn't look so damn sexy. He wore simple attire—jeans and a white T-shirt—but the jeans hugged his muscular thighs, and the shirt did little to hide the solid planes of his chest and the broad expanse of his shoulders. Crimson waves brushed his shoulders, the shade even more striking against his white shirt. She itched to run her fingers through his hair.

Instead, she put her hands on his hips and took a deep breath. The scent of the nag champa soap her mother had recently placed in all the guest bathrooms lingered on his skin. A spicy yet clean scent. She closed her eyes and tried to ignore how wonderful he smelled. She braced herself for the first rush of energy.

Mobius shifted his stance, and his hips moved beneath her hands. One of his palms stroked her cheek. Her eyes flew open.

"A harmonization won't work if you go into it with dread and fear," Mobius said. "You must relax."

"I'm trying!" she exclaimed, frustration seeping into her voice.

His gaze darkened. "Is it so hard to trust me now?"

She bit her lip. "It's not about trust, Mobius. I know now what motivates you, and unfortunately, you're just like everyone else in my life."

He frowned. "I don't understand."

She pulled back from him and raked one hand through her hair, debating with herself over how much to say. *What the hell. What have I got to lose?*

"My entire life is dedicated to being the Earth Balancer. I'm supposed to be strong, invincible, and focus on saving Earth from evil. But sometimes I get tired of being that person. I guess I just wanted someone to see me for who I am. I just wanted to be accepted for myself."

Mobius tilted his head. "You are accepted for who you are."

"No, I'm not. Even my conception was for the sole purpose of creating the Earth Balancer. My own parents conceived me only to fill a role."

"Aurora, that's not true. I know for a fact your mother thought she could not have children and that a large part of her decision to assist in the mission was the promise of a child. Of you." He paused. "You really should talk to your parents about how you feel."

Aurora's lips thinned as his words washed over her. She almost felt ashamed for speaking her secret fear aloud. She knew how much her parents loved her. It wasn't their fault that she was who she was.

Emotions, raw and powerful, washed over her. Her parents were just one issue. There was more. She had to get this out. She'd never told anyone how she felt. Sometimes, she thought she might explode from holding her anguish inside.

"The one boyfriend I had, the one I let see who I really was, found out about my magical life and freaked. My father had to erase his memory. The very thing everyone else in my life wants me around for was what sent him running for the hills." She let out a sarcastic laugh. "Ironic, huh?"

"Aurora, you are more than the Earth Balancer."

She tilted her chin. "What do you know?"

"I know you are a loyal friend, a passionate woman who feels deeply, and a talented artist."

His words squashed the snappy comeback she'd been formulating. Apparently he'd remembered her sketches. And once again, he remarked on her talent. Why that should warm her insides, she didn't know. But it did. And he thought her loyal and passionate. She liked to think that was true.

It seemed Mobius had noticed more about her than she'd thought. Maybe he wasn't so blinded by his obsession with Meri after all.

Don't go there, she silently commanded herself. *Get this harmonization over with and then stay away from the man. He is only going to bring you heartache.*

She cleared her throat. "I'm more relaxed now. I'm ready."

He pulled her close and rested his chin on her head. Her lids fluttered shut, and she snuggled into his chest. The energy rushed up her legs and spine and then washed over her head and limbs, pulsing, fierce, and powerful.

A colorful explosion of every chakra shade appeared in her mind's eye and made her senses reel and her hands tremble. She clenched her fingers in his shirt and held on, grateful for the strength of his body holding hers.

Pleasure pushed through her veins with the rush of her blood. She moaned, the vibrations even stronger than she remembered from the Light Realm. How was that possible? There Mobius had been in god form; here he occupied a human body.

Vaguely, she realized that Mobius was shaking and jerking against her. She had lost control of her own limbs. She arched her back and sensed Mobius's essence move through her as her own soul self passed through him.

Then, they were one being, one giant ball of light and darkness and a kaleidoscope of color and raw sensation. She burned inside. Her breath came in short, quick gasps.

The current spiraled through her and built, becoming more intense until it peaked and rained over her.

After the energy dissipated, her knees buckled. If Mobius's body not been supporting her, she would have fallen. He led her to the bed and lowered her back onto the pillows.

"How do you feel?"

She opened her eyes and gave him a half smile. "Sort of floaty and peaceful."

"Excellent."

It dawned on her that not once had the harmonization taken a turn toward the sexual. She hadn't been consciously trying to stop it from moving in that direction, though if it had gone that way, she'd have halted the process. Or at least she'd have tried. She wondered if Mobius had somehow blocked any potential lustful impulses.

"How about you?" she asked. Mobius blinked as though he'd been deep in thought. His face went pale.

Shivers of alarm pricked her skin. She sat up. "Are you okay?"

He held his hand up and sucked in air. "I'm fine."

Her forehead crinkled in concern. She didn't believe him. "You don't look fine."

His jaw clenched, and he squeezed his eyes shut. When he opened them, what she saw made her blood run cold.

His eyes. His beautiful amber eyes had turned a deep, disturbing, mottled gray.

Chapter Thirty-three

Mobius gripped the bedpost at the foot of Aurora's bed as if it were a lifeline. Images swarmed his brain, violent and destructive, visions of dark deeds committed by evil humans whose souls had been taken by the Umbrae. Nausea claimed his stomach, and he struggled to squash the images.

"Mobius, listen to me. Listen to my voice." He barely heard Aurora's command above the racket reverberating in his head, a buzzing sound like bugs around a streetlight, multiplied by a hundred.

He struggled to push the visions away and succeeded for a moment. Long enough for Aurora's worried face to swim into view. Long enough to realize Axiom, Thumper, and Hillary had entered the room. When had Aurora summoned them? He had been so racked by his sudden illness, he hadn't heard her call out to them.

"Focus on your own light energy," Aurora said.

"Strengthen your aura, push the darkness away." This came from Axiom.

Mobius did as they instructed. He willed his god force toward the insidious evil trying to take hold of him. He sucked in a deep breath and expelled it with force while envisioning himself whole and his aura impenetrable. Almost as quickly as it had appeared, the bizarre illness disappeared. The buzzing in his ears ceased. He could see clearly again.

Mobius rubbed his hands over his eyes, his hands unsteady. "What just happened?"

"I believe you just had a taste of what a Gray experiences on the Earth plane when dark energies become too prominent," Axiom said.

Mobius frowned. "You mean that was some sort of attack?"

"It would seem so."

"I don't understand," Aurora broke in. "How could a Light God be affected like that?"

Axiom shrugged. "I do not know." His brow furrowed, and he peered first at Aurora and then Mobius with keen interest. "What were you doing prior to becoming ill?"

"We were harmonizing. We believed Aurora to be suffering from a focused psychic attack. Willow thought the harmonization would help strengthen Aurora." Mobius did not miss the way Axiom's gaze narrowed at this explanation. No doubt, he assumed the harmonization had been undertaken for more than medicinal purposes.

Aurora must have noticed too, because she touched her hand to her father's shoulder. "He really was just trying to help me," she said.

Before Axiom could respond, Hillary stepped forward with hands on ample hips, mahogany-colored eyes sparking. "Why didn't one of ya'll ask me about this psychic attack? You know I've gotten pretty good at dowsing for that type of thing."

Aurora tilted her head to the side. "I didn't realize."

"Humph!" She reached into her bathrobe pocket and pulled out a silver chain with a star-shaped amethyst crystal dangling from the end. "Good thing I've been keeping this pendulum close by me so I could charge it with my mojo."

The others moved close to watch Hillary's ministrations. She spun around, lips pursed with displeasure.

"Hey, quit crowding me. You act like you've never seen a pendulum."

When Axiom and Thumper backed up, she returned to her task. She held the gadget at different parts of Aurora's body. She kept her hand completely still and seemed to commune with some unseen entity. As if of its own accord, the pendulum swung either left to right or in a circular motion.

After several minutes of this behavior, Hillary cocked her head to the side and regarded the group with a smug smile. "Well, I can tell ya what it is, alright."

"What?" Aurora asked.

"A very lame, badly cast witchcraft spell." She raised one eyebrow. "You let anyone get hold of any personal effects? Hair? Fingernail clippings?"

Aurora shook her head. "No. I'm well aware we need to be careful of leaving that stuff lying around." Then a thought occurred to her. "Shit. The first Gray I fought with in Tampa. He pulled my hair. I thought it was odd he would fight like that."

Hillary nodded. "Hair would do it."

"Who would cast a witchcraft spell against me?" Aurora wondered aloud.

"Beats me, but this curse reeks of the sort of nasty energy a real witch wouldn't dare put out. Especially since it would just come back to him or her," Hillary said.

"Do I need to be concerned?" Aurora asked.

"I wouldn't be. My guess is that whatever effect it was having on you would have dissipated pretty quickly if you'd just focused on strengthening your auric field. Frankly, I'm surprised it was able to affect you at all."

Mobius was surprised as well. And gravely concerned. "The witchcraft spell is no doubt connected somehow to Rhakma. This is more evidence of the Umbrae's hold on Earth. We need to attack soon."

"What's going on?" A very sleepy-eyed Laurell wandered into the room, yawning and pulling her bathrobe closed. "Some kind of meeting I wasn't invited to?"

"I did not wish to wake you. I would have filled you in," Axiom said.

Laurell eyed Aurora and then Mobius, who still sat on Aurora's bed. "Well then, why don't you start now?"

Aurora could not fall back asleep. Like her mother, Lynn and Dawna hadn't woken when she'd cried out for help earlier. She envied them their full night's rest. She glanced at her bedside clock. Four A.M. Several hours since Mobius and the rest of the coven had retreated to their rooms. With a groan of frustration, she swept aside the covers and left her bed.

She tugged on her bathrobe and padded down the hall toward the stairs, thinking to get something warm to drink in the hope it would quiet her mind enough to sleep. She noticed a thin beam of light peeking from beneath the door of Thumper's room. *He must not be able to sleep either. Maybe I'll see if he wants some tea or hot chocolate, too.*

She tapped lightly on his door.

"Come in."

She stepped into the room to find Thumper hunched over a desk in one corner. He was surrounded by vials and mixtures and potions and Goddess knew what else. The room had become his makeshift laboratory while staying at Graves Manor.

He glanced up, pushing his wire-framed glasses back on his nose. His dark hair was spiked in places, as though he'd been running his fingers through it. When he saw her, he sighed, and a hopeful expression was replaced with one of resignation.

"Why so disappointed? Were you expecting someone else?" she teased.

"Yeah. Willow."

She didn't bother to hide her surprise. "Care to explain? You two have something going on?"

Thumper rolled his eyes. "*Had* something going on is more like it."

"Huh." She didn't know quite what to make of that news.

"Is that so surprising?" Thumper pushed his chair back from the desk and the microscope he'd been peering into, and fixed her with a pointed stare. She read the challenge in his stance and shook her head.

"No. Not at all." Thumper was an attractive man, actually, if you liked the bookish sort. She'd always thought of him as she did the other coven members, like family. An uncle. Or a brother. "So where is Willow, anyway? I haven't seen her lately."

"Mobius said she went back to the Light Realm to check on something for him. He wouldn't say what."

"Oh." She couldn't say she was sorry to see the goddess go. The woman still unnerved her.

"I've been doing some thinking," Thumper said.

"About . . . ?"

"Mobius's reaction to your harmonizing."

"You've got some ideas about what is going on?"

"Sort of. A theory, really."

She settled onto the edge of his bed. "Spill."

"Well, the Umbrae turned the Grays by letting them reanimate each other with a harmonization. Then, each Gray performed a process that looked very close to a harmonization with Nilram, only utilizing the opposite energy. More like a deharmonization, for lack of a better term. Which would make sense, since he has no light energy in him."

Aurora nodded. "Nilram is pure evil. It makes sense that merging energies with him would have a detrimental effect. What does that have to do with Mobius?"

"Well, what happens if you merge a Light God with a Gray God?" He didn't let her answer, just kept on talking. "I'll tell you. The dark energies of the Gray deplete the Light energies of the Light God. You and Mobius experienced this firsthand."

Just what was he getting at? "And?"

"So what would happen if you merged a Gray, a Light God, and Nilram?"

Maybe she was just tired, but she did not understand what he was saying at all. Or maybe she didn't want to. "What are you getting at, Thumper? I don't understand."

"I do," came a deep baritone voice from behind. Aurora jumped and spun around. Mobius's large body filled the doorway. His hair was messy, the loose black sweats and black T-shirt he wore were rumpled, and dark circles smudged the skin beneath his eyes.

"You shouldn't sneak up like that. You scared the shit out of me," she snapped.

"My apologies. I was heading downstairs for a drink and saw the light on," he explained.

"You couldn't sleep either, eh?" Thumper offered, glancing between Aurora and Mobius with interest.

"No," Mobius said. "I could not." He stared pointedly at Aurora. "I haven't slept at all well lately."

She squirmed beneath his gaze, knowing full well the reason for his insomnia. *Too bad. I haven't been sleeping. Why should he?*

"So, you said you understand what Thumper means?" She tugged her bathrobe tighter and smoothed her hair with one hand, suddenly self-conscious about her own disheveled appearance.

"I don't know for certain, but I would guess that combining your energy with mine would greatly strengthen your ability to destroy dark energies."

"Okay. But what about you? Why the effect on you?"

He shrugged. "I can only assume that my power is siphoned off by you during a harmonization."

Aurora bit her lip, attempting to make sense of Mobius's words. "Are you saying that I basically sucked the life out of you?"

"Essentially, yes. Apparently, you have more than just the ability to neutralize dark energy. You can also assume light energy and alter it."

"So, what do we do with this? How do we use this information?"

Mobius raked one hand through his hair. "You could attempt a harmonization with another Gray. It's possible that you—or we, actually—could reclaim the turned Grays."

"So, I find a way to harmonize with a Gray? And then, what, you jump in for a three-way?"

"Something like that."

She groaned. "We can't go around grabbing every Gray we find and forcing him to harmonize with us. Besides, that would take forever. We don't even know how many turned Grays exist."

"Um, I have an idea," Thumper said, stepping from behind his desk and striding toward them. "What if instead of striking against each individual Gray, you go straight to the source."

"The source?" Mobius's eyebrows rose.

"The one who turned them. Nilram."

Aurora blinked as realization dawned. "If we destroy Nilram, it's possible his hold on the Grays will end."

Mobius nodded. "This might work."

A sick sensation invaded Aurora's midsection. "Just one problem, though." She glanced at Thumper. "The process would likely kill Mobius. We have to find another way."

Mobius touched her shoulder and shook his head, his jaw hard and his gaze resigned. "No. We don't."

Chapter Thirty-four

"Unacceptable!" The word erupted from Axiom's mouth as he leapt to his feet, knocking his chair to the side.

There was a sharp thud as the chair made impact with the wood flooring, breaking the stunned silence of the coven members. The group sat around the dining-room table, mulling over Mobius's announcement. Mobius glanced at the different members of Hidden Circle Coven.

Hillary sat with arms crossed over her ample bosom, nodding her agreement with Axiom. Lynn and Dawna's expressions were grim. Laurell perched anxiously on the edge of her seat next to the spot where Axiom had been sitting. Thumper and Aurora sat closest to Mobius. Aurora's face was blank. Mobius wondered what she was thinking.

After their conversation with Thumper, she'd grown silent and distant. Even more distant than she'd been since they'd first returned to Earth.

"We've gone over our options many times. This is the only way," Mobius insisted. He'd spent the remnants of last night thinking about Thumper's theory and its implications. If the process worked the way he thought it might, then they could wipe out the leader of the Umbrae and reclaim the Grays at one stroke.

Not only could he make amends for the wrong he'd

done the Grays centuries ago, but also assure that Aurora would be safe. At the moment, the Grays were the main threat against her. He would, in a way, be making up for leaving Meri, for not staying by her side when she needed him most during his previous mission to Earth.

"It's too risky," Laurell said, her hazel eyes filled with concern. "You could die, Mobius. For real. Not just your physical body." She lent emphasis to the last sentence, as if he weren't well aware of the potential hazards of the plan.

It is what I must do, Mobius thought. *For the Grays. And for Aurora.*

He let out a groan of frustration. "I fully understand the risks. We waste time. We should be formulating our plan of attack."

Axiom shook his head. "We must come up with another plan."

Mobius sighed. "We have no other options. The longer we vacillate, the more human lives will be lost and the stronger the darkness will grow. Besides, keeping the Earth Balancer safe is of the utmost importance to our long-term plans. Reclaiming the Grays removes the one true threat to her well-being."

He glanced at Aurora, who watched him with a look of dismay. Could it be that the idea of losing him frightened her? The thought filled him with a strange hope. A hope that he quickly squashed. *If I go to my death, then there is no future for me at all, let alone with Aurora. Best to disengage now.*

Laurell stood then and crossed the room to where Mobius sat. She bent and touched his shoulder. "It's not fair to make us choose between our daughter and our dear friend."

Mobius swallowed, his throat suddenly clogged with emotion. He glanced over Laurell's head to where

Axiom had stopped his pacing and stood rooted to the spot, staring at him with an unreadable expression.

"She is right, Mobius. We cannot choose. Despite our recent differences, you know you are . . . You know how I . . ."

Mobius had never seen his friend at a loss for words. Mobius squeezed Laurell's hand and rose, crossing to where Axiom stood.

"I know, old friend." He placed one hand on Axiom's shoulder. "There is no choice for you to make. I have made up my mind. And you will not change it, so you might as well help me."

Axiom's jaw tensed, and his expression became pained. His shoulders slumped for the barest of moments; then he straightened his spine and nodded briskly. "Very well. We will plan our attack for tomorrow evening. Tonight, however, we will celebrate."

Hillary rose from her seat. "That's right, folks. It's Beltane, remember? Let's not all sit around looking glum. Mobius ain't dead yet."

"Come on, guys," Dawna said, fingering one lock of her shiny black hair. "We've gotta stop thinking about what could go wrong and instead focus on a positive outcome. You know, you get what you expect, and all. . . ."

"I'll get the bonfire ready. And I'll drum," Thumper said.

"I'll drum too," Lynn offered.

"Okay then," Hillary said. "We've got a party in the making, and we're going to celebrate this fertility festival right. Just 'cuz we're all stuck here together and we're feeling the stress doesn't mean we can't have some fun."

Mobius watched the group dismantle and took his seat again at the table as the room emptied.

Aurora paused for a moment in front of his chair. She

swept her ebony tresses from her face and offered a small smile. "I took your advice," she said.

His brows rose. "Oh? What advice?"

"I talked to my mom about what happened before I was conceived. She told me all about how she thought she couldn't have kids until Dad appeared in her life and promised her she'd have me. She told me how much she wanted me. My conception didn't have anything to do with the world needing an Earth Balancer. She just wanted a child of her own."

Her face was open and vulnerable, and he wanted to say something meaningful to her, wanted to respond to her in a way that showed how much his insides warmed to see her resolving an inner fear that had caused her so much turmoil.

Before he could open his mouth to speak, though, she said, "Anyway, I just wanted to tell you that." Then she spun around and made an abrupt exit.

He watched her go, lifting the glass of water he'd brought with him to the meeting and taking a long swallow. The liquid trickled slowly down his taut throat. A myriad of emotions raced through him. He had made his decision, yet he could not help feeling sadness that this was how the story of Mobius and Aurora would end.

That afternoon, Mobius settled in for a nap with the intent of meeting Willow on the Astral Plane. He lay on his bed in the spare bedroom he'd claimed as his own and closed his eyes, willing his breathing to slow and his limbs to relax. The familiar buzzing sensation soon shook his body, and he lifted up and out.

Moments later, the hazy landscape of the Astral Plane filled his vision. He stood on a crystal slab surrounded by vibrant green grass and brilliant lavender-colored skies. He always willed his surroundings on the Astral

Plane to be something pleasant. He never understood the human need to paint the place as dreary and desolate. You got what you expected on the Astral Plane.

He settled down into the grass, waiting.

He smelled Willow's scent before he heard her.

"I learned from the peering pool of your plan to overtake Nilram. I insist you reconsider," Willow said. She glided toward him in a swirl of fuchsia skirts and halted in front of him, forcing him to tilt his chin to look at her.

"Don't bother attempting to change my mind," he said.

"It's foolishness."

"It's necessary."

Her eyes narrowed. "You're doing this for the wrong reasons."

"You know nothing of my reasons," he muttered, anger beginning to burn his gut. He should not have to explain himself to Willow. They had enjoyed a long friendship, but she was pushing the boundaries of that friendship by continuing to question his decision.

"I know you wish to right some wrong you believe you committed against Meri. And I know that Aurora is not Meri. She is not your lost love."

Mobius sucked in a deep breath. He felt as if the air had been kicked from his lungs. *She is not your lost love.* The words reverberated in his head.

"Are you certain?"

"Yes."

It couldn't be true. He knew Aurora was Meri. He'd have bet his life on it. How could his instincts have been so wrong? Did he want to make amends with Meri so badly that he'd convinced himself she'd been reincarnated as Aurora?

Willow's gaze softened. She stepped close to him and placed her palm over his hand. "Please reconsider. Send another Light God."

Mobius lifted his lips in a wry smile. "As if another god's life is worth less than my own?" He shook his head. "No. This is my mission, and I will see it through to the end."

Aurora tilted her head to the sky and drank in the stars dotting the heavens like diamonds as Thumper and Lynn beat their djembe drums in a slow, hypnotic rhythm. She breathed deeply of the night air. The coven members had gathered around a blazing fire. Having completed their group ritual honoring God and Goddess, they had settled into some partying.

Beltane night. One of the two highest holidays of the Wiccan faith. A festival to mark the beginning of summer, a celebration of vitality, youth, sensuality, and the union between the masculine and the feminine. Beltane was Aurora's favorite holiday. One year, she'd attended a public Beltane festival with Thumper, Lynn, and Dawna. The carefree atmosphere, the air charged with laughter and lust and anticipation, had made her dizzy with excitement. She'd sucked up the energy until she'd been giddy.

The past couple of years, as the holiday rolled around, she'd longed for a partner, a man to share the experience with. She glanced across the fire circle through the orange and red flames to where Mobius sat, expression pensive.

She bit her lip. *Oh, the irony!* The first time she might have spent Beltane with an actual boyfriend, and the only man in sight with boyfriend potential might as well have been miles away. Mobius stared into the flames. His hair was wild and unruly around his shoulders, as though he'd fallen out of bed and come to ritual without a glance in a mirror.

His red and orange and copper waves shone gold beneath the light cast by the flames. The messy state of his hair reminded her of how he looked after she ran her fingers through it during their heated kisses and passionate lovemaking. An ache settled in her chest.

She continued to study Mobius, using the fire as a screen. *Why does he have to be so gorgeous?* Even in a simple black T-shirt and jeans, he took her breath away. The clothing hugged his taut, muscular form and made his great shape obvious. That she desired him so much only irked her more.

Damn him. Damn him for being married to a ghost. And damn him for wanting her to be that ghost. A ghost he would risk his life for. Suddenly overcome with anger, she rose and crossed the space between them, circling the fire and Hillary and Dawna as they danced around the flames to the beat of the drums.

She stalked over to Mobius, pausing a second to smooth her trembling hands over her sundress. Her palms were sweaty. Her nervousness only made her more determined to set Mobius straight.

He didn't seem to notice her approach. In fact, it wasn't until she stood directly in front of him and blocked his view of the fire that he lifted his head and looked at her.

"Don't do it," she said.

He blinked as though coming out of a daydream. "Do what?"

"Don't risk your life tomorrow. At least not for the reasons you're doing it."

His eyes narrowed. "What do you know of my reasons?"

She bit back a not-so-pleasant expletive. "I know you, Mobius. Better than you think. I know you want to make amends for what happened with Meri. You think that by saving me, you can make things right, but I'm not Meri."

He sighed heavily. "No. You're not."

Prepared to argue her point, she was taken aback by his sudden about-face. "What are you saying?"

He stood, and his striking amber gaze penetrated her. He seemed to reach deep inside of her and touch all of her most secret, hidden places. She shifted uncomfortably and cleared her throat.

"You are beautiful," he murmured, not answering her question at all. "Inside and out."

She frowned at the turn of topic, and her cheeks heated at the unexpected compliment. "Um . . . thanks."

He touched her face, brushing his knuckles gently across her cheek. "You're fierce and tough as any goddess of the Light Realm, yet soft and tender too. And you have such passion inside you. When it's unleashed you could make any male, man or god, weep with desire for you."

He paused and ran his hand through her hair, fingering her tresses with a reverence that made her squirm, while at the same time she ached to lean into his touch and bury her face in his hand.

"And though you wish the world only to see the Earth Balancer," he continued, "you long to throw that persona away and live a simple life, unfettered by duty and your mission."

Again his gaze probed hers, and he studied her as though digging for some truth in her eyes.

"You're not telling me anything I don't know." Her voice lilted as she attempted to lighten the mood.

"We are such similar creatures, you and I."

His intensity frightened her and threatened to break her tenuous hold on her own emotions. Standing there in the firelight with Mobius, listening to his sweet words while the rhythm of the drums lent emphasis, she realized her current anger, the fury that had driven her across the fire circle, stemmed from her fear that he would be killed tomorrow. Maybe they couldn't be together, but she didn't want him dead. She needed to know that whatever happened, Mobius would be okay.

"Mobius, don't do this. Don't risk your life for Meri. What do I have to do to convince you I'm not Meri?"

"I know," he said. Aurora's jaw dropped, but before she could respond, he leaned forward and kissed her forehead gently, then set her away from him. "But it makes no difference. I will still fight. The plan will go forward as discussed."

And with that, he strode away from her and disappeared into the shadows.

Chapter Thirty-five

I love her. I love Aurora. After his last conversation with Willow, he'd realized pretty quickly that he really didn't care anymore about a past-life connection. The knowledge that Aurora wasn't Meri should have hurt more than it did. Instead, he'd been left feeling hollow inside. Funny. He'd wanted so badly to make things right with Meri, he'd convinced himself Aurora was his lost love. And now it made no difference that she wasn't.

Standing in front of the fire, gazing into Aurora's exquisite eyes, he'd been hit with the force of his love for her. Not Meri. *Aurora.* It didn't matter that she wasn't Meri. He'd give his life for her just as quickly as he would for that woman he'd loved so long ago.

Mobius found himself on the edge of the property, close to where the protection circle ended. He could still make out the orange glow of the flames, and the drums tapped out a rhythm that seemed to move in time with his heartbeat. His vision, heightened as all the gods' vision was, allowed him to scan his surroundings and take in every detail. Though he registered nothing.

He vaguely took in the blackness of the night, the full moon peering from behind one lone cloud, and the trees around the edges of the property. He leaned against a solid, towering oak, and tried desperately to slow his rapid pulse and gain control over his emotions. He was suddenly struck with the irony of his situation.

He had not rediscovered Meri, but he'd found love again. And he didn't want to leave Aurora behind, but he would do so if it meant her life would be spared. He remembered a dark, shadow-laden room. *The flicker of a candle flame. The scent of blood in the air, metallic and acrid. He entered the small log cabin with his stomach in his mouth, fearing the worst, then acknowledging the reality of that fear as he saw her. Meri. Lying on the floor, her neck twisted at an odd angle, her blue dress spattered crimson, tainted by the deep wounds in her chest.*

He knelt beside her, hands shaking, eyes glazed with tears, heart turned inside out as he inspected the wound. Claw marks. The telltale signature of an Umbrae attack. Her dark hair pooled around her like an inky black ocean preparing to swallow her up. He trailed fingers across her cold, pale cheek, and her lifeless eyes stared. Gently, he closed the lids with his fingertips. Meri. Source, help me. No.

The scene played before his eyes, and this time, as he backed away from his dead lover's form, Aurora's face superimposed itself over Meri's. Bile rose in his throat, and he choked it down and shook his head, forcing the memory away.

No. I will not allow Aurora to die.

"I don't need you to protect me, you know." Aurora's voice came from behind him and yanked him from his vile memory. He spun around to watch her approach.

Her red, curve-hugging sundress appeared black in the dim light. He knew that the color matched the lipstick on her full lips, something he'd noticed when the group had first gathered for the Beltane ritual earlier that night. He'd noticed everything about her as they'd stood on the back porch going over their roles for ritual: her shiny onyx mane cascading around her shoulders, her charcoal eyes lined with smoky gray pencil, the arch of her black, perfectly shaped eyebrows. Was there any detail of Aurora he hadn't already memorized? Not likely.

"Mobius? Did you hear me?" she said.

Mobius snapped out of his trance. *Pull yourself together.* "Yes, I'm sorry. I'm not myself tonight."

She halted half a foot away from him. He could smell the bonfire's smoke tangled in her hair. He itched to pull her to him and bury his face in those dark strands.

"I'm not just a mortal woman. I am half goddess, and I'm a witch. I can defend myself even against a Gray," she said, her chin lifted in defiance.

"Yes, but what about two Grays, or three?"

She frowned, pondering the question for a moment, then said, "I'm not alone. I've a coven of powerful witches to come to my aid."

"It still may not be enough," he told her.

"But you just said I'm not Meri."

"No, you are not. Someone I trust was able to confirm that for me. I'm sorry I insisted you were she and that I—" He paused and glanced away from her, suddenly understanding just how much he'd hurt her by calling out Meri's name. Stupid. He was stupid. *So much for being a god, a being of higher intelligence.*

"I regret that I hurt you. More than you know, I regret it."

She tilted her head to the side. "It's in the past. Right now, I'm more concerned you're marching to your death. Reconsider."

"No."

She groaned. Then her gaze softened along with her tone. "Why are you doing this? I'm not Meri, so there's no point trying to right some ancient wrong."

"This is the only chance the turned Grays will have to be freed and welcomed back into the Light Realm. They must be reclaimed for that to happen, and you don't have the power to reclaim a god alone."

She opened her mouth as though to protest, but he held a finger to her lips. "I'm not finished. It doesn't matter that I was wrong about our past-life connection. I loved Meri once, greatly. But I love you here, now, even more. And I would do anything to keep you safe."

Her eyes widened. Wetness shone at their corners. "Mobius." His name fell off her lips on a sigh. She leaned into him, toward his hand, and nudged her face against his palm.

He read acceptance and need in the gesture, and a well of tenderness opened up inside him. He wanted only to be as close to Aurora as possible. He wrapped her in his arms and held her tight, breathing her in.

Mobius reclined against the tree and ignored the bite of the bark against his skin. The press of her body against his stole all thoughts of discomfort. At the feel of her in his arms, his sex hardened and pulsed.

Aurora's hands clenched in his shirt. She lifted her head, and her lips parted in invitation. "I think you should kiss me now," she whispered.

His mouth claimed hers, hot and seeking and with an intensity that overwhelmed him. A brief thought that he might bruise her lips filtered through his brain and drifted quickly away. He couldn't rein in his desire.

She returned his kiss with a passion equal to his own. Her tongue touched his without any hint of timidity. She tasted of honey mead, the homemade wine Hillary had made for the group that night. She tasted of more than that, though. Her sweet lips spoke to him of nights filled with passion, days with laughter, and a heart that had found its home.

Past-life connection or not, his body, his mind, and his heart all ached for this woman with a fierceness like nothing he'd ever known.

Heat spread through his limbs as he rained kisses over her face and neck. He rubbed circles over her bare back and delighted in her goose bumps beneath his fingertips, evidence of her desire.

She pressed herself closer to him, her breasts seeming to burn through the thin fabric of her dress and his shirt. The hard nubs of her erect nipples rubbed his chest. He allowed his hands to drift to her sides and back to her shoulders, where he tugged her dress straps down over her arms.

He pressed his lips to her shoulders, and his tongue darted out to tease the flesh at the hollow of her throat. She shuddered in response. Mobius pulled the dress down until her breasts were completely bared to his view. She wore no bra. For some reason, that knowledge turned him on even more.

He bent and tugged one taut nipple into his mouth and suckled her.

Aurora twined her fingers in his hair and moaned. "Oh God, yes!"

The sound of her pleasure elicited a throbbing sensation in his groin. His blood pounded in his ears, seeming to keep time with the drumbeats. He had to have her. *Here. Now.*

As if on cue, the drumbeat sped up, tapping out a faster rhythm, and seemed to urge a more intimate touch. He released the nipple he'd been laving with his tongue and glanced at her face. Aurora's eyes were shut, her lashes black shadows amid the darker hues of the night. Her lips parted in anticipation as he lifted her skirt with one hand and traced his fingers over her belly, her hip, and then the edge of her panties.

He slid his hand beneath the thin scrap of material and past the triangle of hair, letting her wetness guide him through her folds to the little nerve-laden pearl. He flicked his fingers over it. She gasped and bucked against his hand. He claimed her mouth again with his own, then dipped his fingers deeper and teased her entrance. He rubbed the flesh there over and over again, purposely not delving inside her, trying to prolong the pleasure. She gripped his arms so tightly, her nails dug into his flesh. She broke their kiss with a moan.

"Mobius, make love to me." Her voice was a husky whisper.

The request sent fire raging through his veins, and he turned and pushed her against the tree. Her hands sought his shirt. She yanked the fabric up and slid her hands underneath. Her slender fingers caressed his chest and teased his stomach. Then she made quick work of the button and zipper on his jeans.

She licked and sucked at his neck, sending spirals of pleasure through him. And when her small fingers slid inside his pants and closed around his cock, he sucked in a breath, afraid he might lose control right then and there.

"Mobius, make love to me," she whispered again, this time directly into his ear so that her breath tickled his earlobe.

With one hand, he tugged at his jeans. With the other, he yanked her underwear from her body. The thin material gave way easily and fell to the ground. He braced one of his hands against the tree, but realizing how rough the bark was he pulled back.

"Wait," he said, struggling to get his shirt over his head. He intended to place it behind Aurora's back and use it as a barrier between her bare skin and the tree.

She let out a frustrated groan as he slid the shirt over his head. She didn't want to wait anymore. An urgency had been building within her since the moment he'd first kissed her. She ached to have him inside of her. She needed to experience the deepest joining possible right then. Right there.

Sensing how he intended to use the shirt, Aurora thought to make it easier for him. She twisted around to present him with her backside and rooted each hand to the tree while keeping a few inches of distance between her chest and the tree trunk.

His movement behind her stilled. She arched her back, offering her bottom half to him in a gesture he could not mistake for anything but what it was: a plea for him to take her from behind.

"You are making me crazy with need for you, my beloved. I don't think I can hold myself back."

"Then don't."

The hot flesh of his chest soon pressed against her back. His lips blazed kisses across her neck and shoulder, and her flesh burned beneath her tattoo, this time with the heat of her desire.

He wound one arm around her waist and flattened his palm against the tree. With the other hand, he reached between her buttocks to cup her soft mound. He rubbed the sensitive flesh there again and again. With each sweep of his fingers, her moisture increased until her thighs were damp with it and his hand was slick. A deep throbbing need was building, and she was close to coming. But she wanted him inside her before she let go.

She stood on tiptoe and pushed her rear toward him. He nudged her legs farther apart and teased the crevice of her bottom with his erection. She leaned forward to provide him greater access. A moment later, he slid into her and began slow thrusts that stole her breath away and threatened to send her over the edge.

He kissed her neck and licked a trail to her ear, tugging at her lobe and suckling the delicate flesh there as he continued to move inside her. His erection felt impossibly hard and thick and seemed to reach into her very womb. And still, she wanted more of him. She shifted forward and immediately missed the feel of his mouth on her ear, but the depth of his penetration due to the new positioning made the loss worthwhile.

The drumbeats sped even faster. Mobius's thrusts increased in frequency. She sucked air in and out of her lungs, her breath coming in pants.

She couldn't take it. She moaned aloud with each thrust. Waves of need and desire and a throbbing in her sex that was almost painful built and escalated. But she needed something else. *Touch me. Touch me*— Before she could even finish the thought, his fingers found that sensitive button again and rubbed the nub once, twice, three times, before an inferno erupted inside her and she reached her peak.

At Aurora's cry of release, Mobius could no longer keep his desire in check. He let go. The orgasm rushed through him and over him with all the ferocity of a tsunami. And he roared Aurora's name as he rode the almost painfully pleasurable sensations.

Afterward, he turned her in his arms and cradled her to him while his pulse thudded in his ears. Aurora could hear his heart pumping loudly beneath her cheek. It seemed to beat in time with her own.

"My beloved, let's make our way back to the house. I want you to share my bed tonight. I want to hold you through the night and memorize every luscious curve of your body."

Aurora didn't say the words, but they reverberated through her head, painful and sharp: *Tonight may be the last time we'll ever make love. Tomorrow, Mobius will very likely die.*

Mobius awoke an hour later to the sound of pencil scraping paper. He opened his eyes and leaned toward Aurora, craning his neck to see what she was sketching on the large pad she held in her lap. The dim light from the bedside lamp shadowed the paper and highlighted the outline of a man's face.

"I didn't mean to wake you," she murmured, lifting

her gaze from the pad and eyeing him with intensity. Her eyes shifted from him to her paper and back again.

"Are you drawing me?" he asked, a little embarrassed by the pleasure that spread through his chest at the thought.

She nodded. "Yeah."

"Let me see," he said leaning forward.

She lifted the pad over her head. "No way. I'm not done."

The fact that she didn't want him to see it only intrigued him more. "I don't care if it's done or not. I would like to see what you have so far."

She pouted, her bottom lip slipping forward. "Well, I *do* care."

He was not going to be put off. He flashed his most beguiling smile. "Please?"

She sighed at his obvious attempt to flirt his way into getting what he wanted. Regardless, his pleading worked. Aurora handed him the sketch pad.

He viewed the picture in silence, studying each line, every shaded area. It was an uncanny likeness. Right down to the eyes. Eyes that looked tortured and racked with inner pain.

Mobius swallowed and handed her back the pad. He didn't like being so transparent. Did everyone see him this way? *Or only Aurora?*

"What do you think?" she asked with an anxious expression.

"It's perfect. You have captured my essence well," he said. "I have said it before, and I'll say it again. You are a talented artist."

Her face flushed with pleasure. "Thanks," she murmured. She set the pad aside. Her gaze turned serious, pained. "I can't sleep, Mobius. I love you so much, and all I can think of is . . ." Her words trailed off. He knew she referred to their parting. He could think of little else himself.

He reached for her and gathered her into his arms, pulling her supple curves tight against his body. "Don't think," he said, burying his face in her neck and breathing in her scent.

She reached over and flipped off the bedside lamp before burrowing beneath the covers and snuggling closer to him.

"If only it were that easy," she sighed.

But soon her deep, even breathing was all that marred the silence. And despite himself, the warmth of Aurora's body and the feel of her heartbeat beneath his hand reminded Mobius of another night, so long ago, when he'd held Meri and said good-bye. It seemed almost too cruel that fate would lead him to this place yet again. But fate was ever a fickle fellow. He should know that by now.

Chapter Thirty-six

A dimly lit room, illuminated by two small lanterns that cast shadows over the walls and ceilings. Her gaze swept over the walls of the simple log cabin she called home. The place had an emptiness about it that made her want to weep, but she refused to let the tears fall.

She'd cried so much already. For the loss of her beautiful baby boy. For the loss of her beloved, Mobius. She'd used every argument she had in her to convince him to stay with her, but in the end, she'd known that once the mission was over, he'd go. He'd told her so from the start.

Still, she'd hoped the love he carried for her would win out over his duty to those in the Light Realm. It hadn't. Meri twisted her thick, waist-length hair into a knot atop her head and crossed the room to a small wooden table and chair where an earthen bowl sat. She took her seat, tucking the skirt of her plain brown shift beneath her, and lifted a pitcher of water. She poured the liquid into the bowl, preparing to scry.

"Aimilee, my spirit guide, please come close and share your knowledge," she said. Her voice seemed to echo off the walls of the cabin, emphasizing her solitude.

Aimilee was a spirit being who had passed decades before, barely more than a teenager when she'd been hanged after accusations of witchcraft. She hadn't been a witch. Not that it had mattered to her accusers. She'd *had the wisdom of herbal magic and was a healer. She'd been a threat to the men of her village.*

It seemed somehow fitting that Aimilee chose to hover between the Earth plane and the astral, guiding Meri—a true witch—and providing the knowledge that only one who traveled between the worlds could access.

The air around her shimmered and grew cold. She sensed her spirit guide nearby. "I must see Mobius. I must know how he fares. Does he think of me?" she murmured.

The bowl of water moved ever so slightly, and a ripple appeared across its surface. When the water stilled again, an image appeared. Mobius was addressing members of the Divine Council, telling them he'd changed his mind and would return to Earth for good. Her heart swelled with joy.

"He's coming back for me!" she exclaimed.

Yes. Aimilee's reply resounded in her head. That was how Aimilee spoke to her: she injected her voice into Meri's mind.

A sense of unease snaked its way up Meri's spine, killing the joy. She'd felt the Umbrae near for days now. She knew they wanted her dead. They feared she'd still be utilized by the Light against them. They thought she might yet mother another child of the Light.

The protection circle she'd cast around her home would hold for only so long. Her circle-casting powers were weak from the trauma of childbirth and the death of her child. She could not continue to fortify the invisible fortress on her own.

"He won't make it in time, will he?"

No, Aimilee said.

Meri swallowed hard and once again bit back bitter tears. "But I will see him again someday, won't I, Aimilee?" She couldn't bear to believe otherwise.

In her mind's eye she saw Aimilee's reassuring smile.

Yes. You will see him again. Your time together is yet to come.

"*Show me,*" she commanded. *The water swirled in a clockwise circle, its movement slow and even. When the liquid stilled again, a woman's face appeared. An attractive woman with long black hair and wide silver eyes peered back at her.*

"*Who are you?*" *she whispered to the image.*

The air suddenly became heated and dense. The odor of rotten eggs filled her nostrils. Her chest constricted with fear.

"*Aimilee, are they here, then? Is this the end?*"

They've broken through the circle, *her spirit guide responded.*

A moment later, a crackling noise filled her ears, and the space in front of her split open. Two clawlike hands sheathed in gray, scaly skin reached out and rent the air in two as if it were fabric being split apart.

The Umbra pulled its body through from the dimension where it dwelled to her own. And it stared at her, beady crimson eyes filled with evil intent.

Murky mist filled her nostrils, and she opened her mouth to gasp for air. The mist twisted down her throat. She couldn't breathe. She was choking. Terror arched through her, and she grasped at the creature, her hands sliding on its disgustingly slick skin.

Don't be afraid, *Aimilee whispered.* This is not the end. It's just the beginning. Don't be afraid.

Aurora shot upright in bed, her heart pounding hard enough to burst through her rib cage. Her gaze swept her bedroom. Nothing there but her mahogany furniture, and moonlight-dusted shadows. Mobius sprawled beside her on the bed, his bare chest lifting slightly with each deep breath. He hadn't stirred when she woke. His jaw was slack with sleep, his face crease free. He wore an air of peace about him, and in that moment, she envied it.

She rubbed her arms, willing her pulse to slow, shaking away the terror of the nightmare.

Don't be afraid. But she *was* afraid.

The dream had been more vivid than the others. She'd worn Meri's skin as though it were her own. She'd tasted her anguish, drunk of her pain. Then she'd seen the image of the woman in the bowl of water. *She was that woman.*

The only other time she'd experienced a vision so acutely had been during the one past-life regression she'd had. And that had paled in comparison to this one.

Suddenly she knew, with every ounce of her being, that the dreams she'd been having weren't dreams at all. They were past-life recollections. Mobius was half-right. Harmonization did cause the visions. But not just because she soaked up his energy.

Harmonizing with Mobius was the catalyst for reawakening the part of her soul that had traveled with her through life after life, storing the remnants of those lives in her subconscious. Like the woman she'd met once in a New Age bookstore who'd sworn she had a fear of choking because she'd been strangled in her last life.

It was true. Her body and heart had opened up to Mobius so quickly because they were anything but strangers. Suddenly, it all made perfect sense: her immediate attraction to him, her ability to relax and be herself with him, the fact she was so quick to fall in love with him. Once, they'd shared a love so strong, so deep, so life altering, that not even death could erase it.

I am Meri.

Chapter Thirty-seven

Her tattoo burned and throbbed. A voice cried out down the hall. Goose bumps rose on her arms. She'd been just about to shake Mobius awake and share her news, but first, she needed to see what danger lurked nearby.

Aurora slipped from the bed and pulled on her terry-cloth bathrobe.

She padded down the hall and heard voices. Female voices whispering. Then a woman moaned. Dawna and Lynn.

A thin beam of light spilled from under their bedroom door into the hallway. She knocked lightly on the door. Lynn opened it, her wide brown eyes filled with worry. The lines at their corners, which Aurora thought added to her beauty because they showed how much joy she'd experienced, were now etched deep with shadows of fatigue.

Aurora's gut clenched. "What's wrong?"

Lynn pulled her pink bathrobe tight around herself and ushered Aurora into the room, shutting the door behind them.

"What's going on?" Aurora asked again, with trepidation.

Lynn motioned to where Dawna lay on the bed. Reba, her familiar, was perched on the pillow next to Dawna's head. If a squirrel could look worried, Reba did. The animal, usually seen scurrying around, bright eyed and curious, was motionless. She simply stared at Dawna, her little mouth twitching. A bundle of sage burned on the bedside table; its aromatic scent and tendrils of smoke clouded the room.

Dawna's ebony mane fanned the pillow. Her face was pale and wan, and she lay with the covers tucked beneath her chin. Her eyes were closed, and Aurora pressed a hand to her friend's forehead. Her skin felt cool.

At her touch, Dawna's lids fluttered open. Aurora gasped. Inky blackness clouded Dawna's normally sky blue eyes. Dawna grabbed Aurora's hand and squeezed in reassurance.

"It's okay. It doesn't hurt," she said. "I'm just really tired. And my vision is blurry."

"Okay?" Aurora exclaimed. "I hardly think this is okay! What happened?"

Lynn sighed. "She was meditating."

"I was trying to pick up anything I could about the Field Trip we're planning. The one to Tampa and the Umbrae's hideout."

"In the middle of her meditation, she started screaming," Lynn continued, stroking Dawna's cheek. "I pulled her out of the meditation, and she said she was having a horrible vision."

"Of what?" Aurora asked.

"It wasn't about the Field Trip at all. I saw young people and children dying. I—I don't know what was killing them, but a terrible black cloud appeared to me during the vision, and it started to cover me like a . . . like a shroud, and I couldn't breathe." Dawna gulped air. Reliving the experience was taking its toll on her. Her body trembled with fear.

"She doesn't know what it means," Lynn said. "I don't want to make her talk about it again."

"It's okay." Aurora studied Dawna's eyes and sighed. "I might be able to help her feel better though."

Lynn's brow knitted in question. "Yeah? I was just about to go get Axiom or Mobius."

"Whatever that black cloud was, it tainted you with dark energy. It feels similar to what happens when someone is turned."

"Can you help?" Lynn asked, chewing her bottom lip.

"Yeah. At least I think so." Aurora put her hands on Dawna's head. Dawna looked at her wide-eyed. "Just relax."

Aurora focused inward, on pulling the dark energies inside of her to the surface and using those energies like a magnet to attract the similar force in Dawna. The familiar buzz of current coursed through her veins and seeped out of her hands into Dawna. Dawna jerked, and her eyes rolled back in her head.

"You're hurting her," Lynn cried.

Aurora ignored her, knowing the process was necessary. She willed her power into Dawna, felt it whisper over her friend's skin, and Dawna's body arched, her limbs rigid. One more burst of energy, and then Dawna's body fell back into the mattress.

The current stopped. Dawna opened her eyes and blinked at Aurora. Her eyes had returned to their normal color.

Aurora stroked Dawna's cheek. Her skin was soft and warm to the touch. "How do you feel?"

"Tired. But okay," Dawna said.

Aurora turned to Lynn. "She'll be weak for a day or two. You'll want to keep her hydrated and just let her rest. No more vision-questing for now."

"No worries there," Dawna said with a wry smile.

"Tomorrow, we need to tell the rest of the group what happened."

Lynn nodded. "Tomorrow. But tonight, we rest."

Aurora left the room more troubled than ever. She hurried back to her room, intent on waking Mobius and telling him everything. Her past-life recollection. Dawna's vision. But she swung the door open to find the room empty. Nothing but the rumpled sheets on her bed to prove he'd been there at all. Damn the man, anyway.

The stench of dead corpses smacked Rhakma in the face the moment he entered Nilram's lair. His eyes narrowed. The cave was empty for once. He swept inside. It was dark, as always; he almost tripped over the bodies. The woman Kali, who'd woven the clearly useless spell for him, lay at his feet, her plump body decomposing.

To the side of her, two Grays lay dead, their eyes open, unseeing. The Grays interested him. He knelt and waved his hand over one of the bodies, a blonde female, tasting the remnants of her energy. She was not turned. She was a god in human form.

She must have refused to merge with Nilram, and thus had been able to survive only a few months on Earth. The man beside her appeared to have met the same fate. Rhakma wondered why they would have returned to this cave to die. Perhaps they'd changed their minds in their last moments of life and had wished to be turned.

His lip curled in contempt. *Ignorant Grays.* Though they were currently useful to him, he still had no stomach for the Balancers' mixed heritage. The Grays should never have been allowed to exist at all. They should have been wiped out the moment they emerged from Source.

His contact in the Light Realm had met him on the Astral Plane the evening before, informing him that the spell cast on Aurora had not been strong enough to combat the Violet Fire as well as frequent harmonizations with Mobius. His contact had learned of this from the peering pool. Hmmm. He had not anticipated Mobius harmonizing with the Gray and lending her additional power. The very thought of a Light God and a Gray merging made his stomach twist with nausea. *More inbreeding.*

Reetori, the Gray he'd teamed up with, the Gray who'd released him from the Astral Plane because he had as great a contempt for the mixed blood of the Earth Balancer as Rhakma had of Grays, had been discovered. He had not shown for their last planned meeting. Theirs had been a strange pairing, to be sure. What was the human maxim? *Desperate times required desperate measures.* Even the cooperation of Rhakma and a Gray God.

Fortunately, Reetori wasn't the only god in the Light Realm sympathetic to his cause.

The odor of the decaying bodies and the damp, musky scent of the cave propelled Rhakma back out into the night. He inhaled deeply once outside and breathed in the pleasing aroma of orange blossoms.

"Nilram," he called out. "I am here and await you."

The air in front of him shifted and moved. The night cracked open in a fractured line, and Nilram pulled himself through.

"Why did you insist on meeting here? You could have popped into my hotel room," Rhakma asked. He detested the cave and its vile odors. Nilram's sulfuric stench only served to magnify the unpleasant aromas.

"I like it here," Nilram said in his hoarse crackle of a voice.

"I am surprised to find the place empty," Rhakma said.

"My Finders and the Grays have work to do," Nilram answered.

"Ah, you have discovered more ways to terrorize

humans and increase darkness on Earth?" Rhakma's words were tongue-in-cheek. What else would they be doing?

Nilram's razor-sharp teeth flashed as his misshapen mouth twisted into a grotesque smile. "Always."

Rhakma sighed. "Well, I must report that the spell did not work. And the coven will likely come looking for us now that the Earth Balancer is back."

"They will not find us. Their empath is dead."

Rhakma's brows rose in question.

"He fell into one of our traps. The human Gray came to his rescue, but failed to save him."

At the mention of Axiom, the Balancer who had been the cause of his banishment to the Astral Plane, Rhakma's eyes narrowed. "Too bad one of your kind did not exterminate him as well."

"It is not as easy as you would believe. He still has some of the powers of a god. And he has learned witch-craft from his mate."

Rhakma sneered. "He is mortal. If the Umbrae are unable to kill him, I shall." And Mobius, too. Mobius had assumed human form. He would not be as strong as Rhakma, who still retained god form. Rhakma smiled. He would make Mobius regret banishing him to the Astral Plane.

"They cannot hide in their house forever," Rhakma said. "Sooner or later they will emerge, and we will attack."

Nilram nodded, and his body, constantly shifting from solid to transparent, moved as the smaller Umbrae that made up his form writhed in excitement.

"And as for finding us—" Rhakma paused. "I'm quite certain they already know of this place. It is only a matter of time before they come for us. And we will be ready for them."

* * *

The flight to Tampa seemed to drag on longer than usual. Laurell, Axiom, Mobius, Aurora, Thumper, and Hillary had hopped on a five thirty flight out of Madison. Dawna was recovering from her strange affliction and stayed behind. Lynn also remained to keep an eye on her. The group arrived in Tampa and checked into a local hotel. Laurell had suggested they make sure they had a place where they could retreat for rest and recuperation.

No one knew exactly what to expect from the coming battle. No one knew what to think of Dawna's vision and fleeting illness either, but there had been no time to investigate. It was clear the Dark was increasing its hold on the planet. Every day and every new illness only pointed to the urgency of the situation.

Aurora had been unable to locate Mobius after he'd disappeared from her bed in the early morning hours. Later, when she'd gone to the kitchen to get some breakfast, she'd found him in the kitchen with her father, preparing for their Field Trip. She'd tried to corner him several times throughout the day, but he was always too busy to talk. He was avoiding her. She sensed him pulling away on purpose. Still, she was pissed that he'd decided to run off in the middle of the night. She hated the feeling of abandonment she experienced in his absence.

He knows I'll keep trying to change his mind about the plan. Maybe he's afraid I'll finally convince him. Whatever the reason, she hadn't had the chance to tell him about her past-life realization.

By the time the group checked into their hotel rooms, she was ready to burst. She noted that Mobius didn't reserve a room for himself. Did he intend to stay with her? Or did he assume he wasn't going to be around to need a room? The second possibility brought tears to her eyes. She blinked them away, suddenly overcome with anger at the unfairness of it all. She couldn't have found the love of her life—or *lives*—only to lose him again!

Aurora dropped her duffel bag in her hotel room and rushed out. The door slammed shut behind her, and she hurried to where she'd last seen Mobius. She found him in the hotel's parking lot, leaning against the black Ford van they'd rented, the only vehicle large enough to hold the entire crew.

The night air was muggy and hot, and she was glad of the tank top and shorts she'd donned. The Holiday Inn sign glowed behind him, and the streetlights cast eerie shadows over his tall, broad form. As usual, he presented a stunning example of male beauty in his tight blue jeans and navy blue shirt. His crimson mane was pulled back into a ponytail, a new look for him. She liked it.

Her feet crunched over gravel, announcing her arrival. He turned to her, his amber-hued gaze meeting hers. She saw sadness revealed in those eyes and written across his face. She knew her own face mirrored the sentiment.

She halted less than a foot from him. Her heart thumped against her ribs with a vengeance, and she sucked in a deep breath, then let it out in what she hoped was an inconspicuous manner.

Why was she so nervous? After the declarations of love they'd made to each other last night, both with their words and their bodies, she should be at ease with Mobius. Yet his presence managed to make her react like a silly little girl with her first crush.

"You've been avoiding me," she said.

He tilted his head to the side and took several moments to answer, as though carefully weighing his words. "I've been attempting to keep my distance, yes."

A pang of hurt sliced her, sharp and biting. "Why?"

"This situation is difficult, and I didn't want to make it more so."

Her eyes narrowed. "It's hard for me, too, but treating me like a leper is not going to make it easier! Do you know how I felt coming back to an empty bed last night?"

His gaze softened, and she saw regret reflected in the depths of his golden eyes. "No, I don't."

"Like a pile of shit. Don't ever do that to me again," she exclaimed. *He won't be able to do it again.* She pushed the thought out of her mind as soon as it entered.

"I'm sorry, Aurora," he murmured, lifting his hand to touch her cheek. "I've hurt you yet again. I'm not much good at this."

"At what?" she bit out.

"Love."

That one word sucked the anger from her and made her want to throw her arms around his neck and bury her face in his chest.

Then she remembered her main reason for seeking him out. "I've been trying to get you alone all day to tell you about my dream last night."

"You dreamed again of me and Meri?" he asked.

"Yeah. But you weren't in it. And I realized that you were right! I *am* Meri!"

Mobius's jaw dropped. "You aren't serious?"

"Hell yes, I am."

"You had a dream, and now you're convinced of this?"

She bit back her frustration. "I had a past-life recall. There's a difference."

He shook his head. "No, you picked up one of my memories from the harmonizations."

"No, this wasn't your memory. It was Meri's. Mine."

Mobius started to pace, his agitation clear. "I told you. I've confirmed you are not Meri."

"With who?"

"Willow went to the Hall of Records."

Aurora groaned. "Well, of course Willow would say I'm not Meri! She wants you for herself."

He sighed and rolled his eyes. "She is a trustworthy source."

"Trustworthy, my ass!"

She grabbed his hands, stopping him in his tracks. "Mobius, I'm serious. I *know* that I'm Meri. You were right about us. All of it. I remembered things that you wouldn't have known. Things that happened to Meri when you weren't there."

Mobius arched one eyebrow. "Why are you doing this? All you've done is convince me more that our plan is the right course. That is, if you truly are Meri. And I'm not saying you are."

She bit her lip. This was not getting her anywhere. And time was running short. She wanted to tell him so many things. Like how much he'd touched her. How he'd made her realize that the whole time she'd been worried that no one could accept her for who she was, he had accepted her, loved her. And he'd helped her to see herself more clearly.

She really was the Earth Balancer, the loyal friend and fierce fighter who enjoyed her role—relished it, even. She couldn't imagine being anyone else. Why had she fought her destiny?

She pulled his hands to her lips and slowly pressed a tender kiss to first his left, then his right knuckle. When she raised her eyes to meet his gaze, she hoped her face showed all the love and passion she carried for him.

"I can't lose you again," she whispered.

He sucked in a harsh breath and pulled her into his arms with one quick movement. He held her there, tight against him, and buried his face in her hair. Time seemed to halt, and a million details flooded her brain. His heart made a thudding sound beneath her cheek.

His scent filled her nostrils, fresh with a slight hint of something woodsy. His cotton shirt felt soft beneath her hands. They were all that existed. Just the two of them. After a while, he slowly eased his hold and tilted her head back so he could look into her eyes.

"I would give anything to be able to stay here with you, but it's not meant to be. There are bigger forces, larger issues at stake here. Like the future of Earth and the Light Realm." He paused and looked away, blinking as though he had something in his eyes. Tears?

She knew he was right. She didn't care. Why did saving the world always have to be their first priority? For once, she wanted to be selfish. It was an irrational, impossible desire, but there it was. She wanted Mobius.

"Look, Mobius, I wouldn't ask you to give up your place on the Divine Council. Didn't you say I'd be able to travel there in my physical form?"

He nodded. "Yes, but—"

"That means you don't even have to become human for me. That's the beauty of it!"

"Aurora, stop." He grasped her arms tightly. His jaw hardened, and a pained look took over his face. "You're making this even harder."

"Don't you want to be with me? You came back for Meri. You were willing to give it all up for her!" she exclaimed, suddenly hit with the irony of the situation.

Mobius's eyes narrowed.

"Yeah," she continued. "She . . . I . . . knew you were coming back, but you didn't make it in time."

He dropped his hands from her arms and rubbed them over his eyes, his broad shoulders sagging just a little.

Aurora waited until he focused on her again. She watched unreadable emotions flicker across his features. "She forgave you, you know. She understood your need to protect the Light Realm. You're a protection deity. It's who you are. Your loyalty and determination to help others, even at terrible cost to yourself, is part of what made her fall in love with you."

It was true. She'd picked up these thoughts and more through her last dream vision. These qualities were the same ones that made Aurora love him so deeply now.

Mobius's lips curled into a half smile that didn't meet his eyes. "Aurora, my beloved." She read acceptance in his eyes. He believed her.

He cupped her cheeks with his hands, and his gaze pierced her. "If you knew this about me then, you should know I am the same now. I cannot be other than who I am. Isn't that the very thing you want for yourself? To be seen and accepted for who you are?"

The truth and wisdom of his words hit home. He was right. He was exactly right. And there was no use in her trying to change his mind. He was going to go through with the plan, and there wasn't a damn thing she could do about it.

She could refuse to participate, but what good would that do? She couldn't sit around ignoring the Grays and watch the world self-destruct as the Dark overcame it. It was in her nature to protect the Earth. *Even if it means losing my heart.*

Tears spilled from her eyes, and her throat clogged. She swallowed hard. "We are such similar creatures, you and I." She echoed the words he'd said to her not so long ago.

He leaned forward and pressed his mouth to hers in a gentle kiss.

Chapter Thirty-eight

Moonlight caressed the hill, lighting the entrance to the cave. The group stood outside the entrance, awaiting Mobius's signal to enter. The trek from the van to the cave had been accomplished in silence and had elicited no Finder, Gray, or Umbra activity.

Humidity tinged the air and made Aurora's tank top and shorts stick to her skin. She'd spritzed herself with bug spray before they'd left the hotel, and a good thing, too. Mosquitoes seemed to love the place, and she noticed a couple of the others swatting at their legs and arms.

Anticipatory excitement filled her. She sensed the others felt it, too. Everyone was poised and ready for battle. The aroma of orange blossoms drifted on the wind, mingling with the chemical odor of the bug spray. An odd combination. Still, a much more pleasing scent than the rotten-egg stench of the Umbrae that was certain to come.

Mobius disappeared into the mouth of the cave. Axiom and Laurell, then Hillary and Thumper followed. He'd insisted on putting Aurora at the back of the line, saying she could then defend the group from any sneak attacks.

She suspected he really just wanted to keep her out of danger for as long as possible, but just in case, she periodically glanced over her shoulder: nothing but the chirp of crickets and a slight breeze cutting through the trees. She caught a whisper of the wind on her bare skin, and it provided short-lived but welcome relief from the heat.

Aurora crept into the cave, keeping an eye on Thumper's red tank top in front of her. Soft squishing noises drifted to her ears as she trudged through mud and Goddess knew what else. If she were to look at her feet, she suspected she'd see Umbra slime and, possibly, human remains. The latest odor drifting through the tunnel made the latter seem likely. She chose not to look.

Her shoulder burned and throbbed beneath her tattoo, pointing out the obvious. *Yeah, yeah, I know. Trouble. And I'm walking right into it.*

Once inside the cavern, the group halted.

"No one's home," Hillary remarked.

"Can Nilram come out and play?" Thumper joked, though his voice shook a bit. The hair on Aurora's arms stood. Thumper was right to be uneasy. The place was downright eerie.

Mobius motioned to the lit tiki torches. "Someone has been here recently."

"Must be some Finders. They seem to like hanging out here." Axiom swept his arm in an arc, gesturing around the cavern. "Though I cannot imagine why."

"Where are they?" Laurell murmured. "This feels like a trap."

"Of course it is a trap," came an unfamiliar voice from behind them.

Aurora spun around. A tall, broad-shouldered man with long, thick, blond hair stood in the doorway. He wore a white robe with bits of silver threaded through the fabric. Though she'd never seem him before, she knew this had to be Rhakma. He had the bearing of a god. Confidence seeped from his pores. Or was that arrogance?

Rhakma crossed the space until he stopped in front of Mobius. A small army of Finders and Grays followed him. He tilted his head, and gave Mobius a wry smile. "Mobius, did you think we weren't expecting you? Did you think"—he glanced at Axiom before continuing—"that we were unaware of Axiom's presence here the other night?"

His chuckle grated on Aurora's nerves.

"Why did you not strike?" Axiom asked. His voice was even and measured, but Aurora could make out the pulse at his temple, and his spine was rigid. She knew when her father was keeping his anger in check.

Rhakma's turquoise eyes widened in mock surprise. "You did not think I would waste a good battle just on you and him, did you?" He motioned to Thumper. "Oh, and the old man, the empathic one, he was with you too, yes?"

Rhakma shook his head. "Such a shame, his death. I'm sure you took it quite hard."

Axiom's fists clenched, and he started forward, but Mobius halted him with a hand on his arm and a warning glance.

"No," Rhakma continued. "I much preferred to wait until you brought the entire coven back. Along with the Earth Balancer. How ironic, Mobius, that you, a protection god, should lead them to their deaths."

"The only dead will be your kind," Mobius snarled. "And if you want to talk of irony, how is it that you, also a protection deity, are now only interested in protecting yourself?"

Rhakma's responding grin was rife with sarcasm. "What? The Earth-banished Grays do not count?"

"This is crazy," Aurora exclaimed. "Why would you join ranks with Nilram and help him turn the Grays he captured? You're a Light God! The more the Dark infiltrates, the more all the gods are affected. Do you have a suicide wish?" She guessed it would be hopeless trying to reason with him, but she wanted to stall as long as she could. *There has got to be some other way to end this without Mobius's death.*

Rhakma laughed. "Oh, dear. You think I care about the other gods? The gods who banished me and took from me my rightful place on the Council? Besides, I have already merged with Nilram. The Dark no longer affects me."

"You don't think it has affected you? You're helping the Umbrae kill humans." Mobius's jaw clenched. "Then again, you had no qualms about endangering the lives of humans even when you inhabited the Light Realm. Why should you be any different now?"

Rhakma shrugged. Bemusement flickered across his features. "Why indeed?"

He crossed to where Aurora stood. "The infamous Earth Balancer. Just another Gray." Rhakma's gaze raked her from head to toe, filled with menace. He glanced at Mobius. "I understand you are quite fond of this half-breed abomination, Mobius. You even harmonized with her. Tsk-tsk. You really have sunk low, haven't you?"

"That's it." Hillary pushed forward, hands on ample hips, eyes narrowed with anger. "I'm not gonna sit here and listen to you insult my friends. Time for some ass-whuppin'."

Thumper reached for Hillary's arm and tugged her back. "Easy, Hil," he murmured.

"Where's your slimy friend?" Aurora wanted to know.

Rhakma's lips curled. "Nilram? He'll arrive shortly, I am sure. He will want to witness the end of the Earth Balancer."

Anger coiled in Aurora's belly. She was tired of Rhakma referring to her demise. *I'm not going anywhere.*

"Well," Rhakma continued. "What is it you humans say? Oh yes, there is no time like the present." He swung his hands in a sweeping gesture. Immediately, two of the Grays rushed Mobius and Axiom. Finders lifted their arms, guns cocked, and aimed at Laurell, Thumper, and Hillary.

A bullet flew toward Thumper. Horror grabbed hold of Aurora's heart, and she hurled herself at him, successfully taking him to the ground as it whizzed past. Before she could stand on her own, two large hands clasped her shoulders and yanked her to her feet. She looked up and into two red eyes that glowed with malicious intent. They peered out of the most hideous face she'd ever seen. Nilram.

Her father hadn't exaggerated. He really was disgusting to look at. Nauseating, really. The only thing symmetrical on what you could call his face were his eyes. There was a curved slit that she assumed was a nose and an opening that gaped around razor-sharp teeth. His greenish gray body was both solid and transparent, slick with an unknown liquid in some places and dry and scaly in others. How Nilram managed to be all these things at once, she didn't know, but he did.

"Nice of you to join us," she spat out.

His fingers tightened into her shoulders, drawing blood. Her flesh stung where he touched her.

"I will enjoy watching you die, Earth Balancer," Nilram said, his voice raw and hoarse. The odor of rotten eggs assailed her, and her stomach rolled at the stench.

Her eyes narrowed. "You know, I keep hearing I'm going to die, but I'm still here." She threw his hands off her. His claws scraped her flesh as he withdrew. She winced in pain.

Dank, cool air assaulted her, and when she breathed in, it filled her nose and trickled to her lungs. Nilram was trying to suffocate her. She gathered her power like a ball of light inside of her and pushed back at the lethal air until it dissipated. She crept toward Nilram. The creature's body undulated and shifted as the smaller Umbrae that made up his form cowered back from her.

She smiled. "Yeah, you really should be afraid of me."

"I have no fear of you, witch," Nilram responded. "You may be able to destroy lesser Umbrae, but I am not so easy to dispel."

Still, she noted he made no move to attack her again. He simply watched her with interest. She noticed his gaze directed over her shoulder. The sounds of multiple struggles and battles filled the cave.

She turned sideways, careful not to put her back to Nilram. Mobius and Rhakma battled. Rhakma had Mobius in a headlock, and Mobius grunted and managed to get an arm around Rhakma's leg. He yanked Rhakma to the ground, effectively getting him to release the hold on his neck.

A moment later, shackles appeared in the air and hovered over Rhakma before clamping over his hands. Mobius's ability to create was in full force. Her jaw dropped as a razor-sharp ax appeared and sliced the chains holding the cuffs in two, freeing Rhakma. *Rhakma is a protection deity too, same as Mobius.* She realized with a start that they shared the same powers.

A grunt of effort from the other side of the room drew her attention to where Axiom and Laurell battled two Grays, one male and one female. They seemed to be holding their own, though not with physical strength. As strong as Axiom was, he wasn't a god any longer; the Grays could physically overpower him.

No, the two had cast some sort of witchcraft spell utilizing the air element. The space around the Grays swirled with dirt and debris, and for the moment, they were unable to move.

Thumper and Hillary were dodging bullets and Finders and sending blasts of fire energy at their opponents. Aurora frowned. Why wasn't anyone trying to take her down? Even Nilram simply watched her warily.

As if he'd read her mind, a Gray charged her, his long yellow hair flying. He hit her hard, in the midsection. She fell backward and landed on her rear. He started to jump on her, and she kicked her feet into his stomach. Arms flailing, he hit the ground with a thud.

She glanced to the side of the cave where she'd last seen Mobius. He'd managed to knock Rhakma to his back, and the light-haired god appeared winded and barely conscious. The air to her right pulsed and flickered as if alive. The telltale gut-wrenching stink of more Umbrae on the way wafted past Aurora. Mobius tilted his head toward her, and she nodded. It was time.

Mobius changed course, turned from Rhakma, and charged Nilram. He threw his body against the demon king and held tight. Nilram squirmed, trying to free his arms. He got one arm free and raked Mobius's face, drawing blood.

"Argh!" Mobius grunted and twisted his head away from Nilram, putting all his might into keeping the monster in one place.

"Aurora, hurry!" Mobius cried.

Chapter Thirty-nine

Aurora scurried toward Mobius, but before she reached his side, the blond Gray flew across the room as quick as a blink and snagged her around the neck. He was strong—at least as strong as Aurora. She tugged at his beefy arm to no avail. He was cutting off her airway. She gasped for oxygen and once again willed her power up and out of her core. The blast of current seared the Gray holding her captive, and he cried out in pain and released her.

An Umbra appeared behind Mobius and started to twine its body around his face, cutting off his air supply. The muscles in Mobius's arms and neck bulged with effort, but he did not release Nilram. Aurora rushed to his side and touched her hand to the creature. It hissed and twisted, and quickly disintegrated. But more appeared in its place.

Movement to her left. Cherry red hair and a familiar musky perfume. Aurora's eyes widened. "Fi?"

Fiona, the High Priestess of Hidden Circle Coven, stood at her side, cat green eyes sparking. "Thought you could use some help." She nodded toward someone behind Aurora, and a moment later, Reese, the handsome fair-haired High Priest of Hidden Circle Coven, appeared.

The two stepped back and reached into their pockets. Their hands emerged clasping small, sparkly objects, and both tossed quartz crystals to the ground. The crystals sparkled brilliantly in the dim lighting and moved of their own accord to form a perfect circle around Aurora, Mobius, and Nilram.

A protection circle. Charged crystals. Brilliant. No Finders, Grays, or Umbrae could penetrate. The circle should make it easier for her and Mobius to perform the harmonization with Nilram. Only Rhakma remained in the circle with them, but he still lay on the ground, unmoving.

"Aurora, hurry," Mobius called to her. She quickly dispatched the two Umbrae who appeared next to Mobius, intent on attacking him, then curled one arm around Mobius and one around Nilram. Nilram's skin was icy cold and slick to the touch. Her stomach lurched when she made contact with his flesh, but she forced her dinner to stay put and focused on Mobius.

His eyes had darkened to the color of deep smoky quartz, and his gaze was full of all the same emotions she'd been keeping in check since they'd had their discussion at the van earlier. Her chest ached.

"I love you," he mouthed. And before she could respond, he closed his eyes and the energy surge of harmonization filled her. Bold and bright colors filled her vision, and her body stiffened and held tight to Mobius; her free hand kept a firm grip on Nilram.

She heard Rhakma rousing and opened her eyes to slits, just enough to see him pull himself to his feet. Nilram squirmed and writhed, trying to break free. With tears running down her cheeks, Aurora released her own power to the process. She willed all that she had in her to the harmonization.

There was no pleasure in this energetic mating. Instead, painful twitches claimed her limbs. She dimly registered the same reaction in both Nilram and Mobius. Mobius started to sputter and cough. The energy raged on. Blood leaked from his nose and the corner of his mouth.

Goddess help me. I'm killing him. She wanted to pull away and end the harmonization. Panicked, she even tried, but the current had taken on a mind of its own, and she couldn't stop the power that whirled through and around them.

Suddenly, Mobius was lifted from the ground and sent hurling toward the edge of the protection circle. He landed with a sickening crunch. *Rhakma.*

Rhakma grabbed Aurora's face and pressed. She saw stars. She dug her nails into one of his hands, managing to yank it off her face. She tried to throw him away from her completely, but it was as if her palms had been coated with superglue. She couldn't release his hand. And her other hand still clutched Nilram's arm.

A red river wound its way down Nilram's face. Pain lanced Aurora, more of the power she'd unleashed with the hamonization.

It hurt. Goddess it hurt, but try as she might, she couldn't pull her hands from either of them. A spiral of current built and swirled around the three of them.

Brilliant sparks of light flared as the current moved through their chakras. A roaring sound raged in her ears, growing louder and louder until with a final thrust of searing pain, the room grew silent and the energy disappeared with a brilliant, dazzling burst. She couldn't see. She couldn't hear.

The air whooshed from Aurora's lungs, and she sank to the ground, gasping. She dug at the dirt to push herself up, and the mud squished between her fingers. Finally, when she could breathe again and her vision cleared, she glanced around the cave.

The rest of the coven looked worn, weary, and battle scarred, but alive. Nilram and Rhakma were nowhere to be seen. *Come to think of it,* she thought, *all the Umbrae are gone. The Grays are all lying on the floor. What the hell happened?* She scanned the cave.

Mobius lay on the ground, too—eyelids shut, body still.

Chapter Forty

Aurora stood and shuffled to Mobius's side on unsteady legs, tears blurring her sight. She knelt beside him and touched his face. His skin was cool. He didn't move. She stifled a sob and dropped her head to his chest, burying her face in his shirt and breathing in his scent. She wanted to brand into her memory the smell of his skin.

"Mobius," she murmured. "My love." His heartbeat beneath her cheek made her breath catch. She lifted her head.

Amber eyes peered at her beneath eyelids half-closed. Mobius lifted one hand to her cheek and stroked her skin with the barest of touches.

"You're not dead!" she exclaimed, incredulous, barely able to contain the joy welling inside her.

He gave her a wry half smile. "No, though this body is quite damaged."

"But you—your god self. You're intact, right?"

"Quite."

She threw herself atop him, pulling him into a fierce hug. *Thank you, thank you, thank you, Goddess.*

"Ouch! Be careful," he said when she hugged him too tight.

She sat up again and stared at his face, still filled with disbelief. She'd spent so much time steeling herself for his death, she couldn't quite believe that he was alive.

"It's okay, my beloved," he said, his gaze tender. "This body will heal."

"What happened to Nilram and Rhakma?"

Mobius slowly pulled himself to a sitting position. Before he could respond, Fiona's voice called out, "They both blew up."

Aurora blinked. "Blew up?"

Thumper crossed the room. "You should have seen it. Wow."

Aurora glanced back at Mobius. "How is it Rhakma's dead and you're not?"

Mobius smiled. "When he pulled me away and attacked you, he was sucked into the energy of the harmonization. In essence, he took my place."

"But I didn't think he had any light energy left in him after he merged with Nilram."

"Everyone, no matter how vile, still retains that initial spark of light, the seed of life. Even Rhakma, apparently. It was enough to set off the chain reaction Thumper predicted."

"Then you're going to be okay?"

Mobius nodded. "I can stay in this body for three months, or I can come back as fully human. Though I can most likely get permission to keep some of my powers."

Aurora shook her head. "No. You won't give up your seat on the Council for me. Did you forget that I am half goddess? I can travel to the Light Realm."

Mobius grinned, his delight plastered across his face. "You would do that for me?" He pressed a kiss to her forehead. "My beloved, I will do whatever is necessary to be with you."

She nodded. "I know you would, but I don't want you to. I don't want you to stop being who you are for me."

He gave her a tender smile and pressed a soft kiss to her lips.

Aurora could see her mother and father hovering nearby, but keeping their distance in order to give her some privacy. "We should probably bring Mom and Dad over so I can reassure them I'm okay."

Before she could do that, however, Hillary hurried toward them, tugging one of the Grays behind her. The blond-haired man Aurora had fought earlier.

"I have some more good news, folks," Hillary announced. "Look!" She pointed to the Gray's face.

Aurora peered closely. The Gray's eyes were the normal silver shade of all Balancer gods. "He's healed," she murmured. "Just as we'd hoped."

The Gray touched Aurora's shoulder. "I'm sorry for my treatment of you earlier. I wasn't myself."

"It's okay," she said. "You'd been turned."

"I realize now that I made the wrong choice. I am grateful to be back to myself. Except for the part about dying soon. We won't last long here on Earth in god form," the Gray God remarked with a pained expression.

Mobius motioned to Aurora to help him stand. She did so, gently.

"The Grays are invited back to the Light Realm. My deepest apologies for your banishment. We made a terrible mistake," Mobius said.

The Gray nodded, and a broad smile lit his face. "It will be good to go home." He hurried over to where the other Grays were starting to stir, presumably to give them the good news.

Fiona and Reese rushed over to give her a hug, each in turn. "The crystals were Lynn's idea. Pretty nifty, huh?" Fiona said, her eyes sparkling.

Aurora grinned. Thank Goddess Fiona and Reese had showed up when they did. "I'm so glad you guys are back and were able to find us."

"We got back from Europe this morning. Imagine

our surprise when the entire coven was gone except Dawna and Lynn," Reese said, sweeping his long wavy blond hair to the side.

"Fortunately, Dawna had a general idea where you were headed, and we just sort of followed our instincts the rest of the way," Fiona added.

An image flashed through Aurora's mind. Dawna, pale and weak, as she'd been when Aurora last saw her. "How is Dawna?"

"She's better," Fiona assured her, but a note of worry worked its way onto her face.

"Why do I sense a *but*?"

Reese placed a hand on Fiona's shoulder and answered for her. "There is something else going on. Something beyond the Umbrae. I think Fi has the same feeling I do. There is more battle yet to come."

Aurora sighed. She knew it was true. "Well, when we get back to Graves Manor, we will regroup. We're going to need to find a new empath, for one thing."

Fiona nodded, and her apple green eyes grew moist. "Not that anyone can replace Wayne."

Aurora shook her head vehemently. "No way."

Fiona and Reese wandered away to give Aurora and Mobius some time alone—as alone as they could be in a cave, surrounded by people.

Aurora turned back to her love. "I'm so glad I found you again. Or rather, that you found me."

"My beloved," he murmured, pulling her close to him and rubbing the side of his face against hers. "I would go to the ends of the universe and cross thousands of lifetimes to be with you. You are my heart. You are my soul."

She sighed and melted into him. Her pulse jumped erratically. Even after all the excitement, danger, and adrenaline rushes of the night, just being close to him made her dizzy with happiness.

"That last lifetime was a rough one. I hope this new life with you is better." She tried for a note of wry humor, but emotion clogged her throat.

Mobius tilted her chin up so her gaze met his. "I will spend as many lifetimes as it takes making you happy. I will erase the horror of that time. And when the bloom of youth has faded from your cheeks and you pass on from this life, I will search until I find you again. And again. And again. You will never be free of me."

She grinned. "Some girls might think that's kind of stalkerish. But me?" She pressed her mouth to his in a kiss tender and sweet. "I can't think of anything I'd like more."

For I am my beloved's, and my beloved is mine. And she knew, with every fiber of her being, it was true. He was hers. She was his. And that was exactly the way it should be.

The clear crystalline waters of the peering pool swirled counterclockwise until the liquid stilled and the vision the pool had revealed faded.

Willow lifted herself from her kneeling position and smoothed her hands over her satiny, violet-colored robe. She was grateful she'd chosen the right moment to consult the pool. She'd been just in time to see the final stages of battle and that all had come out of the foray unscathed.

"Assistant Director, I have news," came a deep baritone voice.

She spun around. Helios stood in the doorway, his bald head shiny under the bright lighting of the room. His burgundy gown threaded with hints of gold lent him a regal appearance.

"What is it?" she asked.

"The illness seems suddenly to have fallen away from many of the gods."

"Mobius's mission was successful. The Grays have been reclaimed and will return to the Light Realm. Perhaps this battle destroyed enough of the Dark to make an impact here."

"Yes, but not all of the gods are well," he said.

"We can't expect all of our problems to be solved with this one mission. The Umbrae's leader has been destroyed, but they will appoint a new one. And they are not the only evil that exists."

Helios sighed. "No. They are not." Then, he tilted his head to the side, his gaze questioning. "How do you know the leader was destroyed? Did the peering pool inform you?"

She nodded. "It did."

Helios crossed the room and touched her shoulder, his eyes kind and gentle. "When will you tell Mobius about your findings in the Hall of Records? When will you inform him of the truth?"

"That Aurora is Meri?" she asked.

"Yes."

Willow almost wished she hadn't confided in Helios. She'd been overcome by guilt at her lie and had needed to talk it out. To his credit, Helios hadn't judged her. He had understood her desire to protect their Director.

"When Mobius returns." She recalled Mobius and Aurora's embrace after the battle and their whispered talk of past lives. "Though I think they already know the truth."

"How so?"

Mobius's words of not so long ago drifted back to her. "There are some things the heart just knows."

✂

❑ **YES!**

Sign me up for the Love Spell Book Club and send my FREE BOOKS! If I choose to stay in the club, I will pay only $8.50* each month, a savings of $6.48!

NAME: _____

ADDRESS: _____

TELEPHONE: _____

EMAIL: _____

❑ I want to pay by credit card.

❑ **VISA**   ❑ **MasterCard**   ❑ **DISCOVER**

ACCOUNT #: _____

EXPIRATION DATE: _____

SIGNATURE: _____

Mail this page along with $2.00 shipping and handling to:
Love Spell Book Club
PO Box 6640
Wayne, PA 19087
Or fax (must include credit card information) to:
610-995-9274
You can also sign up online at **www.dorchesterpub.com**.
*Plus $2.00 for shipping. Offer open to residents of the U.S. and Canada only.
Canadian residents please call 1-800-481-9191 for pricing information.
If under 18, a parent or guardian must sign. Terms, prices and conditions subject to
change. Subscription subject to acceptance. Dorchester Publishing reserves the right
to reject any order or cancel any subscription.